Berkley Prime Crime titles by Connie Archer

A SPOONFUL OF MURDER
A BROTH OF BETRAYAL
A ROUX OF REVENGE

A Roux of Revenge

Connie Archer

BERKLEY PRIME CRIME, NEW YORK

THE BERKLEY PUBLISHING GROUP
Published by the Penguin Group
Penguin Group (USA) LLC
375 Hudson Street, New York, New York 10014

USA • Canada • UK • Ireland • Australia • New Zealand • India • South Africa • China

penguin.com

A Penguin Random House Company

A ROUX OF REVENGE

A Berkley Prime Crime Book / published by arrangement with the author

For information, address: The Berkley Publishing Group,
a division of Penguin Group (USA) LLC,
375 Hudson Street, New York, New York 10014.

ISBN: 978-0-425-25242-0

PUBLISHING HISTORY
Berkley Prime Crime mass-market edition / April 2014

PRINTED IN THE UNITED STATES OF AMERICA

10 9 8 7 6 5 4 3 2 1

Cover illustration by Cathy Gendron.
Cover design by Diana Kolsky.
Interior text design by Kristin del Rosario.

For Tom

Acknowledgments

With thanks and much appreciation to Paige Wheeler of Folio Literary Management for her hard work, good advice and expertise, and to Faith Black and Kayleigh Clark of Berkley Prime Crime for their enthusiasm and support of the soup lover's mystery series. And thank you to everyone at Berkley Prime Crime who had a hand in bringing this series to life.

Many thanks as well to the writers' group—Cheryl Brughelli, Don Fedosiuk, Paula Freeman, R. B. Lodge and Marguerite Summers—for their criticism and encouragement. And a special thank you to William M. Walker for his knowledge of bagpipes and Scottish laments and to Adam Smith of the University of Glasgow for his Gaelic expertise. Last, but certainly not least, special thanks to my family and my wonderful husband for their tolerance in living with a woman who is constantly thinking about ways to kill people.

CONNIE ARCHER
CONNIEARCHERMYSTERIES.COM
FACEBOOK.COM/CONNIEARCHERMYSTERIES
TWITTER: @SNOWFLAKEVT

Chapter 1

NATE EDGERTON, SNOWFLAKE'S Chief of Police, reached over and flipped off the siren and flashing light. He pulled his cruiser to the side of the road, slowing and coming to a stop behind a bright blue sports car. Early morning sunlight reflected off the rear bumper of the car where two people, a young couple, sat huddled together. Nate could tell from their expressions there was no need to hurry.

He turned to his deputy. "Cancel the ambulance." Nate heaved a sigh and climbed out. He already knew what he'd find in the ditch—a mangled body or bodies trapped in an equally crushed vehicle. Not how he wanted his day to go. His spirits had been high when he'd left home that morning. He had impulsively hugged his wife and kissed her quickly on the cheek. It was a golden October day. Indian summer warmth lingered over the countryside, and a brilliant glow of crimson and orange covered the trees, leaves unwilling to submit to the coming winter.

He turned back to the cruiser and leaned into the

driver's window. "Get their plate number and run it. And get hold of somebody in Lincoln Falls for a coroner's van."

Bradley nodded and, following Nate's orders, began to make the calls. He really hoped he wouldn't have to see any blood today.

"And after you've done that, talk to those two." Nate indicated the young couple by the sports car. "Get their information, and don't let 'em leave just yet." Nate straightened up slowly, holding a hand against his stiff back, and approached the pair. "You the folks who called this in?"

The man nodded. His arm was slung protectively around the shoulder of the woman who sat next to him. Her face was pale and pinched.

"Did you both go down to have a look?" Nate asked.

"Yes, we . . . well, I got there first. I told my wife to go back, not to look."

"I see." Nate nodded. "My deputy will get your information, and I'll be with you in a few minutes."

Nate doubted the couple was mistaken, but he needed to make sure. He walked to the edge of the road and gauged the distance to a white van tilted forward into the soft earth below him at a twenty-five degree angle. He grasped a sapling that clung to the side of the ditch, and doing his best not to slip or tumble, stepped sideways down the slope. He took note of the footprints in the soft earth, one set larger and deeper than the other. As careful as he was, he was barely able to keep from sliding the rest of the way down into the gully.

The windshield of the van had shattered from the impact. Probably from the victim's head, he guessed. Nate peered through the open driver's window. The body of a man dressed in casual work clothes was splayed over the steering wheel. His face, pressed into the shattered windshield, was striped with rivulets of blood. Sightless eyes were open, fixed at a place well beyond the ditch in which he lay.

Nate sighed and shook his head. Why don't they ever wear their seat belts?

He wrenched the door open and stood back to let gravity do the hard work. The man's left sleeve and shirtfront were soaked in blood. Nate scanned the interior of the van searching for broken glass or a sharp object to explain the blood loss but found nothing. He pulled a pen from his pocket and, using the tip of the pen, very carefully lifted the sleeve of the man's shirt. Humming tunelessly to himself, he replaced his pen and climbed around the van. He studied the ground, noticing a deep footprint at the rear of the vehicle. Stepping carefully over the depression, he leaned close to the bumper for a better look.

"Bradley!" he bellowed.

Nate looked to the top of the rise. His deputy's face appeared over the edge.

"Bring the camera down here." Nate knew the technicians would take plenty of pictures, but whenever possible, he preferred to document the scene himself—too easy for a key piece of evidence to disappear or be overlooked.

Bradley appeared a few moments later, a camera bag slung over his shoulder. He slid down a lot more gracefully than the older man had. When Bradley reached bottom, he passed the camera to Nate, carefully keeping his gaze averted from the front seat of the van.

"Come on over here." Nate scrambled around to the driver's door. "What do you see?"

Bradley followed his boss dutifully. He felt his stomach lurch. "Blood."

"What else do you see?"

"Well, he didn't have a seat belt on. Went straight into the windshield."

"Anything else?"

Bradley shrugged his shoulders. "He bled all over himself."

"Really? So, what do you think caused all the blood?" Nate asked.

Bradley, his face white, shrugged his shoulders.

"Look again." Nate pointed to the dead man's arm and shirtfront and waited patiently for light to dawn in Bradley's eyes.

"This wasn't from the accident?"

Nate slid the pen from his pocket and once again lifted the material of the shirt away from the dead man's arm. "Now what do you see?"

Bradley squinted. "A hole." He turned to Nate, surprise on his face. "He was shot?"

"There's more. Listen and learn." Nate pointed to the rear of the van and led the way. "See this?" He pointed to a clear footprint.

Bradley stared. "Maybe the guy up there . . ." he said, indicating the man by the sports car.

"Oh yeah? What kinda shoes is he wearing?"

"Uh . . . I don't know."

"He's wearing some kind of expensive running shoes. This looks like maybe a small man's size, distinct heel, maybe leather soles—city shoes." Nate indicated dents on the rear bumper. "Here." He pointed to a second spot of damage. "And here? A lot of dings and rust spots, but there's no rust on these. A little paint in there. Maybe they can match it."

"You're saying somebody made sure he went off the road?"

"Yup. Twice, it looks like. Stand over here and help me get this back door open. Whatever you do, don't mess up that print." Nate pulled a handkerchief from his back pocket and wrapped it around his hand. He pulled the door open while Bradley wedged his arm into the opening and pushed. The door creaked and swung open. Gravity did the rest.

Nate stared at the floor of the van. "There's a track of

dirt and leaves—fresh. Maybe somebody was having a look around before we got here. Grab your camera. I want you to get some good shots of this and our man inside, his shirt and these dings on the bumper. But don't touch anything, all right?"

Bradley nodded and began to fidget with the settings on his camera.

Nate climbed into the empty interior of the van. Using his handkerchief, he pushed gently against the panels that lined the interior. One gave slightly, as though loosened. He climbed out, careful to avoid the deep footprint, and jerked his thumb to the top of the rise. "I want to talk to those two up there before they decide to take off."

Nate straightened his back. *Getting stiffer every day*, he thought. *Getting too damn old for this job.* He heaved another sigh and made an effort to climb back up to the road. Taking two steps up and sliding back one, he clung to the thin plantings and branches to give himself purchase.

The man at the car stood as Nate approached. The woman held her hands against her face, leaning over her knees. "Can we go now?" the man asked.

"About what time did you first pull over?"

"Maybe forty-five minutes ago, I think. We saw the top of the van down below. We stopped, thinking somebody might need help, but . . ." He trailed off.

"It was too late." Nate finished his sentence.

The man gulped and nodded.

"Where are you headed, by the way?" Nate made a circuit of the sports car, looking for signs of damage. The chrome bumper was unmarred.

"Over to Bournmouth to visit my wife's parents. We live in Lincoln Falls."

"Did you happen to see any other vehicles when you first noticed the van? Anybody pass by?"

"No. Not a soul. There wasn't any traffic. We came this way 'cause we wanted to take the scenic route." The man shook his head ruefully. "We sure as hell didn't bargain for this."

Nate nodded. "Sorry you had to be the ones. If you've given your names and home address to my deputy, you can be on your way."

Without a word the young woman stood, a look of relief on her face. They climbed into the sports car without a backward glance. The engine revved, and the car pulled onto the road heading east.

Nate watched until the car navigated a turn and was out of sight. He heard the crunch of gravel behind him as another car pulled off the road.

Elias Scott, Snowflake's town doctor and the local coroner, climbed out, a heavy black bag in his hand. Nate shook his head negatively to let Elias know there was no hurry.

"You're sure?" Elias asked as he approached.

"Sorry to drag you out here. Not much you can do now."

"Well, since I'm here, why don't I have a closer look?"

"Be my guest."

Elias stepped carefully down the side of the ditch. When he reached the bottom, he slipped on a pair of latex gloves. Nate followed and watched as Elias looked in the open driver's door. Elias whistled softly.

"What do you think?" Nate asked.

"Well, the accident caused this." Elias pointed to a gash on the man's head and facial cuts. "Might have caused a concussion too. But it doesn't account for all this blood. Looks like it flowed from his left arm. See here." He pointed a gloved finger and then carefully examined the material of the shirt.

"Yeah, I caught that. A gunshot wound."

"He was alive when he went off the road. He could have been in shock from the wound, maybe that's what caused the crash. Could have died from the trauma, the blood loss or even the head injury. Can't be certain yet."

"Have a look back here." Elias followed the path that

Nate had taken, careful not to slip on the damp vegetation. Bradley was returning the camera to its bag.

"Don't walk over there. One good print I noticed." Nate pointed to the area by the rear door.

"Somebody else was here?" Elias asked.

"That's what I think. And then there are two areas of damage. Here and here." Nate indicated the spots on the crushed bumper. "And these are new—no rust. This wasn't caused by the accident. Somebody rear-ended this guy—a couple of times, I'd guess."

"So you think he was shot first? Maybe whoever shot him managed to hit a vital artery."

"And maybe he was able to get away—tried to get help. But somebody didn't want him to." Nate shook his head. "Nothing's simple, is it? I'm gonna have to get the body moved and this thing towed to Lincoln Falls where the techs can have a better look. Let's go back up to the road. I want to get some shots of the tire tracks before everybody messes them up."

The three men climbed back to the road, doing their best not to slip on the soft earth or wet autumn leaves. Nate reached out and took the camera from Bradley. Elias stepped away and watched as Nate shot several photos.

"What can you tell from those?"

"See these right here?" Nate said, pointing to wide tire tracks. "These are the marks from the van. They start right here. No sign of an attempt to brake. This guy just flew off the road. Maybe he was already unconscious. But I still think somebody helped him along."

Elias followed in Nate's wake. "And back here . . ." Nate pointed to another set of marks. "Somebody hit the brakes real hard. See these? And then it looks like he drove onto the soft shoulder."

He turned to his deputy. "Bradley, you stay here until everything's handled and then bring the cruiser back to the station. And make sure you don't touch anything and don't let anybody stop to gawk. And especially right here," Nate said, pointing to a set of tire tracks. "Get some markers out of the trunk and make sure they get an impression of that tire and that one good footprint down there."

Bradley wasn't happy to be stuck on the road for what would be several hours of a mop-up operation, but there wasn't much he could say about it.

"I'll hitch a ride back to town with you, Elias. Bradley can handle the rest." Nate stood for a moment, silently surveying the scene. "Yup. I'd bet my last dollar. Somebody was after this guy. We've got a murder on our hands."

Chapter 2

JANIE SHIFTED THE branches of brightly colored autumn leaves, rearranging them in a wooden cask, one of several placed around the restaurant. "What do you think, Lucky?"

"I think it's fabulous. Maybe you should consider a career in interior decoration, even though I'd hate to lose you." Lucky's compliments were sincere. The restaurant was filled with morning light, filtering through the yellow gingham curtains and reflecting off the wide pine floors of the By the Spoonful Soup Shop.

Janie laughed. "Don't think that'll be happening anytime soon. I'll be stuck in Snowflake for the rest of my life, more likely." She pushed an unruly branch back into place. "But at least we're all dressed up for Halloween."

"I mean it, Janie. Look at this." Lucky waved her arm to indicate the work that Janie had accomplished—bouquets of leaves in brilliant reds and oranges from the autumn chill, cornstalks and baskets of multicolored gourds in the front window. "It really looks terrific."

Lucky's grandfather, Jack Jamieson, had decided to

hold a promotion for the Spoonful—free soup from three o'clock to five o'clock on the afternoon of Halloween. Lucky agreed that would be a great idea. It would cover the time period from when the children were released from school until the sun went down for the children's witching hour. Jack had also decided to sponsor a pumpkin-carving contest. Anyone could enter, each entry was anonymous, and every customer would have one vote for their favorite by secret ballot. The prize would be three all-you-can-eat meals for two at the Spoonful any day of the week.

Janie and Meg, the Spoonful's other waitress, and Sage DuBois, their chef, had each contributed carved pumpkins to get the contest rolling. Janie's jack-o'-lantern sported a smile, with red pepper lips, teeth of seeds and twig eyelashes. Meg had carved one that looked like a tiny demon. Sage's was a leering witch with a parsnip nose. The jack-o'-lanterns were lined up on a long table against the wall. Tiny battery lights twinkled inside each of them.

The holidays were here again, Lucky thought. The first without her parents. Ten months had elapsed since she had returned home to Snowflake to take over her parents' business. Martha and Louis Jamieson had died in a car crash on an icy road, and their death had changed her life forever. Two more months would mark a full year. Somehow she had managed to keep the restaurant afloat. She had been terrified at first of taking over the Spoonful and doubtful about her decision to stay. But now, this path felt the most natural one in the world.

"You can't really see the lights inside the pumpkins during the day," Janie said. Maybe we should turn them off for now and save the batteries 'til it's dark."

"Good idea." Lucky looked up from laying out placemats on the tables.

Janie, a wooden bowl full of gourds in her arms, was staring intently out the front window. Something in her expression caught Lucky's attention.

"Janie? What is it?"

"Nothing." Janie continued to stare across Broadway to the opposite sidewalk. "It's just . . ."

Lucky moved closer to Janie and followed her gaze. "What do you see?"

"That man. I've seen him before." Janie nodded her head, indicating a tall, muscular man with a full head of thick auburn hair streaked with gray. He stood on the other side of the street, in the shade of an awning, as though waiting for someone.

"Maybe he's someone in town working for the Harvest Festival," Lucky said.

Snowflake, Vermont, had been chosen as this year's location for the fall event, hosting a local farmers' market, pony rides and a corn maze for children. Ernie White, a successful businessman from Lincoln Falls, a much larger town, was the moving force behind the festival.

"You're probably right." Janie shrugged and flipped over the sign on the front door to read OPEN. "I just feel like I've seen him around a lot." She turned away, heading for the kitchen to help Sage prepare for the morning rush.

The bell over the door jingled just as Lucky finished laying out the last of the napkins and silverware. Hank Northcross and Barry Sanders, two of the Spoonful's most loyal regulars, came in every morning. Retired gentlemen, they were often together and were usually the first customers of the day.

Hank was tall and thin. His sparse hair, completely gray, was cropped close to his head, and he wore pince-nez glasses that constantly slid down his long nose. Barry, much shorter and very plump, was fond of brightly colored shirts that barely buttoned over his midsection. Today he was dressed in orange and black plaid in deference to the season.

"Morning, Lucky . . . you too Meg," Barry called out. "Jack around?"

"He'll be here shortly. He's picking up some supplies in Lincoln Falls."

"You still let the old man drive?" Hank asked in jest, but there was an undercurrent of worry to his question.

Lucky's grandfather had suffered from wartime flashbacks most of his life. When she had returned home months before, she had realized that Jack had other, more serious health problems. Fortunately these had since been alleviated by medical treatment, but Lucky still worried about him.

"Couldn't stop him if I tried," she answered. Jack was the only family she had now. He needed to feel useful, and she needed his support. There was no doubt in her mind he was essential to the smooth running of the Spoonful.

Lucky approached the corner table where Hank and Barry held court. "Coffee?"

"Yes. Perfect," Barry answered.

She retrieved cups and saucers from behind the counter and poured two cups for the men. She placed them on a tray with a pitcher of cream and a sugar bowl and carried them to the corner table where Hank and Barry were already setting up a game of chess. "Don't forget Jack's pumpkin-carving contest. He'll be disappointed if you don't both contribute."

"We haven't forgotten," Hank spoke. "Wait'll you see mine. I'm quite sure I'll win."

"Not so fast, you old coot. I'm gonna beat the pants off you." Barry looked up. "What do you have for specials today, Lucky?"

"We have three new soups. Sage has a pumpkin rice with Persian spices, he tells me. I haven't tried it yet myself, but it smells delicious. And a zucchini leek with potatoes, and a beet, mushroom and barley soup. I've tried that one, and I really love it."

"Hmm. I'll have to sample every one of those this week," Barry said. "We're going over to the Harvest Festival later.

I want to pick up some vegetables from the farmers' market, but I'll be sure to come back for lunch. Make sure you save me a bowl of that pumpkin soup today."

"I will, and Jack should be back by then." Lucky turned back to the counter. Janie was staring out the window again. Lucky walked closer and stood behind her. The same man stood under the awning across the street. He had disappeared for a short while and now was back.

"You're right. He does seem to be around a lot," Lucky whispered.

Janie had lost her father quite suddenly only four months earlier, just as she was about to graduate from high school. Doug Leonard had been a kindly man who adored his only child. When he died of a massive coronary, Janie was at first inconsolable. Lucky felt a deep empathy for the girl, especially since her own parents had also been taken in an equally sudden fashion. Given Janie's youth, Lucky knew how much more difficult the loss must have been. Lucky tried to always do her best to look out for Janie and make sure she was on an even keel.

"I wonder who he is," Lucky said.

Janie, a troubled look on her face, didn't answer. She turned away from the window and hurried into the kitchen.

Chapter 3

A MOVEMENT AT the front door caught Lucky's eye and the bell jingled as Elias entered. She smiled widely, her heart lifting. She was thankful she no longer blushed furiously when he walked into a room. He had been her mad crush when she was younger and he, older and unattainable. They had reconnected when she had returned to Snowflake and had been seeing each other for the past several months. Elias stopped in for lunch as often as he could. Lucky was surprised to see him at the restaurant this early.

"Elias! You're early for lunch."

He smiled quickly and grasped her hand, then followed her back to the counter. "I just wanted to catch you before it got too busy here." He sat heavily on a stool. He seemed distracted.

"Everything all right?"

"Oh. Sure. I just thought I should tell you first. I've hired a new doctor. Well, it's a trial period to see how it works out. But I thought you should know."

Lucky was thrilled. "That's wonderful!" She knew Elias had been working far too many hours, seeing patients in town, and traveling to Lincoln Falls for his charges who were hospitalized. This would mean they'd have more time together, something they had been missing since Elias's partner at the Clinic had left town.

Elias smiled but made no comment.

Lucky poured a cup of coffee for him. "Some breakfast?"

"No. No. I'm fine. I just wanted to . . . uh . . ." He hesitated.

Lucky waited, but Elias seemed to be searching for words.

The bell over the door rang again. Marjorie and Cecily, two sisters who ran the Off Broadway ladies' clothing store, bustled in.

"Yoo-hoo!" Cecily called out to everyone.

"Hey, Cecily . . . Marjorie . . ." Barry responded from the corner, his hand raised.

Lucky turned back to Elias. He was standing. "Leaving so soon?" she asked.

"Uh, yes. I just wanted to stop in and tell you the news."

Lucky looked at him carefully. He seemed uncomfortable. "Elias, is anything wrong?"

"Wrong? No, certainly not." He smiled in the sisters' direction as they took stools at the counter. "I just need to get back to the Clinic."

"Okay. See you later," Lucky replied uncertainly as Elias waved and hurried through the front door.

"Hope we didn't interrupt anything?" Marjorie raised her eyebrows.

Lucky shook her head. "No. Not at all. Elias just stopped by to let me know he's hired a new doctor at the Clinic."

"Well, that's a good thing. That man has been working way too many hours since . . ." Marjorie trailed off. She didn't need to explain what she meant. Everyone in town knew Elias had lost his partner at the Clinic after the murder of a winter tourist—a woman who had been the doctor's lover.

Lucky poured two cups of tea and carried them to the counter. The sisters' croissants with butter and jam were ready and waiting on the hatch. Sage, working in the kitchen, had no need to ask their order. Lucky delivered the food to the counter. Everyone knew that Elias was stretched thin. But that wasn't why he seemed distracted this morning. Something else was on his mind. What was he about to tell her before the sisters' arrival interrupted him?

Chapter 4

MIRIAM LEONARD RINSED her hands at the kitchen sink, washing off a sticky residue of flour. She dampened a sponge and carefully wiped down her workspace and countertop. All of the pies were set out, ready to be baked. The oven was still warming. She had prepared an apple, a peach and a razzleberry pie—blueberries, raspberries and blackberries— Janie's favorite. Miriam dried her hands on a dish towel as she headed to the front door. She had heard the clunk of the mailbox earlier when the post had been delivered, but she had been in the middle of rolling dough and didn't want to stop. Flipping the towel over her shoulder, she opened her front door. A willow wreath decorated with mini pumpkins rattled against the glass window.

She flipped open the lid of the metal mailbox and, reaching in, retrieved a few envelopes. She stepped back inside and pushed the front door shut with her shoulder and dropped the mail on the hallway table—more bills, she was certain. She turned away to head back to the kitchen but hesitated. Something was different. She picked up the three envelopes—an electric bill, a statement from the dentist and a small blank parchment-like envelope. She turned it over. How did this arrive in her mailbox? It was completely blank. No address and no return address. She ran her fingers over the textured exterior and turned it over. Sealed. She pressed the envelope lightly. Something was inside. She sliced through the top with a letter opener and shook the contents out on the tabletop. One small, delicate flower with petals of tender blue and a bright yellow center lay on the polished wood.

Miriam's heart thumped a heavy beat. The blood drained from her face. The room spun around her. For a moment she thought she would faint. She pressed her hand against the wall to maintain her equilibrium. The blossom was a true forget-me-not. It was him. It had to be. He was the only one who would know what this wildflower would mean to her. She shivered in spite of the warmth of the house. How had he found her? And why after all these years? It must be him. No one else could know that this was theirs—a flower that had once held such meaning for them both.

Miriam dropped the dish towel on the table and, clinging to the banister, slowly climbed the stairs to her bedroom. With wooden steps she approached the bureau and opened a tapestry-covered jewelry box. Pushing a small button inside, she released a narrow compartment at its base and retrieved a yellowing photograph.

He sat in a meadow, sunlight brushing his hair, a half smile on his face that she remembered still. The photo still evoked the same vivid memories. It was late summer. A warm and golden day. They had each slipped away from the campsite and met in the meadow. She had managed to put a picnic basket together, with bread, cheese and meat. Once they were sure they were safe from prying eyes, they made love in the tall grass and fell asleep in the sunlight. She knew, even then, with a knowledge only the young sometimes have, this would be the happiest day of her life.

She had loved him in a way she had never loved since. She had been so full of hope for all that life promised, never imagining her dreams would be torn from her.

She had secretly gazed at this photograph countless times. Now, with the distance of years, she recognized something poignant and knowing in his face, as if he could foretell what was to come for both of them. The real future that would be—not the one they had planned. Her hands were shaking as she slipped the photo back into its secret compartment.

She feared what this message might mean. Why now? What did he want from her?

Chapter 5

LUCKY FLIPPED OVER the sign at the front door. The restaurant was closed. Janie had left for home, giving Meg a ride. Sage was still in the kitchen, organizing pots and pans for the next day. Nate Edgerton sat at a table near the window with Jack. Lucky moved around the room, turning off all but one of the lamps, and then poured herself a cup of herbal tea. She joined the men at the table.

"No idea who he is?" Jack asked. He had grabbed two beers from the refrigerator and poured them into chilled glasses for Nate and himself. The Spoonful never served alcohol, but Jack enjoyed the occasional beer and kept a few at the restaurant.

"There's a name and address on a Maine driver's license. I have a call in to the local PD there to go out to talk to someone—try to find a next of kin. I'm a little suspicious about the license though. The van is registered in Quebec to somebody else. I should be getting something from the authorities there too."

"What's suspicious about the license?" Jack asked.

"Well, I could be wrong, but it just seems a little off."
Nate continued, "He looks too young for his age, at least
the age on the license."

"Usually it's the other way around," Lucky said. "People hang on to old licenses until they have to show up to
have another picture taken. You'd think he'd look older
than his photo."

"You would, wouldn't you?" Nate replied.

"Did you call Elias out to the scene?" she asked.

"Oh sure. Too bad he had to start his day that way, but
I was glad of the company. And glad to get a ride back to
town."

Lucky thought perhaps that's what had been troubling
Elias earlier. He may not have wanted to mention the dead
man in front of the sisters.

"They'll take his prints over at Lincoln Falls just to be
doubly sure." Nate wiped his mouth with a napkin. "I'll
check again in the morning to see if anyone's been reported
as missing, but it might be too soon for that. There arc a lot
of strangers in town right now with the Harvest Festival . . .
and my guy could be one of them."

Jack snorted. "Don't even mention that thing. We've had
Ernie White driving us nuts about setting up a food booth
over there. I told him he could take a hike. If anybody
wants our food, nothing's stopping them from coming into
town and ordering it right here."

"Ernie always gets Jack's back up," Lucky volunteered.
"Jack's right, though. He's definitely been putting pressure
on us to set something up at the festival, but we don't have
that kind of staff. We've done things in the past to help the
town out, but this is different. Besides, most of the festival
folks are coming here anyway. So I'm certainly not going
to close the restaurant just to sell a few sandwiches." Lucky
took a sip of her tea. "Don't get me wrong. I think it's a
great thing he's doing. Some small local farmers get to sell
their harvest. The kids have rides and a corn maze with

scarecrows. I heard they've even booked a Gaelic band from Nova Scotia. It sounds like fun for everyone."

"Speaking of which, that's where I'll be next, asking questions out there. There are a few strangers working those pony rides and stuff. I just hope somebody can identify this guy."

Lucky heard a rap on the glass of the front door. Sophie Colgan stood outside. She wiggled her fingers in greeting as Lucky rose to let her in.

Sophie reached out and gave her a quick hug. "Just here to meet my honey. Is he in the kitchen?"

Lucky laughed. "Where else?" She and Sophie had been childhood friends until Lucky left town to attend college in Madison. A rift had formed between them, mostly caused by Sophie's resentment. Events over the past months had healed the wound, and now their friendship was renewed, stronger than ever.

"Go right in. You know where you'll find him," Lucky answered.

"We have to get together this week—with you and Elias. You have a night that's good?"

"Sure. Any night. No special plans this week. Just give me a call or stop by."

"Great." Sophie beamed.

Lucky sensed there was something on the tip of Sophie's tongue. "What's going on?" She looked at her friend quizzically.

"Oh, nothing," Sophie replied breezily. "We'll catch up later."

Lucky followed Sophie's progress to the kitchen. Something was happening. Sophie was usually upbeat, but now it seemed as if she were barely holding back a happy secret.

A few minutes later, Sage called through the hatch. "Hey, Lucky. I'm taking off."

"Night, Sage. See you tomorrow."

"Need any help with anything?"

"No. We're fine. You two go on," Lucky called back. She heard the back door slam as Sage and Sophie left together.

Nate rose from his chair. "I should get going too. Susanna's gonna wonder what happened to me. Thanks for the sandwich, folks. What do I owe you?"

"Put your money away," Jack replied. "You're not allowed to pay after two bells. You know that." Jack, a Navy veteran, always told time by the bells. Other than Lucky, no one else could ever translate Jack's references. She knew two bells at this time of night meant it was after nine o'clock.

Nate smiled. "You're a stubborn old cuss, Jack, you know that?"

"Who you callin' old?" Jack grumbled.

Chapter 6

THE FOLLOWING MORNING the Spoonful was packed with customers. One of Jack's CDs was playing—this time an upbeat big band sound. Lucky hadn't seen Hank or Barry yet, which was surprising. They were usually the earliest arrivals. She knew most of the residents in town, if not personally, then at least by sight. Snowflake's population was 950 at last count—since one of Elias's patients had given birth. But today it was obvious Nate was correct. There were a lot of strangers in town. She spotted Ernie White, the organizer of the Harvest Festival, at a table with two men who seemed to defer to him. Undoubtedly they were in his employ.

She looked up as Horace Winthorpe came through the front door and waved to her. Horace had become one of the Spoonful's regulars as well. And he was not just a favorite customer; Horace had become a friend. He was a retired professor of history, working on a book about the Revolutionary War. Fortunately for Lucky, Horace had agreed to rent her parents' home on a long-term basis. Horace looked toward the corner table where Hank and Barry usually sat. It was still empty. He approached the counter.

"Good morning, Lucky. Hank and Barry aren't here yet?" he asked.

"No." She shook her head. "Not yet. But I'm sure they'll be in soon."

"Well, I'll just sit here so I can visit with you," he said, sliding onto a stool left by a departing customer.

"What would you like?"

"It's a little early, but I'd like to try that new Persian pumpkin rice. That sounds intriguing. Do you know what spices Sage uses?"

"He told me—not sure if I can remember them all—cardamom, cinnamon, coriander, turmeric, nutmeg and don't quote me, but I heard him say something about rose petals."

"A large bowl, please. That sounds enticing."

Sage knew the pumpkin soup would be a big hit this week. He had prepared three mini sample cups, now sitting on the hatch in case anyone wanted an early taste.

Lucky turned and grabbed one of the small cups. "One large bowl coming right up. But have one of these first, if you like. You haven't forgotten Jack's pumpkin-carving contest, have you?"

"Not at all. I plan to bring my entry over."

"Don't forget to deliver it secretly. You can bring it to the back door, and I'll assign a number."

Sage was tapping at the bell on the hatch behind her. She turned and saw him point to the corridor outside the kitchen. That meant someone had come in through the back door. She nodded to Sage and slipped through the swinging door into the corridor. Hank and Barry were standing outside the door to her office with their jack-o'-lanterns in their arms.

"Hey, Lucky," Barry called. "We didn't want to come in the front door with these. I'm sure I'll win, but I do want the vote to be impartial."

Hank sniffed loudly.

Lucky stood back to admire their handiwork. "Those are great! Thank you." She led them into the small office and took the carved pumpkins from their arms. "Barry, you'll be number four, Hank, number five." She quickly jotted the numbers on two small pieces of card stock with a marker. "I'll bring them out in a minute. You can go right through to the restaurant."

The men nodded and walked down the corridor to the front room. Lucky waited a few minutes more and then carried the two jack-o'-lanterns out to the restaurant and put them on the long table. She placed the cards into holders in front of each pumpkin. When she returned to the counter, Horace was gone. Meg had delivered his order and he had carried his soup to the corner table to sit with Hank and Barry.

JANIE AND MEG bustled between tables, taking orders while Lucky manned the counter and Jack perched on his stool behind the cash register. Meg deftly grabbed dishes from the kitchen hatch and matched them with the order slips. The two girls didn't miss a beat. Janie seemed to fly between tables, while Meg moved slowly, double-checking her orders, but efficient nonetheless. In another quarter of an hour most of these people would be on their way, and the staff could all take a breather.

Lucky peered through the hatch into the kitchen where Sage was lining up plates and rapidly buttering slices of toast. "You need any help in there?" she called to him.

He looked up and smiled. "Nah. I'm fine. Sophie's stopping by again today, and she'll give me a hand."

Lucky was relieved to hear they'd have a little extra help this morning. She hadn't expected such a crowd, but she wasn't complaining. Less than a year ago the Spoonful had been facing bankruptcy when a body had been found behind the restaurant and Sage himself had been arrested for the crime.

During the winter months Sophie worked as a ski instructor at the Snowflake Resort at the top of the mountain. Her off season schedule was light. But Lucky knew that in a month or so, Sophie would be far too busy to stop in at the Spoonful and lend a hand.

Lucky jumped involuntarily when plates crashed to the floor. She scanned the room. Janie stood at a table by the front window. Her face was bright red. She apologized to her customers and rushed toward the kitchen to replace the order. Lucky could tell she was horribly embarrassed.

"I'm sorry," she whispered as she passed by the counter. "It just slipped out of my hand."

"Don't worry about it," Lucky replied. "I'll clean up." She glanced over the counter. Everyone was set for a minute or two. She followed Janie into the kitchen and grabbed a dustpan and broom and a wet cloth. She hurried back to the table, apologized to the couple who sat by the window and quickly cleaned up the spilled food and broken china. As she carried the debris to the dustbin in the kitchen, she passed Janie, rushing her order back. Janie's face was blotchy and red. She looked on the verge of tears.

Lucky returned to the counter and refilled several cups of coffee. She cleared away dishes from patrons who were preparing to leave. She wondered again if most of these people were working at the Harvest Festival in some capacity. They all seemed to be on the same schedule. Once the rush died down and only a few stragglers remained, Lucky peeked through the hatch and spotted Janie in the kitchen. Lucky pushed through the swinging door and approached the girl, who stood at the worktable, slicing tomatoes. "Janie, it's all right. It was just a couple of dishes. It's nothing."

Janie had been crying; Lucky was sure of it. She glanced over at Sage who diplomatically pretended not to notice.

Lucky took her hand. "Come into the office with me?"

"No. No. I'm all right, Lucky. Really, I am."

"You don't look all right. Come on." Half pulling on Janie's hand, Lucky led her down the hall and into her small office.

Janie's eyes were rimmed with red. Lucky gently pushed her into a chair in front of the desk and sat across from her. "Something's wrong. Why don't you tell me what it is?"

"I'm real sorry I dropped that dish and right in front of those two customers."

"This isn't about the dish."

Janie swallowed. "You're right. It's just . . . I saw him again. That man."

"The same man? The one you saw yesterday? Where?"

"Across the street. Watching the Spoonful again. When I looked up, I could've sworn he was staring right at me."

"I think I'm going to have a talk with that guy. I don't like the sound of this."

"Well, that's not the only reason I got so upset. Not really. Although it was kinda creepy. But there's something else." Janie paused for breath. "Yesterday . . . when I got home . . . I mentioned it to my mom—you know, how I've noticed this man a bunch of times around town. It seems like I've seen him wherever I've been."

"I'm sure she's concerned for the same reason I am."

"Well, that's just it. Not really. She got mad. She started grilling me about where I was and what I was doing. She was really angry at me, Lucky." The tears started to flow again. "And I don't know why. It was like I did something wrong. And I didn't."

Lucky was reminded again how young and sheltered Janie was. Seeing her every day at the restaurant, marveling at her efficiency, it was easy to assume Janie was much more of an adult than she really was. The truth was that Janie was a kid just out of high school.

"I doubt she was really mad at you or thought you did anything wrong. Maybe she was just frightened some man might be bothering you." Lucky waited for a response. When none was forthcoming, she continued, "Just remember, she's trying to adjust to being alone." Lucky softened her voice. "Your Dad's passing has been really hard for her. She wants to protect you, and she's probably worrying too much about everything."

Lucky reached across the desk and retrieved a box of tissues. "Here. Blow your nose and wipe your eyes. I'm sure your mom felt bad as soon as she jumped on you. You'll go home tonight, and she'll apologize."

"I guess," Janie replied, not sounding too sure of her mother's apology at all.

"She will. I can't imagine how much I'd worry if I had a young daughter and I was alone in the world. You'll see."

Janie sniffled and wiped her cheeks. "Thanks, Lucky. You're the best."

Lucky reached over and gave her a quick hug. "Stay here for a few minutes if you like. Meg and I will be fine."

Janie nodded sheepishly. "Okay. Just for a minute if that's okay. I'll be out front in a bit."

Lucky slipped out the door and went down the hall to the kitchen.

Sage looked up. The counter was piled with chopped vegetables. "Everything okay?"

"Sure. She'll be fine. Fight with Mom, that's all."

Sage smiled ruefully and returned to his work.

Chapter 7

LUCKY FOUND MARJORIE and Cecily at the counter when she returned. Meg had already filled their order of tea and croissants while other customers had paid and left. Lucky quickly cleared away the cups, saucers and dishes, dropping them into a large plastic bin, and wiped off the counter. She approached the sisters.

"More tea?"

"No dear, we're fine," Marjorie replied. "We need to get to the shop."

"You're earlier than usual today," Lucky observed.

"Yes. We decided that with all these new people coming through town, we'd have a bit more business."

The bell over the door rang, and an older gentleman in casual clothes stepped in. He approached the counter and took a seat one stool away from Cecily. Cecily, always friendly and outgoing, smiled and said hello.

"How do you do?" he replied, smiling in their direction.

"Would you like some coffee to start?" Lucky asked the new arrival.

"Yes. I'd love some." He checked the blackboard on the wall. "How about a bowl of that pumpkin rice soup?"

"Sure," Lucky smiled. "We have some very fresh bakery rolls in today too."

"That would be great." He smiled charmingly, first at Lucky and then again at Cecily.

Lucky noticed Cecily quickly checking her hair as though concerned about her appearance. She sat a little straighter on her stool while her sister Marjorie, on her other side, glanced coolly at the newcomer.

"Are you here for the Harvest Festival?" Cecily asked the stranger.

"Uh, no. But I've heard about the festival. Is it interesting?"

"Oh yes. It's quite fun. Lots of things for the little kids with Halloween and all, but the smaller local farms bring their organic produce and handmade goods—all sorts of things to buy.

"Do you live in the area?" Cecily chirped.

"Actually, no. I live closer to Bennington, but I like to take day trips. Now that I'm retired I have way too much time on my hands."

"Oh, how nice. To be retired, I mean. What sort of work did you do?"

Lucky set the bowl of soup and a bread plate with a roll and butter on the placemat. She caught Marjorie giving her sister a discreet nudge with her elbow. Marjorie, the more reserved of the two, was undoubtedly letting her sister know she was being too forward with a strange man. Cecily ignored the signal and continued to smile.

"Well, I'm an . . . I *was* an insurance investigator. In a way maybe I still am." He smiled sheepishly. "Can't teach an old dog and all that. Can't really let it go." He reached across the empty stool and offered his hand. "Joe Conrad."

Cecily shook the proffered hand. "I'm Cecily Winters . . . and this is my sister Marjorie."

Joe Conrad half stood respectfully. "Very pleased to meet you both. And do you ladies live in Snowflake?"

"Yes, we do," Cecily said. Marjorie sniffed audibly. Cecily continued, "We have the Off Broadway ladies' shop just down the street."

"Ah, I see. Well, you're very lucky. It's a lovely little town."

"It is, isn't it?" Cecily simpered.

Joe picked up his spoon and tasted the soup. He looked up at Lucky. "This is delicious." He continued to sample the soup and broke open the roll. He turned to Cecily. "You know . . . I heard . . ." He trailed off. "Well, never mind that."

"What is it? You were about to say something?"

Joe Conrad cleared his throat. "Well, I overheard a conversation when I stopped at the market a little while ago. Something about a man found dead in a car crash. Have you heard about this?"

Cecily gasped. "No. I haven't. Have you?" She looked at Lucky.

Lucky was privy to the information only because Nate had stopped in at the Spoonful the night before. It was his habit to drop by when the restaurant was closed to talk to Jack. Nate respected the older man and enjoyed hearing Jack's perspective on things. She wasn't about to give out any details of Nate's plans to identify the dead man. "I had heard a rumor, but that's all I know," she answered diplomatically.

"Ah." Joe Conrad nodded. He seemed lost in thought.

Janie returned to the front room through the swinging door. She headed to one of the large tables and began helping Meg clear away dishes.

Joe spoke. "I wonder if you could point me in the direction of the local constabulary? I'd like to introduce myself."

"Be happy to," Lucky said. "Nate Edgerton is our Chief of Police and the station is just a few blocks away at the corner of Ash Street and Green. If he's not there, you can always leave a message for him."

"I'll do that. Can you recommend a place to stay for a couple of days?"

Cecily looked at Lucky for confirmation. "Well, there's always the Resort—the Snowflake Lodge. It's open all year, but you might like the old Drake House better. That's what we call it—it's a bed-and-breakfast. Very comfortable. You can't miss it. It's a big yellow house with white shutters at the edge of town just before you reach the Mohawk Trail."

"Wonderful. That should do fine." Joe Conrad stood. "That soup was excellent, by the way," he said to Lucky. "I'll definitely be back."

Lucky smiled. "We have a fabulous chef. Come back soon."

"Ladies." He turned to the sisters again. "Thanks so much for your good advice."

Cecily twittered. "Do stop in and see us at the shop."

"I will do that. Thanks again." Joe Conrad turned away and headed to the cash register to pay his bill. He spoke a few words to Jack and then left.

"What a nice man," Cecily remarked when the stranger had gone. She leaned across the counter and whispered. "And so attractive."

Marjorie pursed her lips and remained silent.

"Yes," Lucky said. "He seemed like a very nice man. I wonder if he's in Snowflake for some other reason than just passing through?"

"Oh," Cecily gasped. "Do you think he's hot on the trail of a criminal? Is that what he meant when he said he 'can't let it go'?" Her eyes grew wide. "How exciting."

Lucky suppressed a smile. Marjorie had a stern expression on her face, but Cecily had definitely found Joe Conrad fascinating.

Chapter 8

WHEN THE LUNCHTIME rush slowed a few hours later, and Lucky had a chance to breathe, she realized Elias hadn't stopped in. Whenever he could, he would come by for lunch. Perhaps he had been too busy today. But surely if Elias had already hired another doctor, his schedule should have freed up. She cast her mind back to the morning he was at the counter. A sense of unease started to form in her chest. Something had been bothering him that day. She had noticed, but he'd left so quickly she hadn't had the chance to question him further.

"Jack." She called to her grandfather. "I'm taking a break. I'll be back in half an hour."

"Go right ahead, my girl. It's five bells now. Should be quiet for a while."

Lucky pulled off her apron and hung it on a hook in the hallway. The Spoonful's aprons were yellow with the design of a steaming bowl of soup in blue. Her mother, Martha, had designed these and Lucky was determined never to change them. It was their logo, as was the blue and

yellow neon sign in the window that her Dad had created
to echo the colors and design of the apron.

Lucky walked through the short alleyway that led to
Broadway and turned the corner on Maple. The Snowflake
Clinic was close, around the corner and next to her apartment building. When she reached the heavy glass front
door, she spotted Rosemary, the Clinic's receptionist, at
the desk with a phone to her ear. A few patients were waiting in the outer room.

Rosemary raised a hand in greeting when she noticed
Lucky. She was nodding and obviously listening to a caller.
She pointed Lucky in the direction of the door to the inner
rooms to indicate that Elias was in his office and she should
go right in. Rosemary turned away to grab a pen and
started jotting down a message.

Lucky did really want to see Elias, but she also had to
admit to a great deal of curiosity about the man discovered
in the wreck. She tapped lightly on the office door as she
stepped inside. Elias was seated behind his desk, leaning
back in the chair. A beautiful dark-haired woman sat at the
front edge of his desk, facing him. Lucky's greeting froze
on her lips. The woman's position and body language were
so intimate.

"Lucky!" Elias stood, forcing the woman to move away,
which she did slowly and reluctantly.

Lucky stared silently at Elias for a few seconds. She was
taken aback at the scene. Nothing was actually going on,
but there was no mistaking the energy in the room.

"I . . . uh . . . just stopped in to visit."

Elias cleared his throat. "Um . . . good." He stared at her
for a moment. "Lucky, I'd like you to meet Paula Sarens,
our new MD at the Clinic. Paula . . . Lucky Jamieson."

The two women regarded each other silently for a
moment. Lucky nodded. A smile played at the corner of
Paula's lips.

Lucky broke the silence. "Very nice to meet you. Elias

mentioned a new doctor would be coming. I just didn't realize it had already happened." She turned to Elias with a quizzical look.

"How nice to meet you too." The woman's voice was husky and deep. Her smile, Lucky thought, was sleek and feline.

Elias fidgeted. He seemed uncomfortable.

Lucky turned to him, doing her best to maintain a neutral tone. "If you're busy, it can wait. I was just curious about Nate's discovery yesterday."

"Oh. Yes. Well . . ." Elias trailed off.

"We can catch up later."

"That might be a good idea," Elias responded.

Lucky glanced at Paula, who continued to smile. Her look was a cool survey, as though Lucky had been judged and found wanting.

"I'll speak with you later," Lucky replied. She turned away and headed back to the waiting room. Elias followed her.

"I'm sorry, Lucky. We can catch up tonight. I've just been so busy. I'll give you a call."

"Yes, you do seem busy." She did her best to keep a sarcastic tone from her voice but doubted she was successful. She forced a smile and walked through the waiting area to the front door. She didn't bother to wave to Rosemary.

Chapter 9

LUCKY SLOWLY DRIFTED up to consciousness from a heavy sleep. A horrible racket was pulling her from her dream. Groggily, she reached over to the nightstand and felt for the alarm clock. After two attempts, she was finally able to grasp the smooth, round plastic surface. She pushed the alarm button down but the ringing continued. Lucky groaned. It was the phone.

She forced herself to sit up and turned on the bedside lamp, then fumbled in the bedcovers for the alarm clock that had slipped from her fingers. She found it and, squinting, stared at its face. Three a.m. Who could possibly be calling her at this hour? *Jack! It must be Jack*, she thought. Something must be wrong. He might need help.

The phone stopped ringing. She sat for a moment, wondering if it had been a wrong number, wondering if she could lay down and go back to sleep. She definitely needed to get an extension for the bedroom, or at least make sure her cell phone was nearby. She fell back against the pillows and clicked the button on the alarm clock to reset it for the morning. She closed her eyes and soon felt the fog of unconsciousness numbing her brain. The phone rang again. This time she climbed out of bed and hurried to the kitchen, grabbing it on the third ring.

"Hello," she croaked.

"Lucky? It's Miriam. Miriam Leonard."

Lucky wracked her brain. Why would Janie's mother be calling her in the middle of the night?

"I'm so sorry to call you like this. I'm just worried sick. Is Janie with you?" Lucky could hear the tinge of panic in Miriam's voice.

"No. She's not. She's not home?"

It was obvious Miriam was upset and had been crying. "We . . . we had an argument. It was nothing really . . . stupid. Janie got very upset and she went out. She said she was just going for a drive, but she's not back and I'm worried sick."

"Have you tried Meg's house? She'd probably go there." Lucky remembered Janie's friendship with Rosemary, the receptionist at the Clinic, but she had no idea where Rosemary lived. Lucky couldn't imagine what kind of an argument Janie could have had with her mother to cause her to stay out all night. As far as she knew, they had always been close. Until today she had never heard a word of complaint from Janie about their relationship.

"I did. I called Meg's house, but no one there has seen or heard from Janie." Her voice rose an octave. "I don't know what to do." Miriam was barely keeping the panic at bay.

"I'm so sorry, Miriam. Look," Lucky said, "why don't I drive around and maybe I'll spot her car."

"I hate to drag you out of bed."

Lucky didn't want to remind Miriam she had already been dragged out of bed. The mere effort of trying to think of where Janie might have gone had brought Lucky to full consciousness. She knew she'd never be able to get back to sleep now.

"I'm afraid to go out looking for her myself in case she's in trouble somewhere and calls the house."

"You're right. You should stay by the phone just in case. And if you haven't heard from her by morning, then maybe you should call Nate."

"Oh dear God." Miriam breathed. "If something's happened to her . . ."

Lucky quickly jumped in. "I'm sure it hasn't. I'm sure she's just upset about the argument." An image of her own parents' crushed car flashed through her mind. She could imagine the hysteria that Miriam was struggling with. "If she's anywhere in town, I'll spot her car. I'll call you when I get back or when I know something."

"Thank you, Lucky. I just didn't know who else I could call. I thought you might have a clue where she could have gone."

Miriam, a recent widow now, had no family that anyone knew about. Lucky felt a wave of compassion. What would it be like to be alone in the world and have no family? No one to turn to in case of emergency?

"I can't imagine where she'd go, Miriam. But if she's in town, I'll find her. I'll call you back as soon as I can."

Lucky hung up. She was wearing only a flimsy nightie, and the nights were getting progressively chillier. She slipped on a pair of jeans, tucking the nightgown inside the waistband, and slipped on her sneakers. Then she pulled a heavy cable-knit sweater over her head. Grabbing her keys and purse, she touched the nose of her folk art kitchen witch for luck, then hurried out of the apartment and down the stairs. Her car was an older subcompact that had been a gift from Elizabeth Dove, the Mayor of Snowflake and her parents' oldest friend. The apartment Lucky rented was in a building that also belonged to Elizabeth. Lucky felt incredibly grateful to Elizabeth every time she turned her key in the lock of the car or the apartment. Returning to Snowflake would have been so much harder without Elizabeth's generosity.

Lucky revved the engine and started a sweep of the town. Snowflake was a small village. She could cruise its perimeter and then go up and down the interior streets, which mostly ran in a grid. Miriam's house was just outside of the town center, and Janie always drove to work. If Janie were anywhere in town, her car should be easy to find.

Lucky shivered and flicked on the car's heater, hoping it wouldn't take long to warm up. She circled the town slowly. No lights were on in any of the houses or buildings, and a slight dusting of frost covered the windshields of cars parked on the street. Most houses in town had garages, but since the late October weather had been so mild, there was no need as yet to shelter a car. By the time she completed a circuit of the town, the inside of her car was toasty. She drove slowly, hoping to spot Janie's car as she passed. As a ploy to stay awake, she decided to count the pumpkins that sat on doorsteps. She turned the corner on Hampstead, Elias's street.

If Janie wasn't at Meg's house, she could be staying with Rosemary, her other close girlfriend. Rosemary worked at the Clinic, so Elias would probably have her home number, but that would involve calling him at—she checked the clock in the car—three thirty now. She approached the big white Victorian that Elias had bought and spent several years renovating. No lights shone at any of the windows. She really didn't want to wake him. His days were long and busy, and he needed his sleep as much as she did. Besides, she was feeling a nagging sense of anxiety over his somewhat distant behavior, especially after meeting Paula, the new doctor. If she woke him in the middle of the night, it might seem as if she were checking up on him.

She pushed the thought out of her mind. It wouldn't do to call Elias at this hour no matter what the reason, and more than likely, he'd have no idea where Janie was anyway. He might not have Rosemary's phone number handy and would have to retrieve it from the Clinic. Lucky slowed as she passed the entrance to his driveway. A small dark car was parked there. It wasn't Elias's—his was a silver sedan. She hit the brakes and peered out, trying to get a better look at the license plate. It was too dark to make it out, but it wasn't a Vermont plate. Was someone visiting him?

Again, thoughts of the glamorous woman she met at the Clinic flooded her mind. And a fresh wave of confusion tinged with jealousy arose. What was going on? Was Paula staying with him? Was there a real basis for her anxiety? Was she a fool to have believed her relationship with Elias was on solid ground? In her imagination she pictured herself banging on his door, waking him up, using Janie's disappearance as an excuse to find out exactly who was staying with him. Was it jealousy? As much as she hated to admit the possibility, yes, she was jealous, and she felt threatened. Then, remembering Paula's dark, feline smile, she was feeling very threatened.

Chapter 10

SHE WILLED HERSELF to push her angry thoughts away. There were more important things to worry about, namely Janie's whereabouts. Miriam would be waiting to hear from Lucky. She drove the length of Hampstead and patiently cruised up and down every street in Snowflake. She checked every alleyway and parking lot she could think of. There was no sign of Janie's car. There was one logical possibility. Perhaps Janie had headed for the Harvest Festival. It would have still been open and in full swing at the time Miriam said that Janie had stormed out of the house.

Lucky turned her car in the direction of the road out of town. It was only a few miles to the farmer's field where the festival was taking place. Lucky sighed. Best to leave no stone unturned. Once she left the safety of town, a wave of loneliness swept over her. The woods on either side were black against the night sky. Only a sliver of moon glowed above them. The night was playing tricks on her. Twice, she slowed, not sure which way the road turned, even though she knew this route well. Darkness had altered her perception. Either that or she was more tired than she was willing to admit. She yawned widely and rubbed her eyes, flicking on her high beams. When she saw the sign for the festival, she slowed and turned into the parking area. The gate was wide open. Her headlights cut a swath of light across the area. Not a single car, truck or van stood inside the lot. Janie was definitely not here.

Lucky drove a full circle and exited through the opening in the wooden fence. She turned toward town. Where would Janie have gone if she hadn't wanted to go home? And what kind of an argument could she have had with her mother that would have caused her to be so upset? Where did she spend most of her time? The Spoonful! Was it possible Janie had gone to the restaurant? But how could she spend the night there? There was no place to sleep. Lucky mentally kicked herself when she realized she should have checked the Spoonful first before cruising all over the countryside.

Once she reached the main part of town, she drove down Broadway and pulled into the alleyway that led to the small parking area behind the restaurant. Janie's car stood alone behind the restaurant, parked in the same spot she used every day. Lucky shook her head. *Stupid!* Why hadn't she thought to check here first? What was wrong with her brain? Hopefully, she could blame the oversight on lack of sleep.

She turned off the engine and climbed out. She snuggled into her sweater and hurried to the back door, turning her key in the lock. The hallway interior was dark, except for the glow from a small nightlight in the kitchen. Lucky flicked on the switch by the back door and illuminated the hallway leading to the front of the restaurant. She called out. "Janie? Are you here?"

No answer.

She walked to the door of the large storage closet and

pushed against it. It opened without a sound. She reached for the cord that controlled the overhead light. The storage space was brightly illuminated. Janie was curled up in a fetal position inside a sleeping bag on the wooden floor. Lucky saw a slight movement. Janie turned her head and squinted. When she realized she had been discovered, she sat up quickly.

"Lucky!" she exclaimed.

"Janie, what are you doing here?"

"Please don't be mad, Lucky." She rubbed sleep from her eyes. "I just didn't have anyplace else I could go. Without a lot of explanation anyway."

"Your mother is worried sick about you."

"She called you?" Janie squeaked.

"Yes. You shouldn't let her worry like that, no matter what happened."

Janie's jaw tightened. She looked like she was about to give a sharp retort but thought better of it. "I'm sorry, Lucky. I didn't mean for you to have to go looking for me."

"Well, I'm just relieved you're all right. But you can't spend the night like this—what's left of it. And you'll feel wretched in the morning. Besides, our insurance policy is very clear. We're not covered for employees who love us so much they can't go home."

Janie nodded sadly and climbed out of her sleeping bag. "Okay. I'm sorry. How did you know I was here?"

"I didn't. Didn't even occur to me you might come here. I spent the last hour driving all over town before a lightbulb went off in my brain." Janie groaned in response. "Don't ask me why I didn't think of the Spoonful first."

"I'm so sorry, Lucky. I didn't mean for you to get dragged into this. I figured I could get up and wash and get dressed and stash my sleeping bag in the car and no one would know I had even been here."

"Janie, you should go home. I'm sure the argument with your mother can't be that bad."

"It was. I'll leave, but I'm not gonna go home."

Lucky heaved a sigh. "If you're not going home, then you're coming back with me. I have a very comfortable sofa you can sleep on until we sort this out."

"You mean that?" Janie looked up hopefully.

"Sure. It's fine. On one condition though. You have to call your mother and let her know you're safe. She's out of her mind right now."

"I don't want to talk to her. Can you call her?"

Chagrined, Lucky bit her tongue. She was losing patience as well as sleep, but she didn't want to say anything that would push Janie over the edge. Better for the girl to sleep on her sofa than be wandering who knew where all night.

"All right. I'll call her. Grab your stuff. We can walk back to my place. Just leave your car where it is."

"Thanks, Lucky. Thank you so much." Janie threw her arms around Lucky's neck and hugged her.

"What did you two argue about that was so awful? You've always gotten along great with your mom."

Janie's face fell. "You'd never believe me if I told you."

Chapter 11

THE FOLLOWING MORNING at the Spoonful Lucky kept a close watch on Janie. So far, she seemed to be doing fine. She was a lot less nervous than she had been on the previous days, but Lucky noticed she would occasionally stare out the window, as though expecting the stranger to be there. Miriam had been relieved and grateful when Lucky had called the night before to let her know Janie had been found and was safe. Miriam sounded rather sheepish on the phone and apologetic, but offered no further explanation as to why Janie had stormed out.

The Spoonful was crowded. The din of the restaurant made it impossible to hear the bell, but movement at the door caught Lucky's attention. She looked up to see Ernie White. He entered, accompanied by two men who more than likely worked for him at the festival. Ernie, overweight and not in the best of shape, wore an expensive gray suit while the two men were in jeans, boots and work shirts. Meg seated them at a table and passed out menus.

Lucky glanced over at Jack. She could tell he had

spotted Ernie. She hoped Ernie didn't decide to approach her grandfather again about setting up a booth at the festival. Jack turned in her direction and shot her a meaningful look, indicating Ernie with a jerk of his head. Lucky nodded in response.

She heard the clatter of dishes behind her. She grabbed three orders from the kitchen hatch and placed them on trays for Janie and Meg to deliver. She looked up as Elizabeth Dove came through the front door. Lucky waved to her and pointed to an empty stool. Since Elizabeth had become Mayor of Snowflake, her schedule was so busy that Lucky rarely had a chance to visit and chat with her.

"Early lunch?" Lucky asked. She knew Elizabeth always had breakfast at home and started her day at the municipal offices early.

"Yes. I have a meeting in an hour, but I'm starving now." Elizabeth smiled. Lucky thought the older woman looked healthy and completely back to normal. A few months before Elizabeth had been held prisoner on the orders of a man she had trusted. Elizabeth looked up at her questioningly. "What is it?"

Lucky smiled widely. "You just look so fantastic."

"I am perfectly fine." Elizabeth laughed. "Now stop worrying about me."

"What can I get you?"

"I'd love to try that new beet and barley soup with maybe a bakery roll?"

"It's delicious. How about a rosemary roll from Bettie's Bakery? The flavor would go nicely with that soup."

"Can I get it to go?" Elizabeth asked.

"Of course." Lucky placed the order slip on the hatch. She turned back to Elizabeth and leaned over the counter. "So tell me, how is everything?"

"It's fine . . . I have a meeting about the . . ." Before Elizabeth could complete her sentence, Ernie White slid onto the stool next to her.

"Elizabeth! How are you?" Ernie managed to make his greeting sound as if he were holding court and Elizabeth was a supplicant for his favors.

"I'm fine, Ernie. And you?" Elizabeth's tone was pleasant but, to Lucky's ears, distant. She knew Elizabeth's guard was up. Ernie had the knack of affecting a lot of people that way. And Lucky was sure Ernie's intent related only to his own agenda, not just to passing the time of day.

"Lucky, I'm glad I caught you." Something oily and overly friendly in Ernie's tone raised her hackles. "I've been talking to your grandfather about the Spoonful providing food at the festival—you know, a nice little booth. Chance to expose more people to the restaurant. I'd even be willing to negotiate my percentage."

"Jack's been over this before with you, Ernie. It's not worth our while."

"I'd go sixty-forty with you. Forty for you, sixty for me."

Lucky was nonplussed. "What part don't you get, Ernie?"

Elizabeth watched the exchange with amusement.

Lucky glanced over at Jack, who had started to rise from his stool behind the cash register. She shot him a look to let him know she had the situation under control. "Why would we split anything with you? Assuming we even had the staff to run a concession, which we don't. We're doing just fine as it is."

"Well . . ." Ernie smiled. "It wasn't that long ago you were almost belly up. I wouldn't be so quick to get on my high horse if I were you."

Elizabeth was silent, but her eyebrows raised a notch. She was well aware Lucky had a temper, and if Ernie hadn't already experienced it, he was pushing real hard to expose it.

Lucky's face flushed deeply. She knew it was happening and couldn't do much about it. The pitfalls of having such fair skin. "I'll tell you what, Ernie. I'll keep your very generous offer in mind. Now, is there anything else you'd like? If not, Jack's right over there to collect your money."

Ernie's face shifted from oily to mean. "Have it your way. But don't come begging for a shot at a booth next year." He rose quickly and headed to the cash register, slapping some bills in front of Jack. He walked out the door without another word, the two men in work clothes trailing behind him.

Lucky shuddered. "He just always manages to bring out my worst side. I'm with Jack on that one," she said to Elizabeth.

"I don't blame you," Elizabeth responded. "Seems there's always a dagger under that insinuating tone. He's managed to make some enemies since he's been in Lincoln Falls, or so I've heard."

"I can believe that." Lucky hesitated. "What did you say? Since he's been in Lincoln Falls? I thought he was from there originally."

"I don't think so. He comes from . . . actually, I don't really know where he's from. Someone told me, but I don't recall offhand. He's been in Lincoln Falls for maybe five or six years. He's been very successful, but I don't think he's made a lot of friends. The sooner he goes back to wherever he came from, the better, I say."

Marjorie slid onto the empty stool next to Elizabeth. She stashed the shopping bag she was carrying under the counter at her feet. "Elizabeth. Haven't seen you for a while. How have you been?"

"Oh, just fine, Marjorie. Where's your sister today?"

Marjorie pursed her lips. "She's very busy. Couldn't make it."

Lucky's ears went up. She couldn't recall a day when the two sisters weren't together.

Elizabeth picked up her order. "Have to run." She stood and blew Lucky a kiss. "Marjorie, good to see you too.

We'll have to catch up some other time." She smiled and walked over to the cash register.

"Tea and a croissant, today?" Lucky asked Marjorie.

"Yes, dear. That would be fine." Marjorie was never talkative, but today she seemed nervous and upset.

Lucky carried the cup of tea and buttered croissant to the placemat. "Is everything all right?" she asked. Marjorie looked close to tears.

"Oh . . ." Marjorie shrugged her shoulders and took a deep breath. "Cecily isn't speaking to me right now. We had a terrible row."

"I'm sorry to hear that." Lucky had always noticed the differing personalities between the sisters, but never remembered a disagreement between them.

Marjorie leaned over the counter and whispered, "That man we met here . . . he stopped in at the shop yesterday, just as we were closing. And he asked her to have dinner with him! Can you believe that?" Marjorie's tone was indignant. "I didn't say anything in front of him, but I told her later she was taking an awful chance having a date with a strange man."

"Ah." Lucky nodded seriously, in what she hoped was a neutral tone.

Marjorie continued. "After all, he's a complete stranger in town. We really know nothing about him." Lucky was relieved no one was sitting close to Marjorie who could overhear her remarks. Marjorie took a sip of her tea. "Cecily became very upset with me. And when I reminded her . . . you know, she had a terrible blow years and years ago. She . . ." Marjorie leaned closer. "She was jilted, almost at the altar. Well, not exactly, but another few days and it would have happened that way quite literally. Well, she just blew up at me. That's the only way I can put it. Told me what she thought of me and my opinion." Marjorie sniffed back a tear. She looked truly wounded to have her good advice rejected so vehemently.

"I didn't know. What an awful experience for her to have. I'm so sorry," Lucky commiserated.

"I realize my sister isn't like me. I'm perfectly happy as a spinster. Never met a man I would have wanted to share my life with. Who really needs 'em, I say. But Cecily . . . she's such a trusting soul. I just couldn't bear it if my sister got hurt like that again."

Lucky was torn. She wanted to remind Marjorie that her sister was a free agent and shouldn't spend her life in a bubble, but at the same time she could understand an older sister's desire to protect a vulnerable sibling from hurt. "Oh, oh." Lucky touched Marjorie's arm. "Here comes Nate with that insurance investigator in tow." Joe Conrad had obviously been successful in locating Nate.

Marjorie took a last bite of her croissant. "I'm leaving now." Without futher ado, she gathered up her shopping bag and purse. "I'd rather not have to deal with the man who caused our argument last night." She stood and headed for the cash register.

Lucky watched as Nate paused on the sidewalk before coming into the restaurant. He was staring at Ernie White, who stood on the sidewalk talking to the two men who had been with him at the restaurant. Nate leaned toward Conrad and made a remark. Conrad nodded in response, and then together the two men entered the restaurant.

Chapter 12

ONCE THE LUNCH rush died down, Lucky joined Jack, Nate and Joe Conrad at their table where they lingered over coffee. Janie manned the cash register while Meg cleared off the remaining tables.

"I guess you two have already met Joe," Nate said.

Jack reached across the table to shake Joe's proffered hand.

"Hello again," Lucky said. "I see you found Nate."

"Joe's been retired for a while, but he was telling me about his last case. Very interesting," Nate said.

Joe smiled sheepishly. "It's my ego, or maybe pride, I guess. It just galled me that I had to retire—company policy—before I could close this one out. The young guy that took over my caseload couldn't do anything with it either."

"What company are we talking about, Joe?" Jack asked.

"I was with Union Fidelity my whole career. And not to brag too much, but I had a great record as an investigator.

All except for this one last case. I guess that's why I can't let it go."

"You think your company might be willing to share their records?" Nate asked.

"I don't know. I can ask, if you like, but they might want a subpoena to do that."

"Well, if it turns out this might be related, I'll give them a call."

"You have no connection with the company anymore?" Jack asked.

"Nope. But I sure would like to bring this one to them on a silver platter. Not for any reward or anything, but who knows, maybe they'd rethink their strict retirement policy."

"What's it about?" Jack asked.

"About seven years ago, there was an armored truck robbery. You may remember it—over at Bennington."

"I do remember," Jack said. "It was all over the news."

"It was pretty terrible. There were two guards on duty in the company's office early that morning. Another man, dressed in a guard's uniform with a ski mask, busted in. One of the two guards resisted and was killed. He was a young guy with little kids. Very sad."

"And they never caught the man who did it?" Lucky asked.

"Nope. Never did. The company had to pay out on the loss after all. What happened was this . . ." Joe said, taking a last sip of his coffee. "It's pretty definite it wasn't just the one man involved. It was a pretty secure bunker, so one of the two guards in the facility had to be in on it. Although it took the police a little while to get suspicious of him. He may have even masterminded the heist. What I think, and the police at the time came around to thinking, was that the inside man, one of the guards, turned off the alarm and left the outer door unlocked. The other guard, the young

guy who got killed, must have been completely unaware
that it was a setup. The police went over his life with a
fine-tooth comb, but they never turned up anything suspicious. Nothing to indicate he had been involved."

Joe looked around the table, sure he had piqued the
interest of his listeners. "The intruder had a weapon and
ordered the two guards to transfer a shipment of cash to
the armored truck out in the lot. They didn't have much
choice, so they followed his orders. Once the cash was
loaded, the guy with the gun grabs the keys to the truck
and orders the two guards back into the building. It's early
in the day, and there's no one else around, no other guards
on duty. At first, we thought the young guard foolishly
decided to be a hero and got shot for his trouble." Joe shook
his head. "After that happened, the man with the weapon
took off in the armored truck."

"Was it the other guard who was the inside guy? Who
turned off the alarm?" Lucky asked.

"I believe so. He claimed complete innocence. Said he
didn't know what was happening, but he didn't turn off the
alarm. He said the other guard must have been in on it and
was shot by his cohort . . . The more the police sniffed
around, the more his story didn't hold water. He was questioned a few more times, and eventually his version of
events didn't make sense. Sadly, no one thought to do a test
for gunpowder on his hands.

"The detectives finally came to the conclusion that the
guard who was still alive had to be the inside man. He had
turned off the alarm, left the door unlocked and shot his
coworker. Possibly the man who broke in with the weapon
didn't shoot at all, maybe because he was never attacked.
Maybe . . . and this is just speculation . . . maybe the young
guy realized that the other guard had to be in on it. Maybe
he said something, maybe he indicated suspicion, who
knows? And the inside guy decided to get rid of him. Why
leave a witness alive? So, to answer your question, we

never found out who the man that drove away with the armored truck was, although I had some ideas."

"The guard you believed was guilty, did he ever give up the name of his partner?"

"He never did. Initially, with all the commotion, no one checked the remaining guard thoroughly enough. When they finally got suspicious and started to question him, he took off. Disappeared. They later discovered his identity was false. The company wasn't large, and they were a little sloppy with their due diligence, and this guy was slick. The police later matched his photo to a guy who was wanted in another state for armed robbery."

"So, if either one of them is found or picked up for some reason, they could still be prosecuted, right?"

"Not unless that happens within the next month."

"What do you mean?" Jack asked.

"Statute of limitations. There's a seven-year statute of limitations for robbery in our state. And in another month, it'll be seven years."

"But surely not for murder?" Lucky asked.

"That's right. Not for murder." Joe nodded.

"Quite a story," Jack said.

"My company had to pay off on the loss. I know it's not my job anymore, but I sure would love to see those guys apprehended. You see . . . the young guard who died . . . he was the son of one of my neighbors. So I guess you could say I have a personal interest."

"That's why Joe stopped in to see me," Nate said. "He suspects the man we found on the road might be one of the two responsible for that armored truck heist."

Jack whistled. "What makes you think that?"

"Long story, but as I mentioned, the guard who disappeared had a record. Getting that job under a false identity was a lot easier to do even just a few years back. So the police started looking at his known associates, looking hard, but nothing led back to any of his partners in crime.

They picked up the people who had been involved with
him in the past and grilled them, but they never got a thing.
It led the police to think that none of them knew anything
about this robbery. They never even got a clue where to
start looking. Nothing.

"However," Joe smiled, remembering his glory days,
"there was a carnival in town at the time, and I have always
suspected we might have found our guy there. Oh, I almost
forgot. The armored truck was eventually found in the
woods a few months later, and the lab found sawdust and
animal hairs. That just confirmed my suspicion. These
people move around a lot—travelers I guess you'd call
them. Impossible to trace. By the time the police were
ready to start questioning some of those men, they had
moved on." Joe shrugged. "I have a lot of time on my hands
these days, and I like to drive around. So I always try to
stop at some of these festivals and carnivals around the
state in the summer months. I heard about this festival,
that's what brought me to Snowflake. I thought maybe
there'd be a chance some of the same people might be
working out there at the kiddie rides or the farmers' market. I've always suspected our guy was someone who just
wasn't on the radar in any real way."

Nate listened silently as Joe talked.

"Nate can't get a bead on who that guy was they discovered on the road, and Nate thinks . . ." Joe hesitated, looking to Nate for permission to speak further.

"Go right ahead. We're among friends here," Nate
replied.

"Nate thinks there's something hinky about that driver's
license. This guy could very well be a traveler—a gypsy."

"Even if he is, why would you think he was the same
man involved in that robbery years ago?" Lucky asked.

Joe Conrad shrugged. "No solid reason. It's just a hunch.
When I heard about a dead man with a bullet wound that
nobody knew, my ears went up. Just thought I'd check it out

as much as I could. And even if by some long shot the dead man is the same guy, I don't know what good that would do. Oh, one thing I forgot to mention—there was a witness to what happened, although she was pretty shook up. She was going through an intersection on a green light when the armored truck barreled through. Almost wiped her out. She hit the brakes and managed to avoid the accident. She was in a bit of shock, but she did get a close look as the guy pulled off his ski mask. Eventually she was able to give the police artist enough for a sketch. Here, I'll show you."

Joe pulled a well-worn piece of paper out of his inside jacket pocket. A wanted poster showing a black-and-white sketch of a man with a long face, high cheekbones and receding hairline. "How accurate this is, I can't say, but it was the best we could do at the time. I've shown this to Nate." Joe passed the poster across the table to Jack.

Nate spoke. "It's real hard to be certain. His face was pretty messed up, and I wasn't about to move the body till the techs could get there. Besides," Nate shrugged, "I don't know what good it'll do anybody if this guy turns out to be involved. He's dead, the other guy's disappeared, and I'm sure the money's long gone."

"How much did they get away with?" Jack asked.

"Pretty good sum as these things go. Eight hundred and some odd thousand."

"That's huge," Lucky remarked.

"You can say that again."

"I'm gonna take Joe over to Lincoln Falls to have a better look at this guy," Nate said. "If his driver's license and van registration don't check out, he could very well be a traveler—we get 'em through every so often. Some of 'em come down from Canada. As long as they don't cause any trouble, I have no objection. Wouldn't be my choice of a lifestyle, but I guess it suits them."

"What was this guy driving?" Jack asked.

"An old customized van, pretty beat up though. It's at

the impound lot in Lincoln Falls for now." Lucky heard the
bell over the door ring. She twisted in her chair and saw
Miriam standing on the threshold. Miriam stepped into the
restaurant and headed to the counter where Janie was
working. She leaned across and spoke softly to Janie.
Janie's cheeks suddenly flushed. She flung a dish towel
down on the counter and ran through the door to the corridor. Miriam followed.

   Lucky excused herself from the group at the table. So
far, the small drama hadn't caught anyone's attention. She
hurried down the hallway and found Miriam at the rear
door, crying. Janie's car tires squealed as she pulled out of
the lot behind the restaurant.

Chapter 13

JANIE SAT HUDDLED at one end of the sofa. Lucky placed a mug of tea on the table in front of her and curled up at the other end of the sofa. Janie finally mumbled her thanks and picked up the tea.

"Look, Janie, I don't want to pry into your business, but from where I'm sitting, your mother hardly seems like a monster."

"You think I'm crazy, don't you." It was a statement not a question.

"I don't think any such thing. I just don't know what's going on. You and your mother . . . well, you two have always been so close. I don't understand."

Janie looked on the verge of tears. She clamped her jaw shut in an effort to control her feelings. "You'd never understand. You'd never get it."

"Try me." Lucky's heart was torn just looking at Janie's face. It was obvious she was suffering terribly. Earlier that day, Meg had done her best to offer comfort to Janie and had been rebuffed.

"You remember a couple of days ago when you saw me looking out the window at the Spoonful?"

Lucky nodded but didn't say a word. She was afraid to interrupt Janie's narrative now that she was willing to talk.

"When I went home that night, I mentioned it to my mother. I thought it was kinda creepy, 'cause I remembered seeing the same man in the market and the same man walking down my street, outside my house."

"I remember."

"I told you my mom had a real weird reaction. I could understand if she were concerned some stalker was around, but it wasn't that at all. She started yelling, like she was blaming me for something. Like I caused it. That's the best way I can put it. I was mad at her after that, so I just hid out in my room." Janie took a sip of her tea. "Later, my mother came to the door and said she was sorry, she didn't mean to get so upset, but she just had a lot on her mind. I was still kinda mad at her, so I pretended to be asleep."

Janie took a deep shaky breath. "The next evening, my mom was at a neighbor's for a little bit." Janie looked over the edge of her mug at Lucky. Her expression seemed slightly sheepish. "There was something about him—the man I mean. Something like . . . like I'd seen him before, before all this, or . . . something about him seemed familiar, I guess. I opened my mom's jewelry box. It has a secret compartment. She didn't know I knew about it, but I've seen her open it before and take out an old photograph. I never let on I knew. So . . ." Janie took another sip of tea.

Lucky was silent, listening. This was the best thing that could happen. Janie was finally ready to open up.

"I pulled out the old photo she kept in there." Janie took a deep shaky breath. "Lucky, it was the same man! A lot younger, but I'm *sure* it was the same man. Then I heard my mom come home. The front door slammed, and I heard her coming up the stairs. I should have just put the photograph back in the secret slot, but I didn't. I wanted to know what was going on.

"She came into the room, and she saw me holding the old photo. Her face turned all white. I thought she was going to faint. But I was still mad at her from the night before. I held it out, and I . . . I was yelling. I didn't mean to, but I was so . . . confused, I guess, upset and all." Janie fell silent for so long Lucky wondered if she would continue. "That's when she told me."

"What did she say?" Lucky whispered.

"That man is my father. My real father," Janie wailed. Her hands started to shake so badly, Lucky reached over and took the mug from her, placing it safely on the table. Janie burst into angry tears. "I started screaming at her. 'You're a liar! I have a father. You're a liar,' I said."

Lucky could imagine the shock Janie must have felt. She couldn't think what to say to calm the girl. She had been so attached to her father—the man she knew to be her father. His death had been very hard on her and surely difficult for her mother. But to learn that the man she loved was not truly her father . . . Lucky shook her head in disbelief.

"She tried to explain, but I guess I was yelling at her. She said this man was someone she had loved when she was young, but they were torn apart. At least I think that's what she was trying to say. She was crying by then, and I was yelling at her, and it was just awful. I freaked out. She was trying to tell me stuff, but I just covered my ears and ran out of the house." Janie reached over for a tissue, wiped her nose and eyes, and looked over at Lucky. "What does this mean? Was I an accident, Lucky? Was I an illegitimate child? What?" Janie demanded.

Lucky reached over and held Janie's hand. "I don't know. Obviously, there's a lot more to this story you just weren't ready to hear. It doesn't sound like you were an accident or illegitimate, whatever that means. It sounds like you were conceived because two people were very much in love. The fact that something happened to them, that they couldn't be together . . . well, that must have been out of their control. Stuff happens in life, Janie. Things people can't control. Lovers go off to war and never come back. But certainly, you were loved. You're the most important person in your mother's life. She's a lovely woman, no matter what happened to her when she was younger, and she's done her very best for you."

"And my father? Or the person I always loved and thought was my father—did he know I wasn't his child? Or was he just like my mom—lying to me my whole life? Or did she lie to him? When he died, I thought I would die. It was so terrible to lose him. Everybody else has a family, a mother and a father, except me. You—you couldn't possibly imagine what this feels like."

"Maybe I couldn't, but you know what? You have a mother that loves you with all her heart, and she's still on this earth. And the man who raised you *is* your father, even if he's not your biological parent. He loved you, and he was always there for you. My parents aren't here anymore. They're both gone. You have every right to know the truth, but Janie, you're so young. You can't even begin to imagine the things she might have suffered in keeping you and raising you. And she did. She didn't abandon you. Maybe you're right. Maybe your father, the father who raised you, knew the whole story and loved her and you just as if you were his own daughter? Maybe he wasn't free to tell you more."

"No," Janie snuffled. "I mean, I don't know. I don't know what the truth really is. And who is this man? Has he been following me around? And why? And where has he been for the past eighteen years? Why is he around now? And if this hadn't happened, would my mother have *ever* told me the truth?"

"Only your mother can answer those questions. I

think . . ." The sound of the phone ringing interrupted her train of thought. "Janie, hang on a minute. I'll see who it is and call them back."

Lucky walked back to the kitchen and grabbed the phone. It was Elias. What bad timing.

"Can I come over to see you?" he asked.

"Now?" she asked. This was an odd preamble to their evenings together. Usually Elias suggested dinner at his house or at a restaurant.

"If you're free," he answered. There was something in his tone that sounded as if he were making a business appointment.

"Actually, I'm not. Janie's staying with me right now. What about tomorrow night?"

"Uh . . . Lucky, I'd really like to talk to you, in private, if I could." Lucky felt a sinking feeling in her chest. This was so unlike him. They had been seeing each other for eight months. They were never formal with each other. In fact, Elias had virtually proposed on several occasions. She felt as if she had been suddenly relegated to the position of a third-circle friend. And it had started the day Elias told her he had hired another doctor. Another doctor—Paula Sarens. This had to have something to do with her! Lucky had disliked her the moment she set eyes on her. It was time to get to the bottom of whatever was bothering Elias.

"Why don't we have a drink at the Pub? I can meet you there in half an hour." She kept her tone reserved. There was nothing friendly about this meeting. She could feel it in her heart. Something had changed. Elias had changed— at least toward her.

Lucky returned to the living room. "Janie, I'm so sorry. Something's come up, and I have to go out for an hour maybe, but I'll be back, and we can talk some more, if you like."

"That's okay, Lucky. I'll be all right. I don't think I can talk about it anymore anyway. I'm just gonna crash. I didn't mean to dump all this on you. I've just been carrying it around for days it seems."

"You didn't dump on me. Don't say that. I *wanted* you to talk to me. Getting it all out is the best thing. And finding the answers to all your questions is the next step."

"I'm not really ready for that part just yet. I know you're right. I just appreciate your letting me stay here. I need some more time on my own right now."

"I understand. You can stay here as long as you need. If you're still up when I'm back, well, I'm a good listener."

Janie nodded. "Thanks."

Chapter 14

LUCKY FELT A knot forming in her stomach as she walked the length of Broadway to the Snowflake Pub. She hated to cut her conversation with Janie short, but there didn't seem to be another alternative. Elias hadn't pressed, but she could feel his determination to talk to her tonight. Whatever it was, it wasn't good; she could feel it in her bones. Elias had been distant and distracted the other day when he had stopped in at the Spoonful. She thought at first that he was just tired. He had been working long hours with no backup, and she had been thrilled when he told her he had hired another doctor, but there was an undercurrent of . . . what? Something not spoken? Something hidden? He didn't sound relieved about his decision. More as though he were dreading something. Since that day, he hadn't called or stopped by to see her at the restaurant for lunch as he usually did. Again, that was very unlike him.

Maybe it was best that they meet on neutral ground. They had been so close for so many months, and now something was wrong, but she didn't know what. As hard as this might be, it would be better to talk to him and find out exactly what was going on.

She felt a hot rush of anger rising in her chest as she approached the Pub. She knew she had fallen head over heels in love with Elias in the early days, and she believed he felt the same way. This ambiguous behavior on his part was confusing her. Normally, she would have brushed her hair and put on some lipstick, maybe even a little blush. After all, wasn't everyone always telling her she should be more feminine? No one denied she was good-looking, but she knew she was never one to care about fashion or her appearance. So be it. He'd get her as she was—tired, no doubt looking dragged out after her talk with Janie and a long day on her feet.

A noisy crowd was gathered at the near end of the bar as she pushed through the door. The overhead television was turned on, and the loud drone of a football game filled the air. She pushed past the group and spotted Elias sitting near the rear, behind the central fire pit that hadn't been lit for the winter yet. She slid into the booth across from him.

He looked up and smiled. He was nursing a beer. He reached across the table and took her hand. "What can I get you?"

"Red wine would be nice." She forced herself to smile in return. No point in being a downer right off the bat.

Elias slid out of the booth and headed for the bar. The waitress, the one that always flirted with him and made Lucky uncomfortable, was busy with her loud customers at the other end of the room. He returned with a glass of wine and a napkin. "Cabernet. A good one."

Lucky took a sip. "Sorry I couldn't invite you over. Janie's going through some stuff, and she's staying with me for a few days."

"She all right?"

Lucky shrugged. "Upset about some family matters, but

I think she'll be fine." *Although I may not.* She waited a few moments for him to speak. When he didn't, she finally said, "What's going on, Elias?"

He took a deep breath as if to steel himself. "I wanted to tell you this the other day, but I realized the Spoonful wasn't the place to talk."

Lucky waited, watching him carefully. There was nothing to criticize in his behavior, nothing concrete that is, but she knew she was right to feel the ground had shifted beneath her feet, an earthquake of the heart.

"You met Paula at the Clinic. The day you stopped by."

"Yes." *And, in fact, I didn't like her very much,* Lucky thought, but for once kept her mouth shut.

"The part I didn't mention is that Paula and I . . . well, we did our internships together and . . ."

"Elias, spit it out, please." Lucky could feel her face flushing.

"We had a relationship—years ago."

"A relationship." Lucky felt her eyebrows reaching toward her hairline. She did her best to keep her tone neutral. "What kind of relationship?"

"We were involved . . ."

Lucky felt her heart sink. What was he trying to say?

"We were planning to be together."

"Engaged? To be married?" Lucky was sure her voice had risen two octaves.

"Yes." Elias finally looked her straight in the eye.

"I see. And now you're working together?"

"Lucky . . . it's not like that. It was over years ago. As time went on, we realized we wanted different things in life. Paula was interested in a specialty practice, and I . . . well, you know how I feel about my work here. I love Snowflake. Paula never wanted to leave the city."

"And she does now?" Lucky couldn't keep the skepticism out of her voice.

"She's had second thoughts. And to be frank with you,

not a lot of what I would consider experienced, qualified people have applied."

This explained a lot. The feeling she had when she walked into Elias's office. The energy in the room. The fact that Paula had been so close to him, almost in a sexually suggestive way. Elias's embarrassment. She hadn't misread the signals.

"I just don't want you to be upset. I don't want anything to interfere in our relationship. You know how I feel about you."

Lucky felt as if she had been punched in the stomach. "Elias, I don't know what to say. All this time we've been together, you never once mentioned you were ever engaged to anyone. This is all news to me."

"We were never officially"—Elias shrugged—"engaged. We were close; we just assumed that's where it would lead."

"Did you love her?"

"I suppose I did. I felt that way at the time. It just dissipated slowly as I realized how different we were as people. It was amicable when we finally broke up. I just hope you're not upset about this. I'd really like this to work out for Paula too."

Lucky remembered the strange car she had seen parked in Elias's driveway the night before when she was searching for Janie. "Where is Paula staying?"

"Uh . . ." Elias hesitated. "She's actually . . . uh . . . she's staying in the spare room at my house until she can find her own place."

Lucky stared at him silently. She felt torn between tears and anger. She took a deep breath, not trusting herself to speak at first. "Elias—I'm just really feeling confused and trying not to be upset. First of all, you have never, not once, ever mentioned this relationship that was so important in your life. And now, you've actually hired an ex-fiancée, whatever she is, to work closely with you at the Clinic. And she's staying at your house? How else would you expect me to feel?"

As the words poured out, Lucky realized she sounded like an insecure, jealous lover, but she couldn't stop herself. What would the mature response be? The civilized one? *That's fine, I'm glad this is all out in the open?* Lucky was well aware of her own temper, and she could feel it gathering strength now.

"There's nothing for you to be jealous about." Elias's expression was smug.

"I'm not jealous," she replied hotly. "I'm just dumbfounded that you would choose to hire her."

"Whatever we had was over a long, long time ago, Lucky. We're friends now." Elias's face took on a superior look. "I would have expected you to understand."

"And how does Paula feel about you?"

"She's great. She knows that we're just friends. And she really wants to work hard and fit in here—in Snowflake. Her goals have changed. Can you understand that?"

"Yes, I think I do understand." *Elias, how can you be so blind*? It was obvious to her that, assuming Elias was being completely honest, Paula had another agenda. The fact that Paula was staying at his house meant that he and Lucky wouldn't have that space to themselves. He had to be deceiving himself about Paula's intent, and his cavalier attitude was making her angrier.

"I just didn't want you to feel that I hadn't been honest with you."

Lucky twirled her wineglass around in a pool of condensation that had formed on the tabletop. "Well, actually, you weren't honest with me."

"What are you saying? I've never lied to you."

"There are lies of omission, Elias." She stood, leaving her wine untouched.

"Are you leaving?" He looked shocked.

"Yes. I'm very tired. I'm going home."

"Let me walk you back, then."

"Don't bother. It's not necessary." Lucky stood and slipped on her jacket. Elias followed suit.

"I'm walking you back to your apartment. After all, I'm the one who dragged you out."

She had no choice. It was obvious he was going to insist. Frankly, she would have preferred some private time to sulk and feel justifiably angry on the way back to her very nonprivate apartment. Elias quickly threw some bills on the table and followed her as she hurried through the pub and pushed through the door to the street. She was silent as they walked along Broadway, passing by the darkened Spoonful. It was just as well Elias didn't try to make conversation, because she wasn't sure what would pop out of her mouth next.

When they arrived at her building on Maple Street, Elias followed her up the flight of stairs to her apartment door. "Lucky, look, it's obvious you're upset with me. We should talk about this."

She took a deep breath. "I don't know what I am right now, Elias. I feel . . . disoriented, I guess. It doesn't make me feel comfortable that Paula is staying in your guest room. I mean, how would you feel if the situation were reversed?"

"You mean if you hired a former love from your past and they were staying in your apartment?" Elias was silent for a moment. "Okay, maybe I wouldn't be thrilled, but I do think I'd have a bit more faith in you than you're showing me right now."

Lucky hated to admit it, but Elias had a point. "I'm sorry. It's just . . . if Paula were a different person . . ."

"Different how?"

"There's something about her that just gives me the willies. I can't explain it." Actually, Lucky thought she could probably explain it quite well to anyone but Elias.

She recalled the slow smile and the movements that reminded her of a cat preening itself.

"Now you're being silly." Elias smiled and leaned down for a kiss.

Lucky turned her face up to him. The kiss, when it came, felt like a perfunctory action, a necessary chore. It bore no resemblance to the heat and ardor he had shown on her threshold on prior nights.

"This week will be crazy for me. I've got to get Paula acclimated to our procedures. I have three patients scheduled for surgery in Lincoln Falls over the next few days, and all the rest of the stuff that goes on in the Clinic, but I'll give you a call in a day or so. We can go someplace special for dinner, if you like."

Lucky nodded. "Sounds great." She was glad the light from the hallway sconce was dim. She hoped the worried expression on her face didn't show. "Good night." Lucky turned away and slipped her key into the lock.

Elias hurried down the stairs and out the front door. Lucky leaned over the banister and watched his retreating back. *Damn, Paula*, she thought. *You don't fool me one bit.*

Chapter 15

LUCKY HEARD THE front door of the apartment slam as Janie left for work the following morning. She groaned and buried her face in the pillow, unwilling to face the day and embarrassed at her behavior the night before. She felt as if she had carried on the argument with Elias in her sleeping state. She cringed when she reviewed her words to him. As much as she was angry at his comment about her jealousy, she had to admit he was right. She was angry. She was jealous, and no doubt with good reason. She hadn't misread Paula's intent that day in his office—the strange woman's familiarity with him. Lucky was certain Paula had designs on Elias, a desire to renew their past relationship, for whatever reason. She was certain of it.

It wasn't that Elias had actually *done* anything unforgiveable. She didn't believe he had. It was just that in all the time they had been together, he had never even mentioned a prior important relationship. What else hadn't he mentioned over the past eight months? She took a deep breath. Her blood pressure was probably rising, and she hadn't even crawled out of bed. In fairness to Elias, she had never actually *asked* about his love life before they were together. In truth, because she didn't want to know. She was well aware she had been falling deeply in love over the past months. She wanted to leave the past unspoken. She had had boyfriends in college and after, and never felt any of her relationships or friendships worth mentioning to him. They simply weren't important anymore. What was significant was the fact that this striking, educated, urbane woman who had sat so close to Elias in his office the day before had actually been heavily involved with him. And now she would be working with him every day.

Lucky wanted to cry. She felt a heaviness in her chest. No matter how she covered up her feelings, the fact remained that Elias couldn't help comparing the two women. And she, Lucky, would definitely be found wanting. She wasn't sophisticated. Pretty, yes, in a girl-next-door sort of way, but highly educated, no. Involved in the same profession? No. She ran a restaurant. A restaurant in a small town. How could she possibly compete with the glamorous, accomplished Dr. Paula Sarens?

She knew she had to stop obsessing about the situation with Elias. There were other things to take care of this morning, getting her apartment to herself again for example. As much as she loved Janie and didn't really mind the fact that Janie was staying with her for a few days, the breach between Janie and her mother needed to be healed. This couldn't go on forever. It was time to have a real heart-to-heart with Miriam Leonard.

MIRIAM SAT AT the kitchen table, nervously wringing her hands. Her eyes were rimmed with red. She had obviously been crying on a regular basis. Her face was swollen, and now she was doing her best to maintain some semblance of control. Two cups of coffee were on the table along with a pitcher of cream and a sugar bowl. Miriam sat, stirring her coffee. She stared into the mocha-colored mixture for several minutes, lost in thought.

"Janie told me," Lucky spoke.

Miriam looked up quickly. Her hands started to shake.

"In all fairness, I more or less pried it out of her. I hope you'll forgive me, but I just had to get to the bottom of it. I couldn't watch her sulk and carry on needlessly."

"There's no need to apologize." Miriam took a shaky breath. "You had every right, Lucky. I'm sure it's been a burden on you, having her there."

"No burden. But I wish she'd talk to you. I'm sure it's breaking your heart."

Tears sprang to Miriam's eyes. "You have no idea. I'm sure you'll think I'm foolish, but I really never thought this day would come. That my past would come knocking on my door so to speak. She caught me in a vulnerable moment; otherwise, I never would have told her. You see, the other day, I found an envelope in my mailbox. A blank envelope, nothing written on it at all, and inside was a forget-me-not. You know those little blue flowers with the yellow centers. It was from him. He must have left it. Only he would know about that flower. He knows where I live— where Janie lives. Her father . . ." Miriam hesitated. "Janie's father has found us and . . . well, he must know that she's his daughter." She laughed ruefully. "How could he not? The resemblance is striking."

"And your husband—Doug? Did he know?"

"Oh, yes. Douglas saved my life. Literally. You see, my family . . ." Miriam looked at Lucky, a frightened look on her face. "We were travelers . . . gypsies, I guess you'd call us. It's impossible for you, or anyone like you, to understand."

Lucky could feel Miriam closing down, guarding her words. "Why do you say that? Someone like me?"

"You . . . you had a home, a real home. A real identity. A birth certificate, a driver's license, an education, for God's sake. The way I grew up, none of that was possible.

We lived under the radar. None of us had . . . has . . . a real identity in the outer world. Oh, we knew who our parents were, our brothers and sisters, and we were given names, but that was all."

Miriam stared out the kitchen window at her garden. Her face had taken on a far-off look. "My name was Morag. We moved constantly. We were always warned to stay away from strangers —people who weren't like us— anything to avoid involvement with the outside society, particularly the authorities, border guards, police, school systems. Someone like you, you have a real history, so did your parents. You had ancestors, official records, lives that were lived aboveboard. We had nothing like that. Truly we were second-class citizens or worse—not even citizens."

"You didn't know where your family came from?"

"We knew our ancestors were from Nova Scotia. Originally Scottish. And we always maintained a connection with that place, but we traveled constantly. The men would pick up work wherever they could, and every few years we'd return to Cape Breton. We speak . . ." Miriam caught herself quickly. "They speak Gaelic, our dialect. We would always speak Gaelic when we were with our own people. But we also spoke English and French—had to in order to survive, especially traveling through Quebec and New England."

"But if you had no identity papers, how were you able to cross borders?"

"That was nothing. Our people knew all the byways, all the small roads and fire trails. We usually knew which country we were in, but it didn't matter to us. Countries, nationalities, those things had no meaning for us."

"How did you come to leave? Was it not the life you wanted?"

Miriam laughed ruefully. "I never knew there was any other kind of life. There were 'us,' and there were 'the others' that we must at all costs not become involved with. We were told we'd be taken from our parents; the police would arrest us; we'd be put into homes with strangers. It was drilled into our heads. Our only safety was in obeying the rules." Miriam took a sip of her coffee and looked around her kitchen. "This," she said, indicating the walls of her home, "this was unheard of, unthought of, something that we could never hope for. In truth, something we should not even want. It was a strange, xenophobic mentality. To me, now, it feels as though I was raised in a time period that would have made sense several centuries ago."

"And you left that life?" Lucky asked.

Miriam shook her head. "I never intended to. I never knew anything else. We didn't have books to learn about the outside world. I could speak three languages, but I couldn't read or write any of them. Can you believe that? How helpless we really were in terms of the real world." Miriam paused to take a sip of coffee. She seemed calmer now that she was speaking of her past. "It was a strange world, stranger than you could ever imagine. We . . . we had certain rituals." Miriam pursed her lips, as though aware she had gone too far.

Lucky's curiosity was piqued. "Rituals?"

Miriam stared into her coffee. "I never realized until many years later how strange this tradition was." She paused for a long moment, lost in thought. "Once a year, at the winter solstice, someone, one of the adults, would be chosen to be the Keeper."

"The Keeper?" Lucky asked.

"Yes." Miriam nodded. "The keeper of the secrets. It was considered an honor but it was a terrible burden as well. Every adult in the clan had to confess one secret to the person chosen as the Keeper. Something they had never told anyone else. Something that they never *would* tell anyone else. And the Keeper could never, upon pain of shunning, reveal those secrets. When I look back on that now, I am horrified. When or how this practice started among us, I don't know. Perhaps it was invented as a form of confession, a method of chastisement. If someone knew a terrible secret about you, something shameful you had done, something dishonest, something you had lusted after in your heart, then you'd be forced to admit to yourself you could no longer commit that transgression. I imagine it had the effect of keeping everyone in line. The purpose of everything we did was to keep our clan together."

"I couldn't even imagine being put in that position," Lucky said. "And you're right. What a terrible burden to bear, and to never be able to speak of it."

"I never intended to leave," Miriam continued. "I fell in love . . . with Eamon. Eamon MacDougal, Janie's father. And he with me. We were so young, but we loved each other with an intense sureness that only the young can experience when they know nothing of life. We were so certain we would be together." Miriam took a deep breath. "But it was never to be.

"Our clan . . . our extended family if you will, was, simply put, a completely patriarchal society." She looked up quickly. "I don't mean to say that women were held prisoner, nothing like that. The women supported this structure. What else could they have possibly done? They all grew up like me; they knew no other life." Miriam sighed deeply. "You see, I had been 'promised' to another man. My father had arranged the marriage. I begged and pleaded with him, but he had made up his mind. He didn't know about Eamon. It wasn't easy, but we were able to keep our involvement secret. Although, when I look back on it now, I think my father suspected, and for whatever reason he insisted I must marry another man. I was out of my mind with grief, with rage, and no amount of argument could change my father's mind. He was set in his ways. He wasn't violent, but he was . . . a throwback, you'd consider him."

"How awful!" Lucky tried to imagine what it would be like to have your life choices irrevocably set by another.

"Yes." Miriam smiled slowly. "How awful." She was silent for several minutes. She took another deep breath and continued. "Eamon and I hatched a plan. He was as determined and rebellious as I. We decided that if our families wouldn't allow us to be together, we'd run away. We'd leave, and for better or worse, we'd make our way in the world. At least we would be together." Miriam closed her eyes. "I loved him so very much. He was my life, my future path; I was sure of it.

"When the day came, I slipped away into the woods. We were camped about a hundred miles north of here. I know that now, but I didn't at the time. Eamon was to follow. But he never came. I waited at the spot we had agreed upon. I waited for three days. I had taken only water with me. I had no food. And after three days, I was growing weaker."

"Had he changed his mind?"

"I thought so at the time. I cried bitter, bitter tears. On the last day I finally had to admit to myself that Eamon would not be joining me. Something had gone wrong. He had lied. Or he had changed his mind. I didn't know why, but I was devastated. I was starving, half frozen during the night, and terrified as well. Eamon had abandoned me. There was no other explanation. I couldn't go back. If he didn't love me, there was nothing left for me. I didn't want to live any longer and . . . I'm ashamed to admit this now, but in my delusional state, and I'm sure I was delusional with hunger and grief, I decided to kill myself.

"What I can remember now is stumbling out to the road. A car pulled up. College kids. They offered me a ride and asked me where I was going. They must have thought I was hitchhiking. I wasn't in my right mind, and I'm sure they thought I was sick or stoned or something, but at least they were kind enough not to leave me in the road. They were heading for Bennington, and they asked me where I was going. I told them I'd had a fight with my boyfriend and my name was Miriam. I just made that name up on the spot. I was afraid if I told them my real name, it would sound strange to them and they would know who and what I was. I told them I wanted to get home to Lincoln Falls. It was the only town I knew the name of. There were three boys and two girls. They looked at me strangely, but they bought me food and promised to take me to my home." Miriam laughed. "Home. What a joke that was, but I knew it was safer to tell them a lie."

"What happened then?"

"I was very lucky. We stopped for gas in the town. I told them I could walk from there. I was stronger by then. I'm not sure they believed me, but they didn't argue, and we said good-bye. I owed them my life I guess. When I think what might have happened to me all alone out there . . ." Miriam trailed off.

"I wandered around Lincoln Falls for several days. I was hungry again. I had no money, of course, and I looked like a street urchin. One night I waited in the bushes behind a restaurant. The cooks who worked there were tossing food away in the garbage can. I was so desperate. I waited until I was sure no one was in the parking lot and went to the bin. I opened the lid." Miriam looked up. "I'm sure you're horrified to hear this. That someone could stoop so low as to eat garbage from a restaurant. But I was starving, literally. Just as I reached for a discarded chicken leg, I felt a hand on my shoulder. I almost jumped out of my skin and tried to run away, but this man had grasped my arm. He told me not to be frightened. He had no intention of hurting me." Miriam pressed her lips together in an effort to stem the tears. "He . . . he had a bundle of food from the restaurant that he was taking with him. He asked me if I wanted his food. All I could do was nod. Something in his voice made me trust him. He told me again not to be frightened, but I should sit in his car to eat. If I was afraid, I could leave the door open. He told me again he wouldn't hurt me or even touch me. I knew he was telling the truth. That man, that wonderful kind man, was Doug Leonard, my husband. May the heavens keep him and bless him."

Lucky reached across the table and squeezed Miriam's hand. Tears had sprung to her eyes.

"He told me he lived in Snowflake with his elderly mother whom he cared for, and the house had an extra bedroom off the kitchen. He said if I didn't have a safe place to stay, I should come home with him. I was freezing and decided to try it for one night." Miriam looked out the window, remembering. "One night, that's what I thought then . . ." She laughed a little at herself. "That was the beginning of my real life. Doug was a good ten years older than I. He worked in sales and sometimes had to travel. He had been paying for home care for his mother when he couldn't be there, so he offered me a job. I could keep the room as my own." Miriam smiled at the memory. "I'll never forget that. It was a beautiful room with lovely wallpaper, flowers all over the walls, and expensive sheets and pillows, a bureau and everything. In exchange, I took care of the housework and the meals. His mother, my future mother-in-law, was a very sweet lady. She was barely ambulatory, but she was no problem. I took care of bathing her and of her laundry and meals and medications. She was very bright. Age hadn't dimmed her mentally. Millie taught me to read. At least enough to get by at first and then later, I could teach myself a lot, simply by reading. I was afraid to go into town, to buy groceries and things, for a long time. I was afraid my family would be looking for me, and I knew I couldn't return to them. I couldn't marry someone I didn't love, someone my father had chosen, and if the man I loved had abandoned me, then there was nothing for me there.

"Doug always picked up groceries, and eventually, after a long time, I wasn't too frightened to leave the house. It was an odd arrangement, but it saved my life, and they were both such good, loving people. I was very blessed.

"It didn't take Millie Leonard long to realize who and what I was. I had been hungry for so many days before Doug found me that at first I didn't realize something wasn't right. It was Millie, Doug's mother, who knew when she saw the changes."

"Knew what?" Lucky asked.

"That I was pregnant. Here I was, the same age Janie is now, and I was about to become a mother.

"When Doug found out about the baby coming, he asked me to marry him. He promised to somehow get me a birth certificate to legitimize my identity. He said that once we were married, no one would be asking questions, no one need ever know, unless I wanted them to. I was so very grateful." Miriam wiped her eyes on the dish towel. "So . . . you can guess the rest. We were married in a civil ceremony in Bennington. We thought that would be safer, and we made up a past history for me to tell when people asked questions about how we met. Once Janie was born, life went on as usual. Janie had just turned three when Doug's mother died. I consider Millie my real mother. I barely remember my true mother. And I'm sure my father is dead now. I had a dream one night in which he came to me to ask me to forgive him. I woke with a start, and I knew then. I knew he was dead. I cried the rest of the night. For him, for me, for Eamon, for all of us."

Lucky spoke softly. "You're a remarkable woman, Miriam. I have nothing but admiration for you. And I think when Janie knows the whole story, she'll feel differently."

"When Janie told me someone had been watching her, I was terrified. The people who would have controlled my life are all gone by now, I'm sure, but my childhood fears came rushing back. I know I didn't handle it very well when I questioned Janie at first. And now, I'm sure Eamon really is here. I've been overwhelmed with feelings. I hardly know how to make sense of things. Complete terror they will try to pull me back, rage that Eamon abandoned me, that he left me to starve and die. What if those college kids hadn't found me on the road? What if it hadn't been Doug Leonard who found me behind that restaurant? Part of me has always been afraid my clan would travel through here. When I first learned about the Stones near Snowflake, I realized that could be a possibility."

"The Stones? Why?"

"My clan has a belief about the Stones—that they are very ancient. That they were constructed by our ancestors thousands of years ago."

"I always thought the Stones were old Indian dwellings.

Didn't people believe the original colonists used them as
root cellars?"

"They're not. I don't know what the archeologists would
say today, but the people of our clan believe they were constructed by our long-ago ancestors. Not just the structure here
in Snowflake, but the ones all over New England and other
places in the country too. It's a pilgrimage for them to return
every few years to the spots they consider sacred. The experts
really haven't agreed, although I know there are a lot of theories. Bear in mind, I had never seen a map. So I didn't connect the Stones and Snowflake when I first came here. But
that must be why they're traveling through this area now. And
work at the Harvest Festival probably brought them to town.
I can't face any of them. It's fear, embarrassment, shame, all
those things. I've spent my life being terrified of being found
out in this world and found by the old world."

"Miriam, you have nothing to be ashamed of and nothing to be afraid of. They can't hurt you now. They can't
spirit you away. You should be proud of yourself. You
made your choices. You built a good life. You have a beautiful daughter who loves you. Never forget that."

"But will she ever forgive me?" Miriam said. "In my mind,
I've confessed the truth to her a million times. It was Doug
who wanted to be honest with her when she was younger. But
I held him back. I always planned to tell Janie the truth one
day. When I imagined doing so, it never looked like this.

"I really appreciate that you're taking care of Janie right
now. I'm not happy about how this all came to light, but at
least I know she's in a safe place."

"She is safe. And I plan to talk to her some more. She
will come around; I'm sure of it."

"I COULD TELL the minute you walked in the door that you
had been talking to my mother." Janie's tone was more
resigned than accusatory. Lucky sat next to her on a stool

at the counter. The morning rush had ended, and only a few straggling customers remained in their seats.

"Yes, I did talk to her."

"Did she come to the apartment?" Janie's voice held a hint of sarcasm.

Lucky was losing patience trying to break through Janie's walls. "No, she didn't come to the apartment," Lucky replied. "I went to see her."

Janie looked up quickly. "Why?" she cried. "Why would you do that?"

Lucky needed to put an end to the "us against Mom" attitude. "Because you're just eighteen. Because you can't support yourself. Because she's your mother. Because she loves you. Because you're all she has in the world. How's that for starters?"

Janie's anger melted a bit. At least she had the good grace to look embarrassed. "It's like . . . I feel like I'm turning my back on my dad. Like I'm not being loyal to him. Can't you understand how I feel, Lucky?"

"Yes, I can, Janie. I mean I can't totally imagine how I'd feel if I found out my dad wasn't my biological father. But the man who raised you was your father in every sense of the word. And you know who your mother is. You know she loves you and she did everything she possibly could for you. You have to talk to her. You need to hear the whole story, how her life came to be. Do you have a right to be angry? Okay, maybe you do. But you need to talk to her, to give her a chance to explain why she did what she did. I think you'd feel differently if you heard everything."

Janie didn't respond. She stuck a spoon into her mug of cocoa and swirled the creamy topping around until it dissipated. "My whole life has been a lie, Lucky. I loved my father. He was the greatest guy in the world. When he died, I wanted to die too. But now I'm sure he must have lied to me, just like her. How could he have done that all those years? If you love someone, how can you look them in the face and *lie* to them?"

Chapter 16

NATE SPUN A pencil around on his desktop. Soothing music, undoubtedly designed to calm nervous claimants, emanated from the receiver balanced on his shoulder. To his relief, the music stopped and a pleasant female voice spoke, professional and distant.

"This is Amy Thorsen. How may I help you?"

Nate identified himself and the reason for his call.

"We're happy to be of help. Can you tell me what this is in regard to?"

"Uh . . ." Nate thought quickly. "It's nothing serious. Just a background check. We have a situation here in our town that might be related to a case a Mr. Joseph Conrad once worked on. He gave Union Fidelity as a reference, as a former employer."

"That's right. Mr. Conrad was one of our investigators. But he retired several years ago."

"I see. And were you his supervisor at that time?"

"No. Unfortunately, I did not know Mr. Conrad personally. I transferred here from another location. But I do know he had an outstanding record prior to his retirement."

"Is there anyone with your company at the present time who actually worked with him?"

Ms. Thorsen was silent for a moment. "I believe so. Perhaps I can have one of his colleagues call you back. Can you give me your full name and position again, and I'll ask him to call you right away."

"That would be great. I'd appreciate speaking to anyone who actually worked with Mr. Conrad. Thanks."

"You realize, of course, we can't divulge any personal information. Not without a subpoena. That would be against the law and against company policy."

"I understand completely. Just like to get a feel for the man." Nate recited his cell phone number. He'd rather not make Bradley aware of his call.

"Fine. I'll have Mr. Isaac Brewer call you back."

"Thanks."

Nate hung up the phone and waited. The photocopy of Joe Conrad's license lay on the desktop in front of him. He wasn't quite sure why he wanted to talk to one of Conrad's coworkers at the insurance company. Was it because he found it hard to believe the man could still be obsessed with an old case he hadn't successfully seen to completion? But then, maybe investigators were just like cops. Couldn't let a thing go until it was neatly sorted. The driver's license was in order; the home address checked out. There were no outstanding warrants on the man, but all the same Nate knew he'd feel better if he talked to somebody who actually knew Joe when.

His cell phone finally rang. "Thanks for calling me back. I won't take much of your time. Just wanted to speak to someone who worked with Joseph Conrad."

"Oh, no problem. I knew Joe. He trained me, in fact."

"Is that so?"

"Yeah. Smart guy. Everything I know I learned from Joe. Although I haven't talked to him for a few years now."

"Guess he wasn't happy about retiring."

The man laughed. "No, he wasn't. He was fit to be tied, in fact. Felt bad for the guy. His work was his life. Plus his wife had died a few years before."

"So you were with him when that robbery in Bennington happened?"

"I had just started with the company. I did my best to carry on after Joe was forced out, but . . . I couldn't make any headway. Neither could the police. You weren't involved in that investigation by any chance, were you?"

"Oh no, not at all. But it was all over the news at the time. Couldn't avoid hearing about it." Nate paused. "Who would I talk to about looking at your company's files if I need to?"

"That'd be the Legal Department. Hold on. I'll get you their information." Nate was put on hold to the sound of music once again. "Got a pen?" Isaac Brewer recited the information, and Nate quickly jotted it down. "You can send your subpoena to them."

"Thanks."

"Has something new come to light about this?"

"No. We're working on something here that might have a connection, but I don't have enough information as of yet. If it looks like it pertains to your case, I'll give you a call."

"Thanks," Brewer said. "I'd appreciate that. That case drove Joe crazy."

"Would you say he was the kind of guy to keep trying to chase it down? After his retirement I mean?"

"Oh, hey, is that what's he up to?"

Nate remained silent.

"Yeah, I could certainly see Joe doing just that, now that I think about it. The guy was so thorough. If there was anybody who couldn't let something go, it was Joe. We used to call him the pit bull—behind his back, of course. But don't repeat that."

Nate chuckled. "I won't. I appreciate your time, Mr. . . . uh . . . Brewer. Thanks a lot."

"Hey, if you talk to him, tell him I said 'hi' and to give me a call."

"Will do," Nate replied.

Nate clicked off. He glanced at his desk where he had doodled triangles all over the blotter. He wasn't sure yet if he'd mention this call to Joe.

Chapter 17

THE LATE-AFTERNOON DINNER rush hadn't started. There were only a few customers at the tables. Lucky looked forward to a break of her own. Other than a piece of toast she had grabbed in the morning, she hadn't eaten all day— that and the coffee Miriam had offered her. The bell over the door rang. She sighed and pushed the thought of a break away for another half hour. Guy Bessette stood on the threshold and waved to her. She smiled and indicated he should grab a stool at the counter. He headed her way, and when he entered the restaurant, Lucky noticed a small figure behind him, following in his wake.

"Haven't seen you for a while, Guy. How is everything?"

"Just great, Lucky. I've been pretty busy with the shop and all; that's why I haven't come by." Guy, a mechanic, had inherited Snowflake's only auto shop when its prior owner was murdered.

"But," Guy said, smiling, "I have a new helper, so things should go a lot smoother now." He indicated the young boy who had followed him in. "What would you like to have, Tommy?" Guy asked.

Tommy wore a loose sweater and a pair of threadbare corduroy pants. He couldn't have been more than nine years old. The boy shrugged. "I don't have any money, Guy," he said, studying the list of daily specials.

"Don't you worry about money. You've earned your keep today. I'm buying, so order whatever you want." He turned to Lucky and winked. "Tommy wants to be a mechanic when he's older, so I'm startin' to train him now. He's a big help."

Lucky smiled at Tommy. Before she could ask for his order, he solemnly informed her, "I would like a chicken salad sandwich and a small bowl of beet and barley soup, please."

"Same for you, Guy?" Lucky asked.

"Sounds good."

"Coming right up." She placed the order slip on the hatch, and Sage grabbed it quickly.

"Excuse me," Tommy said. "What's the pumpkin contest? I saw a sign in the window."

"Well," Lucky replied. "The jack-o'-lantern that gets the most votes wins three all-you-can-eat meals for two at the Spoonful."

"Really? Wow!" Tommy's eyes grew wide. "I'm not eighteen yet, but can I still enter?"

"Of course. We're open to all ages," Lucky replied, doing her best to keep a serious expression on her face.

"What's in there?" Tommy asked, pointing to the hatch behind the counter.

"That's our kitchen, and Sage is our chef. Would you like to meet him?"

"Sure."

"Go in and say hello. He's very friendly."

"Okay." Tommy spun the stool around and hopped off, heading through the swinging door to the kitchen.

"I like your young friend," Lucky replied to Guy.

Guy leaned forward and spoke in a quieter voice. "He comes to see me after school just about every day. Poor kid's lonely. His mother's been very ill. She's the only family he has. She's still recovering from surgery, and she can't really take care of him or do much with him. I keep an eye on him in the shop and teach him whatever little things I can about cars. Keeps him busy, and when I quit for the day, I take him home. His mother is getting stronger, but she's got a ways to go. He mentioned her birthday's coming up. Between you and me, I think he's asking about the pumpkin contest so he can treat his mother to some fancy dinners."

"Oh, how sweet!" Lucky exclaimed. "And how kind of you, Guy. That's really wonderful."

"Hey, Harry did the same for me. I'm happy I can repay it a little bit. Even if Tommy's only turning nine now. 'Course he could change his mind ten times before he hits sixteen, but he's good company for me too."

Tommy returned to his stool just as Sage placed the two orders on the hatch. Lucky reached over and delivered the dishes to Guy and Tommy at the counter.

Tommy said, "I told Sage I wanted to enter the contest, and he told me he'd help me do the carving if I needed help. My mother doesn't let me have a knife yet. She said someday she might."

"That's good," Lucky replied.

"You know, Tommy. I think I'll do a pumpkin too, so if Sage is busy, let me know. I've got some good carving knives at the shop."

"Thanks." Tommy grabbed his sandwich and took a hefty bite of it. "I don't wanna tell my mother about it. She wouldn't like me using knives, and if I win, I want to surprise her for her birthday."

Lucky and Guy nodded their agreement. Guy winked up at her when he was sure Tommy wouldn't notice.

Chapter 18

"COME IN, COME in," Sophie trilled happily when she opened the door. "I'm so glad you made it. Finally. How many nights have we invited you over for a drink but you're always so busy. Where's Elias?"

"He, uh. . . . It's just me."

"He couldn't make it?"

"No." Lucky smiled, but didn't offer any further explanation. "Sorry. I should have let you know."

She had called Elias's office at the Clinic that afternoon to invite him to come along to see Sophie and Sage's new apartment. Their conversation had been stilted to say the least. After what seemed to her a long silence, Elias said he had made some other plans but perhaps next time. To be completely truthful with herself, she was relieved. She was still disturbed about seeing him in his office with Paula. It would have been too hard to pretend that everything was fine, especially with Sophie and Sage looking on. And then there was the evening at the Pub. She had been upset and was sure Elias had been as well. But she had come away feeling she was being chastised for her reaction. She had turned it over and over in her mind, and she was still convinced she had a right to be, if not angry, then at least put out that he had hired someone with whom he had been involved in the past. Not to mention the fact that Paula was actually staying at his house, however temporarily. Was she acting like a jealous lover? Probably, yes. Was she jealous? Well, yes and no. Intimidated might be a better way to explain her feelings. And threatened. There was that. Paula was accomplished and striking, and Lucky was sure she hadn't been mistaken about the tension she had felt when she walked into Elias's office. Even if he were being honest with himself, she suspected Paula had other plans.

"That's too bad." Sage appeared behind Sophie, a towel thrown over his shoulder.

Lucky smiled. "You look like you're still working."

"Yes, my girlfriend is a slave driver. Here, let me take your jacket." Lucky shrugged her shoulders out of the sleeves and handed it to Sage. He hung it on a peg in the hallway. Both Sophie and Sage had given up their respective studio apartments and moved to a larger two bedroom in a small building on Chestnut Street. Sophie had been decorating and picking up odds and ends of furniture. They were excited to show off their new space.

Sophie grasped Lucky's hand. "Let me give you the quick tour." She led Lucky down the hallway to an open door. "This is our bedroom here and . . ." She pulled Lucky further down the hallway to a second room. She reached around the doorjamb and flicked on a light. The lamp illuminated a much smaller room that was dominated by a desk and a filing cabinet. "We're going to use this as an office. Don't mind the mess. We still haven't unpacked all our boxes. Right now it's more of a storeroom."

She beckoned Lucky to the end of the hallway. "This is the kitchen. This is what sold us. Check out that fabulous stove. Sage just loves it. He made some hors d'oeuvres for us tonight. What would you like? Red or white? We have a great Chilean import. Want to try that?"

Lucky nodded, and Sophie reached up to a wineglass holder over the sink and pulled down two delicate crystal glasses. "I found these at a yard sale years ago, and I've saved them for ages. This was the right time to bring them out, I thought." The wine was already decanted. Sophie poured two small glasses, one for Lucky and one for herself. "Here you go."

Sage scooped up a tray from the counter. "Let's sit in the living room, it's far more comfortable there." Lucky and Sophie, carrying their wineglasses, followed him to the other end of the apartment. A CD of soft jazz instrumentals was playing on the stereo.

Sophie sat and kicked off her shoes, curling up at one end of the sofa. "Sage mentioned that Janie's been staying at your place."

"Yes." Lucky took a sip of her wine. "This is delicious by the way. Thank you. I feel bad for her. She's fighting with her mother right now. She disappeared one night after they fought, and Miriam was hysterical. I finally found her sleeping in the storeroom at the Spoonful in her sleeping bag. I couldn't let her stay there. So I offered my sofa, rather than have her wandering around all over the place. I'm just trying to figure out how I can get her to talk to her mother and make it up."

"What in heaven's name is her problem? Her mother's such a nice lady. I thought they were real close, especially since her father died."

"Well, they are, or rather they were, but something's come up that's really upset Janie."

"Like what? Does her mother have a new boyfriend or something?"

Lucky laughed. "No, it's not that. It's . . . something from the past that has Janie so upset, but Miriam confided in me, and I can't talk about it. It's really their business."

"Okay." Sophie nodded. "Fair enough."

"Hey," Sage said. "Try some of these." He placed a small dish and napkin on the coffee table for Lucky and held out the tray of several different hors d'oeuvres.

"These look tempting and I am hungry." Lucky chose three different ones and began to nibble.

Sage watched her expectantly. "What do you think?"

"They're fantastic," Lucky mumbled, her mouth full.

Sage passed the tray to Sophie and she took one. "I've been picking at these for the last hour before you arrived." She turned to Sage. "I hope you'll still love me when I weigh three hundred pounds."

Sage smiled but said nothing. He reached over from his chair and grasped Sophie's hand. They turned and smiled at Lucky. "We invited you over because we have some good news," Sophie said.

Lucky was already anticipating what their news would be. "It'll be the only good news I've heard all week. Tell me. Tell me."

"We're getting married!" Sophie exclaimed. Their faces were wreathed in smiles.

"Oh, that's wonderful!" Lucky placed her wineglass carefully on the table and slid closer to Sophie to give her a hug. "I am so happy for you!" She stood and hugged Sage awkwardly across the coffee table as he rose from his chair, still smiling. "I am so very happy for you both."

"Yup. We decided," Sage said. "We're actually gonna tie the knot. We figured, why not? We've moved in together. We love each other. And it just felt right. And, of course, now that I'm not sitting in a jail cell, I need to get on with my life."

"I couldn't be happier for you both." Lucky grinned. "Can I volunteer to be a bridesmaid?"

"Of course. I'd love that. We don't have the money for a big wedding, but we can figure something out that will be inexpensive and fun. We thought in the spring might be nice. Early or middle of May perhaps. And I would love you to be my bridesmaid. What am I saying? You're it. There's no one else. You'll be my maid of honor," Sophie gushed.

Lucky smiled, marveling at her friend's happiness and the joy that could have been so easily destroyed only months ago.

"We'll probably just have a civil ceremony in Lincoln Falls and then maybe go out to a fancy dinner. It'll just be you and Sage's brother, Remy, after all. We really don't have anyone else—either one of us."

"That would be fine, but wouldn't you rather have something a little more romantic?"

Sophie shrugged. "Like what?"

"Well," Lucky thought. "Jack has a beautiful garden and a gazebo, and maybe we could find a harpist or a violinist to play a little music."

"I could organize a dinner and take care of the food," Sage said. "That's if Jack wouldn't mind."

"Jack would love that!" Lucky said. She laughed. "Here I am volunteering Jack's house, but I know he'd love to be included."

"This sounds like a lot of work for you," Sophie offered.

"No worries. I'll take care of it. After all, if I'm the maid of honor, it's part of my job."

Sophie looked at Sage. "Well, then maybe I could invite a couple of friends from the Resort."

"Fine with me," Sage agreed.

"Then it's settled," Lucky said. "I'll talk to Jack and figure out what we need to do."

"Not to be a nosy girlfriend and pry, but what about you and Elias?" Sophie twinkled.

Lucky strained to smile. "Oh, we have no plans." *In fact, we may not even be speaking to each other,* she thought. But this was hardly the time or place to bring that subject up. The last thing she wanted to do was rain on Sophie and Sage's parade.

"Uh . . ." Sage cleared his throat. "I don't want to drag you two away from the girlie bit, but I couldn't help overhearing some of the talk at the Spoonful yesterday—about the robbery and the guy from the insurance company saying he might have found his man?"

Sophie grabbed a cushion from the sofa and hit Sage's shoulder playfully. "You *are* a downer. I want to talk about wedding dresses."

Sage smiled. "Not for me I hope?" He reached over to tickle Sophie who tried to block his efforts with the pillow.

"Stop!" she cried. "Stop it!" Laughing, she scooted away from him.

Lucky was starting to feel like a third wheel. She wondered if she should claim tiredness and leave the two of them alone.

"I was in the kitchen. I only heard bits and pieces, but it made me curious," Sage said. "Did you hear the whole story?"

"Pretty much. Although Joe didn't totally explain how he got from A to Z and focused on this guy. He may have been deliberately holding back. What makes matters worse is that Nate still has no idea who the man he found on the road really was. Nate's suspicious the license may be a fake. He's called the other jurisdictions asking about missing persons, but no one's been reported. They've taken the man's fingerprints to see if they match up with any available in the database. That's everything I know. But here's the really weird part, Nate says he actually looks younger than the photo on the license."

"That's easily explained," Sophie said. "I'll show you mine. Worst picture I ever took."

"Joe says there was evidence the other man might have been a carnival worker or a traveler, and Nate's starting to think the dead man might be one too. If he is, the documentation could very well be fake or stolen. Nate feels like he's on a wild-goose chase just trying to identify the guy, never mind who shot him."

"The insurance guy, what's his name? Joe Conrad?"

Lucky nodded.

"Had he actually ever seen the dead guy—in life, I mean?" Sage asked.

"He wouldn't have. There was an eyewitness report when the guy ran a red light taking off with the armored truck. The only man he did meet during the investigation was the guard they later decided was in on the robbery. And he did a disappearing act when the police got suspicious."

"So what led Conrad to think the dead man might be the one he's been looking for?" Sage asked.

"Well, he admits it's just a hunch that he wants to check out. There was a carnival in town at the time of the robbery, and Joe suspected the second guy might have been working there. The forensics clinched it, but by then the carnival was over and the casual workers were gone. Joe admits he's a little obsessed with the one case he couldn't complete. He said when he heard about the dead man who was shot, it piqued his interest. Now that he's retired, he makes it his business to check out men working at these places."

"Interesting. And they've never caught either robber?"

"Apparently not. They both disappeared. Of course, there may be more Joe knows that he's not telling us."

"Hmmm," Sophie said. "If Joe's right and the dead guy might be the one Joe's been looking for, maybe he never shared the money and it's a falling out among thieves. Maybe that's what got the guy shot."

"That's one theory at least. I'm sure Nate doesn't tell us everything either, but he likes to talk to Jack and I like to listen in." Lucky took a last sip of her wine. She glanced at the tray and realized she had eaten all but one of Sage's hors d'oeuvres. "Hey, you two, I've been a bit of a piglet."

"Better you than me," Sophie yawned and stretched like a cat.

"You're tired, aren't you? I should probably head home. I'm wiped out too."

"Well, I'm glad you had time to stop by and hear our news. Tell Elias we miss him. No excuses next time."

"I will." Lucky smiled and rose from her chair. "This was nice, and my congratulations again!"

Sophie jumped up. "I'll walk you downstairs. Do you need a ride?"

"No, I'll be fine. I walked over. No point in driving." Sophie and Sage's apartment on Chestnut was just a few blocks from Lucky's own place on Maple.

Lucky slipped on her jacket, and Sophie followed her to the door. Sage busied himself picking up wineglasses and napkins, and clearing off the coffee table. Sophie was silent as they left the apartment and walked down the flight of stairs to the front door. When they reached it, she said, "All right. Fess up. What's going on?"

"What do you mean?"

Sophie shook her head in frustration. "Don't play that with me. What's going on with you and Elias? Something's wrong. I can tell."

Lucky sighed. "I don't know. He seems . . . strange, distant. And then last night he told me . . ." She trailed off. Sophie waited. "This new doctor—Paula, whatever her name is . . ."

"Get to the point, Lucky."

"They had a relationship years ago. Apparently a very serious one."

"Hmm. Well, that's no surprise. I'm sure there were women in his life."

"It's not that, Sophie. It's that he never, and I mean *never*, mentioned that there was someone he was terribly serious about, that he thought about marrying. And now he's hired her." Lucky felt all her jumbled emotions rising to the surface.

"So? It doesn't matter what happened years ago before you met him. The only thing that counts is now. Are you saying you think he might still have feelings for her?"

"He says he doesn't. He says he wanted to tell me about the past and he doesn't want it to interfere with our relationship."

"Well, then, it doesn't sound like he's confused."

"What he says and what he really feels could be two different things. Besides, have you seen her?"

"No," Sophie replied hesitantly.

"She's drop-dead gorgeous. And she looks at Elias like he's a piece of candy."

"Lucky"—Sophie grabbed her by the shoulders—"in case you've failed to notice, so are you. Take a look in the mirror. You might be hopeless when it comes to makeup, and you certainly could use some fashion advice, but you're beautiful . . . inside and out. Of course he's crazy about you. He'd have to be nuts not to be."

Lucky felt close to tears, admitting her insecurities to Sophie. But who else could she tell? She smiled ruefully. "You are a very good friend and I love you."

"Yes, I am. And I'm also right. Now go home, get some sleep and stop worrying about nothing." Sophie stood at the top of the stairway and watched Lucky as she headed to the sidewalk. Lucky turned back to wave good night, and Sophie blew her a kiss.

WHEN SHE REACHED her apartment, she turned the key carefully in the lock and very quietly shut the door behind her. At one end of the hall, the living room was dark. Janie must be sound asleep. Lucky tiptoed in the other direction toward the kitchen and flipped on the overhead light. She

gasped. The kitchen was a disaster. The sink was full of
pots and pans and unwashed dishes. Spilled food was
crusted on the stove. Dirty dish towels hung off the back of
a chair. More dishes were on the kitchen table, unwashed.
All she wanted more than anything was to crawl into bed,
but she couldn't bear the thought of waking up to this mess
in the morning. She glanced at the answering machine on
the counter. No blinking light. Elias hadn't called. Then
she spotted a note in the midst of the heap on the kitchen
table. A slip of paper was held down by the saltshaker.
*"Lucky—I made a vegetable barley casserole. There's a
plate in the refrigerator for you."*

She sighed. It was a lovely gesture for Janie to prepare
food for them both, but it would have been lovelier if she
had cleaned up after herself. Lucky slipped her jacket off
and hung it on a chair. Inside the refrigerator was the promised plate. It was wrapped in plastic with a heart drawn in
magic marker. Lucky wasn't particularly hungry, not after
eating all the hors d'oeuvres that Sage had prepared, but
she thought she should at least have a taste. Janie had obviously worked hard preparing the dish. She scooped up a
bite with a fork. Not bad, not bad at all. She ate a few more
bites, discovering she was hungrier than she realized. She
cleaned the plate and carried it to the sink.

She stared at the heap of dishes in the sink and heaved
a sigh. These would be caked solid if they were left all
night. She rolled up her sleeves and filled the sink with
soap and hot water and started scrubbing. There were so
many she had to stop to dry the pots and pans and put them
away before tackling the next batch of dirty dishes. What
in heaven's name had Janie cooked to make such a mess?
When everything was washed and stacked in the dish
strainer, she dried her hands on a towel and headed to the
bathroom.

The counter there rivaled the kitchen. It was littered
with crumpled tissues, spilled makeup and hair curlers. A

smear of toothpaste dribbled down the mirror. Janie's clothes hung from the hook on the back of the door and the towel rack. Couldn't the girl make an attempt to be a little bit neater? Lucky felt a sudden rush of sympathy for Miriam. This is what life with a teenager must be like. Were they all like this? How could Janie, who was so efficient and neat at her job, function in such a mess? She was almost out of her teen years. Very soon teenage-hood wouldn't be an excuse. Lucky wiped the toothpaste off the mirror, moved the hair curlers and makeup out of the way, cleaned off the countertop, then washed her face and attempted to brush her teeth. The toothpaste was almost gone. She had to use all her strength to squeeze out the last of it. She was positive the tube had been half full this morning. Not only was Janie a messy roommate, she was an expensive one. Lucky'd definitely have to do something to move this situation along. Janie needed to return home.

In the bedroom Lucky slipped off her clothes, pulled a nightie over her head and collapsed on the bed. She snuggled under the comforter for warmth. The nights were getting chillier. Winter was coming. With luck, maybe they'd have another month before the first snowfall. She reached up to turn off the light. If only Elias had called, she might not feel so empty and lost. But what did she expect? She had given him a hard time at the Pub. She suspected he was angry at her for reacting the way she did. Perhaps he said he couldn't be with her tonight because he just really didn't want to. Perhaps he was only making an excuse, or maybe he really did have other plans. Maybe those plans involved Paula. Lucky struggled to recall Sophie's vote of confidence in Elias. She hoped against hope that Sophie was right.

Chapter 19

"HEY, LUCKY," SAGE called through the hatch. "There's a strange man here asking for you."

Lucky turned and peeked into the kitchen. Sage had a grin from ear to ear, and next to him, also smiling widely, was his brother Remy.

"Remy! Where have you been?" Lucky cried. She slipped from behind the counter and pushed through the swinging door into the kitchen. Sage's younger brother seemed to have grown taller and sturdier. Remy had always depended on Sage for security after surviving a tough childhood. Months before when Sage had been arrested, Remy had had an emotional meltdown. In an effort to keep him busy and grounded, Jack had put him to work at the Spoonful, and both Lucky and Jack had done their best to offer him moral support. Once Sage was free and the dust had settled, they hadn't seen very much of Remy.

Lucky was thrilled to see him again. "Sage said you were working on a farm. I meant to get your phone number from him. We miss you!"

Remy, slender as he was, was strong. He threw his arms

around Lucky, picking her up off the floor, and spun her around.

"I miss all of you too. But I have a real job now. I figured it was about time I settled down. I'm not getting any younger."

Lucky's eyebrows raised. "How old are you now?"

"Twenty-two."

Lucky struggled to keep a straight face. "Almost a senior citizen." Sage winked at her behind Remy's back.

"Well, I can't mooch off my brother forever." He turned and grinned at Sage. "But it's not exactly a farm. I'm working with horses."

"Really? That's great. Taking care of them?"

"Training them."

"No kidding."

"Can you believe that, Lucky? Me! I'd never even come close to a horse before, but for some reason—and it was just luck I showed up at the right time 'cause they needed somebody—for some reason, horses really like me. And I like them too—sometimes better than humans. There's an older guy at this place that's been doing this all his life, but he wants to retire, and he's teaching me. He says I have a knack."

"Oh, Remy. That is really wonderful. What a great thing to be doing." Lucky gave him a hug in return. "You've got to visit a bit and tell Jack all about it too."

"I plan to. I'll be based over at the festival for a few days. The owners have rented some of their ponies to the festival people for the kids to ride. So I'll be keeping an eye on them and taking care of them at night."

"That sounds like a dream job!" Lucky said.

"Well," Remy shrugged. "It would be if it weren't for all the tension over there. Not a happy place."

"What do you mean?"

"Ah, nothing serious, really. Just that guy Ernie. I don't trust him as far as I can throw him. Never does what he says he's gonna do. I had a run-in with him just the other day. I overheard him talking to this big guy that works for him—Rory—about pulling off the panels. I told him he couldn't touch anything in the barn. It was all modified for the horses. The owners were very specific about how the stalls should be set up, and I don't want my horses to get upset."

"Ernie bugs us too when he comes in. I just hope the rest of the week goes better for you. You know, Sophie's stopping by any minute. We were planning to go over there for an hour or so this afternoon, just to see what's going on." She turned to Sage. "We might take Janie with us, just to cheer her up. Jack and Meg'll be here though. Is there anything I can pick up for you at the farmers' market?"

Sage's brow furrowed. "Uh, yes, actually, there is. See if they have any late-season blueberries and blackberries. There's a soup recipe I've been thinking about. And would you mind picking up one of those fairy-tale pumpkins? I promised Tommy I'd get him one for his project. He thinks it'll make a real spooky jack-o'-lantern."

"Sure. How many berries do you need?"

"Not a lot. Maybe just a pound each. That'll give me plenty in case anything goes wrong with my experiment."

The bell over the door jingled. Lucky peeked out to the restaurant. "Sophie's here now," she said, slipping off her apron.

Sophie waved to Jack on her way through the restaurant and rushed into the kitchen. She kissed Sage and reached over to pinch Remy on the cheek. "Are you sure you don't want to stay with us while you're in town?"

"You'll be seeing me, but I'm gonna sleep in the trailer out at the field. I need to be close to keep an eye on the horses. I'm not crazy about the guys Ernie hired to run the pony rides for the kids. They know less about horses than I do about nuclear physics."

"Well, if you change your mind, we have a very warm sofa and an extra pillow and blanket. But come to dinner every night at least, okay?"

"Thanks." Remy grinned. "I plan on that." He turned

to Lucky, "I have to head back now, but I'll come by to visit with you and Jack again."

"You better."

"See ya." Remy slipped out to the corridor and left by the back door.

Sophie turned to Lucky. "Want to go now? While things are quiet? Where's Janie?"

"She's stacking cans in the storage closet. I'll go get her."

Lucky walked down the corridor and hung her apron on a hook in the closet. She tapped on the storeroom door and pushed it open. "Hey, Janie. Still want to come with us? Sophie's here."

Janie was squatting near the lower shelf, counting cans of corn. Just about all the ingredients in Sage's soups were fresh, but occasionally, if some item was out of season or hard to come by, Lucky always made sure there were plenty of supplies on hand.

Janie placed her clipboard on the shelf and slipped off her apron. "That sounds like fun."

"Let's escape for a bit. Sophie's got her car. We can drive over with her." Lucky was hoping a break in the routine would be good for the girl's spirits.

"Have you been to see your mom?" Lucky watched Janie's face carefully.

Janie averted her eyes and mumbled, "No."

"You're gonna have to sooner or later. Don't you think sooner would be better?"

Janie looked up, tears in her eyes. "I will, Lucky. I just can't right now."

"But you will?"

Janie sighed. "I will. I will."

Janie couldn't go on being angry at her mother forever. Sooner or later she'd have to return home. She was sure time would heal the wound and Janie would eventually get over the shock.

"Okay, let's go, then."

Chapter 20

THE PARKING LOT was almost completely full when they arrived. Sophie drove up and down the rows and finally found an empty spot. A lush Indian summer had lasted well into the month, and the afternoon sun filtered through brilliant red and gold leaves. Nature's sensuous treat, one last tantalizing kiss before the bitterness of winter swept in. Inside the gate, the tables of the vendors were laid out in two long rows. Their overhead canvases flapped in the gentle wind. Behind the vendor stalls an area was carved out for a small carousel painted in brilliant colors. Young children filled every seat and calliope music played as the carousel turned round and round. Another gate straight ahead led the way to the pumpkin patch and farther on the corn maze. Inside a fenced corral two handlers watched over the children riding ponies. Lucky saw Remy leaning on the fence, watching the men and the horses carefully. Doting parents stood on the periphery taking snapshots. Another sound, a haunting note from a stringed instrument, reached the women's ears.

"Do you think I could pass for six years old?" Sophie

asked. "I'd love to ride one of those ponies, except I wouldn't want to stay inside the corral."

"That's why they don't want you on their horses, and no, I doubt you could pass," Lucky replied.

"I'm with Sophie. Maybe the horses would like to escape." Janie giggled. "I know if I were a horse, I would."

"I see Remy's keeping a close watch." Lucky turned to Sophie. "It's great that you and Sage are staying close. I'm sure it means an awful lot to him."

"And to Sage too. That's his baby brother. He's struggled his whole life to get to a place where he could keep Remy safe. It took a while, but I think Remy's turned it around. He's standing on his own two feet now."

"Listen," Lucky said. "I'll be right back. I have to find the fruit sellers. I want to pick up Sage's order before I forget. I'll meet you back here?"

"Okay. We'll be around. Maybe Janie and I will do the corn maze. What do you say, Janie?"

"I'd like that. It'd be fun. Let's go."

Lucky was relieved to see Janie smile and forget her troubles for a moment. "Don't get lost," she called out as Sophie and Janie headed for the entrance to the maze. "I'll meet you after."

Lucky heard a stringed instrument playing again. She looked to the far end of the field and saw musicians setting up on a stage under the trees. A small audience had started to gather. She turned away and wandered in the other direction toward the stalls, glancing over each table piled with the harvest of the season—squash, corn, artichokes, and the last of the strawberries, thanks to a longer than usual summer. Handmade wares—candles, crocheted coverlets, knitted scarves and pottery—covered many of the tables. She browsed past several vendors and finally decided to purchase a trio of large handmade candles for Sophie and Sage—a small early engagement present.

She continued down the main pathway and spotted a table

with oddly shaped, fantastical pumpkins. Tommy would need a good-sized one for carving. She studied each one carefully and finally purchased one with the best carving possibilities. It was heavy and too big to fit into her carryall. She'd have to lug it around, but it was all for a good cause, she thought. At the end of the row of stands she found a fruit stall with luscious-looking berries. Just what Sage needed.

"Could I have a pound of those and those?" she asked, pointing at the bins of fruit. "They look delicious."

"They are," the woman behind the table said. "You'll love them." She scooped the blueberries and blackberries into paper bags. Her arms were heavy and tanned. She had probably farmed the berries herself. Lucky paid for the fruit and tucked the bags into her carryall with the candles. She slung the straps over her shoulder and, holding the heavy pumpkin, headed back toward the pony corral, wondering if Sophie and Janie would be done with the corn maze. As she left the shelter of the tents, she spotted Nate's cruiser pulling into the parking lot. Was this just a casual stop to pick up vegetables? Or to make sure no one was breaking any laws? She watched as Nate and Bradley climbed out and headed toward the corral. Sophie and Janie were nowhere in sight.

Nate gestured to one of the men at the corral. The man glared at Nate and reluctantly approached. Lucky recognized the big man she had seen with Ernie White at the Spoonful. She moved closer, close enough to hear the conversation but not so close it was obvious she was eavesdropping.

"Anyone else working with you here?"

The man shook his head negatively. "No. Just me and my guy over there." He indicated a young man who stood in the center of the corral watching over the children, making sure no child was having trouble staying on his or her pony.

"And how 'bout the ride over there? Anyone who was here and hasn't shown up lately?"

"Nah," the man said. "Just the three of us and a mechanic from Lincoln Falls who checks the ride occasionally. And the farmers who come every day, but I don't know any of them."

"Who hired you then?"

"Ernie White," the man answered in a surly tone. "You got any questions, you should talk to him."

"I plan to. What about the band, the musicians?"

The man shrugged. "You'd have to talk to Ernie. I don't know where they come from. He hired 'em."

Nate nodded his head in the direction of the younger man who stood in the center of the corral. He had studiously avoided looking in Nate's direction. "And that guy? Did you hire him? Or Ernie?"

"He's with the bunch playing music. I give him a few bucks to help me out." The man turned and called out. "Hey, Danny Boy, get over here."

The young man looked over quickly and stood stock-still. For a split second, Nate was sure he would approach the white-railed fence. Instead, he bolted in the other direction, climbed over the fence and took off across the farmer's field.

"Damn," Nate muttered under his breath. "Go get him, Bradley."

"Me?"

"Yes, you. Get a move on."

Bradley shot a frustrated look at Nate but ran around the corral and took off after the runaway.

"What the hell's goin' on? Why'd he run?" Nate barked at the big man.

"Can't tell ya. Maybe he's got unpaid parking tickets. Look, I gotta keep watch over those kids."

Nate waved him away and, peering across the distance, watched Bradley as he closed in on the fugitive.

Lucky had watched the scene play out and finally approached Nate. "What's happening?"

Nate turned suddenly. "Lucky! Didn't see you there." He glanced back to make sure Bradley was hot on the trail of the runaway and smiled. "He'll catch him. Bradley's fast. I'm just trying to make the rounds and talk to everyone around town. I need to get some kind of a solid ID on this guy we found. So far, nobody's claiming him."

"What about that driver's license from Maine?"

"No luck there. That man died ten years ago. Can you believe it? Who the hell is this guy? And I'm still waiting for the results of those paint scrapings and any fingerprints or anything else that turns up."

"Sorry you're having such a tough time."

Remy stepped down from the railing and walked toward them.

"Tough ain't the word. Somebody shot this guy. He died of blood loss and shock. How the hell can I find who did that if I can't even identify the victim?" He nodded toward the musicians setting up on stage. "That's my next stop. But I doubt I'll get very far there."

"Why do you say that?"

Nate shrugged. "Look at 'em." Nate indicated the other end of the festival area where the stage sat under a stand of trees. "They're travelers, I'm sure. Even if they know who the dead guy is, they probably wouldn't tell me anyway." He grumbled.

Remy had remained silent, listening to their exchange. Four people moved around the wooden stage, three men and a woman, preparing to begin their set. The woman moved to center stage. She wore a long flowing skirt and balanced a stand-up bass against her shoulder. She played long slow notes with her bow as she deftly adjusted the tension in the strings. One man sat on a stool behind a keyboard, another picked up a banjo, and the third took his place at the side with a violin.

Nate watched the activity on stage. "Looks like I missed my opening. I'll have to wait for a break," Nate said.

Lucky spotted Sophie and Janie exiting from the gate to the corn maze and waved to them to catch their attention. Sophie waved back. She and Janie walked toward them.

"Janie's here?" Remy asked. He stood straighter and ran a hand through his hair.

Lucky nodded, aware that Remy had done his best to attract Janie's attention months before.

The woman on stage coaxed long, slow notes from her instrument. She began to sing. The keyboardist and the violinist played quietly in the background, supporting her plaintive song. The words were unrecognizable. Lucky listened carefully. She was sure she was listening to Gaelic. Something about the music tugged at her heart. Without understanding the words she knew it was a song of yearning, perhaps of love lost. Sophie and Janie stood quietly next to her. The rhythm of the song picked up, and the man playing the violin moved downstage, out of the shadow of the trees. Janie gasped and grabbed Lucky's arm.

Sophie was instantly aware of Janie's reaction. "What is it?" she whispered to Lucky.

Janie's face was pale. "It's him," she breathed. "Lucky, that's the man I've seen."

"Are you sure it's the same man?"

Janie nodded.

Lucky sensed someone behind them. She turned and saw Ernie White tap on Nate's shoulder.

"Trouble, Nate?"

Nate's face was a closed book. "No trouble, Ernie. Just talking to a few of your people here."

"I'd appreciate it if you'd talk to me first or let me know you're coming."

"Oh? Why's that?" Nate asked. Beneath his casual reply Lucky heard an undertone of Nate's official voice.

Ernie laughed suddenly. An effort to make light that came off as an angry bark. "People get nervous when they see cops around. Especially cops asking questions. I don't think a police presence is good for business, Nate."

Nate was silent, showing no reaction. "You better rethink that, Ernie, because you wouldn't have these concessions without a license, and that license can be easily revoked. My job is to make sure this town is safe, and if I think you're harboring any undesirables, then I'm gonna start asking questions. Do you get my drift?"

Ernie's face flushed a deep red. "Now don't go accusing me of anything. Everything here is open and aboveboard."

"Then you shouldn't mind my sniffing around." Nate glanced down at Ernie's feet. Lucky noticed his eyes harden.

Bradley was approaching from the direction of the horse fence, pushing the young man forward. His wrists were secured behind his back.

Nate called out, "Put him in the car, Bradley. We're taking him to the station."

"Hey," Ernie shouted. "You can't do that. We need all the help we can get here."

Lucky saw the tall violinist on stage turn slightly to watch as Bradley walked his charge to the cruiser. The man caught the eye of the keyboardist and indicated with a subtle nod of his head the action occurring in the parking lot. Lucky turned to watch. In the parking lot Bradley opened the rear door of the cruiser and, placing his hand on the head of the young man, pushed him into the police vehicle. No one on stage changed their positions or their expressions, but Lucky was certain every one of the musicians was aware of the young man's capture.

"Are you arresting him, Nate?" Remy asked.

"I'll let you know if I charge him with anything. Right now I just want to talk to him, find out why he tried to run."

Another man with weathered skin approached from the open field and walked in their direction. Ignoring Nate, he spoke directly to Ernie. "I'm planning on harvesting that corn before the week is out."

"You can't do that. Not now," Ernie shouted. "This festival runs till Halloween. The kids have to have the corn maze."

"I told you before, Ernie. I couldn't promise I'd hold off all week. I gotta harvest that corn now."

Ernie's face grew red. "Like hell! You told me you could wait till *after* Halloween. I put up ropes and everything."

"They can have their corn maze; I'll hold off on that section till later. But I can't have anybody in there or anywhere around when we come through with the combine. You know that, Ernie."

"Damn it. You said you were gonna wait."

"I said I'd try. And I have waited. I can't wait anymore. We're gonna go through that field in a few days—very early at first light. Just you make sure no one's around when we do. I don't want any accidents. Besides, you told me you were gonna fence off that area, and you didn't do it. We agreed on a temporary fence, not stakes and ropes."

"What are you talking about? I never said that. That's not part of our deal."

"Like hell, Ernie White. It may not be written in the contract, but you gave me your word. Don't ask me to trust you next time you want to use my property."

"There won't be a next time," Ernie snarled. "I'll find another field."

"Fine by me." The man turned and headed back toward the cornfield. "You got today and two more days and then we're going through that corn," he shouted over his shoulder.

Ernie fumed. "Son of a . . ." He muttered under his breath.

"Watch it," Nate said. "There are ladies here." Nate had remained silent during the exchange between Ernie and the farmer. "And I want to see *you* first thing tomorrow at the station with your employment records and proof of insurance. And make sure you provide home addresses for all these people you hire and a list of the farmers' and vendors' concessions. You got that?"

Ernie looked furious but didn't say a word. If it was possible, his face grew redder and a vein throbbed in his forehead. He took a deep breath and made a conscious effort to quell his temper. "Sure thing, Nate," he said through gritted teeth. "Not a problem." Ernie stormed away in the direction of the vegetable sellers.

Remy looked as if he wanted to say something to Janie, but she had taken no notice of him. "I'll see you all later," he said. "I better lend a hand with the horses." He hurried away toward the corral.

"Ladies," Nate said, "it's been a delight." He smiled and headed toward the cruiser where Bradley waited, his prisoner locked in the back.

Sophie squeezed Lucky's arm to get her attention. Janie was white as a sheet, still staring at the man playing the violin.

"Janie, are you okay?" Lucky asked.

"No," she replied angrily. "I'm not okay. That man is a . . . traveler. I heard all about them in town." She turned to Lucky, a stricken look on her face. "How awful is that? My father is a *homeless* man. And my mother slept with him!" she cried.

Sophie's eyes grew wide, shocked at the meaning of Janie's words.

Lucky placed her free arm around Janie's shoulders. Her whole body was trembling.

Janie turned back to look at the stage. Her face shifted as realization dawned. "Oh no," she whispered. "Was my *mother* one of them?"

Lucky opened her mouth to speak, wanting to be honest, but unsure what to say. Miriam would have to be the one to reach her daughter. If only Janie would break down and talk to her.

Hot tears spilled down Janie's cheeks. "Please, can we go? I don't want to stay here. I don't want anything to do with these people . . . these *gypsies*." She spat out the words. She pulled away from Lucky and ran toward the parking lot.

Lucky sighed and turned to Sophie. "Let's go. I think we just made a bad thing worse."

Chapter 21

SOPHIE SLOWED TO a stop in front of the Spoonful. They had ridden back in complete silence. Janie sat in the backseat, her cheek pressed against the glass staring up at the sky. She looked completely miserable. Sophie was confused but careful not to ask any questions. Lucky was forced to remain silent, unable to offer any information to Sophie or solace to Janie without risking another outburst. As soon as the car came to a stop, Janie jumped out and headed inside the restaurant to return to work. She hadn't spoken a word since leaving the festival.

"Well, that went well," Sophie remarked.

Lucky sighed. "No good deed . . . as they say."

"Uh, can you fill me in?" Sophie drummed her fingers against the steering wheel impatiently. "What was all that about?"

Lucky closed her eyes and leaned back against the headrest. "I'll give you the broad strokes, but you have to promise never to tell this to anyone, even Sage, and you can't let Janie know I've told you."

"It's a deal," Sophie replied.

Lucky conveyed the gist of Janie's dilemma in a few short sentences. When she had finished, Sophie let out a low whistle. "Well, that must have been a shock to the poor kid."

"It was . . . it is. However, she's sleeping on my sofa, and I'd really like to see her make it up with her mother and go home. I thought today might cheer her up a bit. Boy, was I wrong!"

"Well, that's no reason for her to act like a total little brat, especially where you're concerned."

"She's a good kid, Sophie. She's just had a big shock, and she's so young she doesn't have any experience of real life or what can happen to people—people like her mother. Miriam's the one I feel bad for. I'm sure this is breaking her heart. Her whole life's revolved around that girl. She must feel like she's been kicked in the stomach."

"Frankly, I don't know what she's so upset about. I would have traded my whole family any day for a tribe of travelers. I used to dream about running away with the circus when I was thirteen."

Lucky laughed. "You think you'd trade 'em in. But trust me, you wouldn't."

Sophie grew still for a moment. "Speaking of trading in . . ." She looked carefully at Lucky. "What you were telling me last night about Elias? There might be some-thing to it."

Lucky felt a sinking feeling in the pit of her stomach. "What are you talking about?"

"A couple of little birdies have been chirping in my ear."

Lucky waited, her heart beating heavily. This was not going to be good news.

"The word is that you and Elias have broken up and that he's seeing the new doctor at the Clinic."

"Whaaat?" Lucky said. "Where did you hear that?"

"One of the bartenders at the Lodge saw them having dinner last night. They seemed very cozy."

"Last night?" The night that Elias said he had other plans. The night he didn't come with her to Sophie's. "So who said we were breaking up?"

"I can't remember, Lucky." Sophie looked apologetic.

"Come on, Sophie. Of course you can remember."

"No. Honestly. It was *really* thirdhand. And where it originally came from, I don't know. I think it was one of the waitresses from the Resort who's friendly with a woman who's a patient at the Clinic, who heard something from someone there." Sophie held up her hands in surrender. "That's it. That's all I know."

Lucky bit her lip. "If that's true, it might have been decent of him to at least let *me* know." A heavy feeling settled in her chest. She felt as if the world she knew was spinning around too fast.

Sophie reached over and grasped her hand. "Look, maybe it's not at all true. You know how rumors start. Everyone in this town is so damn nosy. Maybe somebody noticed an attractive woman working there and jumped to conclusions. It could be as simple and as stupid as that."

"Or not." Lucky could barely choke out the words. She felt hot angry tears forming.

Sophie hit her in the shoulder. "Cut it out. It's not true unless it comes from the horse's mouth. I know what I'd do. I'd march myself right over there and get in his face and ask him point blank what's going on."

"I can't do that."

"Oh, you have too much pride, I suppose? Well, it's a better idea than imagining the worst and suffering in silence."

"But what if it is true? What is there to say? I'm in love with Elias, have been for months, maybe my whole life, and he's falling for somebody else? Sophie, she's a doctor!

She's probably brilliant. She's gorgeous. How could I ever compete with that? What do I do? I run a restaurant for heaven's sake!" Lucky felt her face burning.

"Don't you *dare* put yourself down!" Sophie shouted. "I'll slap you silly. I swear I will. You're an amazing person. You're beautiful too, just in a different way. You have a heart as big as the world. You've helped so many people, and you have so much to offer as a person." Sophie heaved a great sigh. "And if it's true, I'll kick his butt and tell him exactly what an idiot I think he is."

Lucky snuffled back tears. "I have to get back to work. Jack'll be wondering what happened to me." She reached down and lifted the heavy pumpkin onto her lap.

"Don't forget what I just said. Otherwise, I'll have to paint it on the front window of the Spoonful so you'll see it every day and not forget."

Lucky laughed in spite of herself. "Thanks for saying all that. I appreciate it. I really do, but I have to get back." She leaned over and hugged Sophie. Fighting off a heavy feeling of misery, Lucky climbed out of the car and waved as Sophie drove away.

Chapter 22

"I WASN'T TRYING to keep you out of the loop, Jack." The Spoonful was closed for the night, and Lucky wanted to fill her grandfather in on everything she knew. She had no desire to betray Miriam or Janie, but Jack had certainly noticed the changes in Janie's behavior, and it was obvious to him that Miriam and Janie were not on good terms. He needed to hear everything, if only to be on the alert. Lucky wasn't entirely sure that the man who watched the restaurant was really Janie's father. Miriam had never identified him. It was only Janie's opinion that the man in her mother's photo was the same man who had been watching from across the street. Miriam had received a forget-me-not in her mailbox, but that wasn't actual proof that the person who left it and the man who was watching Janie was Eamon MacDougal. And if he wasn't Eamon, what was his motive for hanging around and keeping the restaurant under observation?

"Janie is upset. I guess she's angry and ashamed. And Miriam told me everything in confidence. She's the one I

worry about more; she's a complete wreck right now."
Lucky passed the sugar bowl to Jack and watched as he
stirred a tiny spoonful into his mug of tea. "So now you
know everything I know."

"I'm glad you're not keeping any secrets. That could be
dangerous."

"And I am worried about Janie. She doesn't seem to be
handling this any better. I thought after a few days she'd
calm down and reconcile with her mother, but she just
seems to be more entrenched in her anger. Besides . . ."
Lucky smiled. "I sure would like to get my apartment back
to normal."

"She's young. She'll get over it. Don't forget, she's just
lost her father. I mean the man she thought was her father,
so that's a part of it too."

"You're right."

"I do have a question though," Jack said. "Is Miriam
sure that man we've seen across the street is Janie's father?"

"That's exactly what I've been wondering. Miriam
seems sure. But what evidence does she have? She says
when she found the flower in her mailbox, she knew right
away he was here in Snowflake. It was something very
significant to them when they were young. So to answer
your question, unless Miriam actually sees him and talks
to him, which she doesn't want to do, we won't know for
sure that the man hanging around *is* Janie's father.
Although there is a resemblance between him and Janie.
By the way, his name is Eamon MacDougal."

"Might be a relative of his?" Jack speculated.

"Could be. Even assuming the guy we've seen is
Eamon, we still don't know anything about him. The man
Miriam knew when she was young could have changed.
How do we know he isn't the killer of our mystery man?"

"We don't. We don't know anything. I'm not willing to
trust him, even if he fesses up to being Janie's father," Jack
said. "Not until Miriam sees him and says it's him."

"Too bad he wasn't hanging around when Miriam came in a couple of days ago to talk to Janie. We know he's working at the festival, he's a musician and he's a traveler, but I have a sneaky suspicion he's around a lot more than we realize. If he really is Janie's father, then I can understand it at least. If he's not, then in my opinion, his motives are definitely sinister."

Lucky nervously fidgeted with the salt and pepper shakers on the table. "And the man who was shot to death may have no connection to the group that's here now. Just because he has a false ID, doesn't mean he's a traveler. He could be on the run. He could have been the inside man at that robbery, the one who disappeared. And whoever shot him could be the guy who took off with the cash."

"Or the other way around. If one guy took off with the cash, maybe he didn't share the loot. And maybe the guy on the inside was after him. We could guess till the cows come home, but it's all speculation. Why don't we talk about what's really been on your mind these last few days?"

Lucky blushed furiously. "You don't miss much, do you?"

"Nope," Jack replied. "Keepin' watch from the fo'castle is part of my job. Where's Elias been?"

Lucky shrugged. "I don't really know. I haven't heard from him."

Jack waited while Lucky struggled with how much to tell her grandfather. "We had an argument, I guess you'd call it. You know he hired a new doctor?"

Jack nodded. "I heard."

"She . . . I met her at the Clinic. She's very beautiful, and I think she's making a play for Elias."

"So? The world's full of beautiful women. I'm sure lots of 'em have been taken with him. And by the way go have a look in the mirror if you're feelin' wobbly."

"I don't feel wobbly!" she exclaimed.

Jack raised an eyebrow. "Coulda fooled me."

"All right." Lucky sulked. "I feel wobbly. I feel threatened. I feel jealous. Happy now that I've admitted it?" she replied grumpily.

"That's a start."

Lucky took a deep breath. "I'm sorry. Didn't mean to bite your head off. I know you're just trying to help. It's just . . . Elias was worried that I would be upset. He wanted to tell me that he had had a relationship with this Paula . . . whatever her name is . . . years ago. He wanted me to know, and he *said* he didn't want it to interfere with our relationship."

"That sounds pretty straight to me." Jack took a sip of his tea. "But you don't buy it."

"It's not that. I think he meant what he said at the time. But I got really upset because he had never mentioned this relationship before. And then to go and hire her to work at the Clinic. I just don't get it. They split up because she didn't want a small town practice, and now she's supposedly changed her mind? I kinda lost my temper and wanted to storm out of the Pub."

"Hmmm." Jack ruminated for a moment. "Hope you didn't give him a right hook." Jack was referring to the time she had broken the nose of an elementary school bully. Jack had nicknamed her Lucky after his favorite Navy boxer, Virgil Lukorsky. The nickname immediately stuck until eventually only her mother called her Letitia, her given name. Jack had always been very proud of her pugilistic abilities. "Sounds like he just wanted to clear the decks and be honest with you. And he must've meant what he said—that he didn't want anything to come between the two of you."

"Sometimes I feel stupid that I reacted like I did. But to make matters worse, she's staying at his place until she can find something on her own, and the night I was looking for Janie I saw a strange car parked in his driveway."

"He told you this? Or are you just jumping to conclusions?"

"He did. He told me himself."

"If that's the case, I can see why that'd make you uncomfortable. So what happened after that night at the Pub?"

"Nothing. Absolutely nothing. I think he's angry at me, and he thinks I'm an idiot. He couldn't make it to Sophie's with me. I just found out he was out to dinner with Paula."

"Then it's time to go after him. Fight for what you want, my girl."

"Easier said than done, Jack. I have no idea how to do that."

Chapter 23

NATE EDGERTON LEAFED slowly through the haphazard stack of papers piled in front of him, his glasses resting at the end of his nose. "Well, Ernie, I appreciate you bringing in all this information. I do see you've got liability insurance and agreements with the owner of the field. What I don't see is any information about your employees. I don't see tax withholding information; I don't see employment records with social security numbers; I don't see any of that."

"Uh, well, I haven't had any time, Nate. You didn't give me much time to gather up all my records. And," Ernie started to bluster, "I need to get back out there to the festival. The day's starting, and I need to be there."

"Uh-huh," Nate agreed. "Well, when do you think you can get me that information, Ernie?" Nate asked patiently but with a hint of a threat in his voice.

Ernie frowned. "Aw, come on, Nate. Let's stop kidding each other here. A lot of this is casual employment, just an agreement between friends, a handshake, a little cash under the table. I don't have time for all that record keeping. You know that." Ernie ran a finger around his shirt collar. His expensive suit looked a little more rumpled this morning.

"So you're tellin' me you have no employment records? How many people you got out there, Ernie?"

"Well, not many. There's the guy who runs the pony rides, and the stupid kid who's taken off now, after I went to the trouble to pick him up, but he's with the band anyway. I got a few day laborers who've done odd jobs, settin' up and stuff like that, and a guy who runs the little kiddie carousel. The mechanic who takes care of the ride works for the company, not me. The farmers are on their own. My bookkeeper in Lincoln Falls keeps track of them; they have to sign up for their spots."

"What kind of records do you have for the Gaelic band?"

"Nothing. Why should I? They're independent contractors. I pay them in cash."

"No 1099s for them either?" Nate asked quietly.

"No," Ernie sulked. "Why should I? They're happy to get paid in cash, and I'm happy not to have to do all that paperwork or report to the government."

Nate nodded. "Nice little setup you got, Ernie. You declaring income tax on the proceeds? Or is that too much for you and your bookkeeper?"

Ernie flushed a deep red. "You'd have to talk to my accountant."

"Ah, good idea," Nate said, a dark tone in his voice. "Maybe I will do just that. You make sure you leave his information with my deputy on your way out, will ya?"

A vein throbbed in Ernie's forehead. "Why are you hassling me, Nate? I don't get it. Here I am," a whining tone crept into his voice, "bringing people into Snowflake, putting this du . . . putting the town on the map and making money for businesses here. It's a win-win situation."

"I'm sure the village of Snowflake deeply appreciates your efforts on its behalf," Nate replied sarcastically. "But there's something else I'd like you to have a look at." Nate slid the photo of the dead man across the table.

Ernie glanced down. His complexion had lost all its color. "What the hell . . . ?"

"You tell me. You recognize this man?"

Ernie's jaw tightened. He didn't look up. Finally he said, "Never seen him before. Who is he?"

"He's the victim of a shooting. He's the man we found in a van in a ditch outside of town."

Ernie looked up, his expression closed. "Why would you ever think I knew him, then?"

"Just a hunch." Nate leaned back in his chair. "You see, we found a pretty good footprint out there. And we found it behind the van. Now, obviously our dead guy didn't rise from the dead and walk behind his van after he went into that ditch." Nate waited, studying Ernie's face. "So, it's reasonable to assume that somebody else was there after the van went off the road."

"Very interesting. Terrific detective work, but why are you tellin' me all this?"

"Well, I guess I'm passing this information on to you so that," Nate shouted across the table, "you stop screwing around with me and admit you were there."

Ernie jumped involuntarily. "What the hell?" he spluttered. "That's crap. I don't know anything about this dead guy or the van or the accident. I didn't have anything to do with it. Why are you hassling me?"

"Because Ernie, we've matched your footprint." Nate's voice boomed. "I'm sure when we search your room at the Resort, we'll find the exact shoes you were wearing that day."

"That's crazy." Ernie was sweating profusely. "I wasn't there. That can't be my footprint. It just can't."

Nate sat back and raised his eyebrows. "How many men do you think have small feet like you, Ernie? And how many of those men with small feet wear expensive Italian leather shoes?" Nate relaxed even further. "Why don't you make it easy on yourself? Just tell me what you were doing there."

Ernie's breathing had become shallow. Nate realized he was hyperventilating. His face had turned a beet red. Ernie, overweight as he was, was already a prime candidate for a heart attack. Nate just wished that if he were going to have one, it wouldn't be at the police station.

Nate's tone became warm and friendly. "Just tell the truth Ernie. We're gonna find everything out anyway."

Ernie looked as if he were about to burst into tears. "All right," he shouted. "All right, I was there! Okay? Are you happy now?"

"Tell me all about it," Nate replied in his warmest avuncular tone.

Ernie took a deep breath. His shirt collar was soaked with perspiration. "I saw the van, okay?" he replied truculently. "I was drivin' into town, and I spotted it down below. That's all. I pulled over and went down to see if anybody needed help."

"That's real big of you," Nate replied.

Ernie shot Nate a look, the sarcasm not lost on him, but he refused to rise to the bait. "But . . . there was nothin' I could do."

"So how come you just told me you didn't recognize this guy?" Nate shoved the photo closer to Ernie.

"I never did. I never . . . I didn't look at his face; I didn't want to. Besides, his face was in the windshield, I couldn't see it very well anyway."

"Did you by any chance check to see if he was still alive?" Nate replied gently.

"Uh . . . well, no, I mean I figured he was dead."

"I see. Then what?"

"Well, I wanted to check if there was anybody else in there. So I looked in the back of the van to see. And there was nobody there."

"And did you by any chance climb into that van?"

"No. Of course not. Why would I? It was empty."

"You didn't climb into that van and remove anything? That's what you're tellin' me?"

"That's right," Ernie said firmly.

"Then what did you do?"

"Huh?"

"Then what did you do?" Nate repeated.

"Well, nothing."

"Nothing," Nate said flatly. "You didn't think to report the accident? You didn't think to make sure the man was still alive? And you didn't search the van just to see what you could find?"

"You got no right, Nate. You got no right to accuse me of anything." Ernie's voice had risen. "I didn't do anything wrong. I didn't kill anybody. I didn't steal anything. All's I was doin' was making sure nobody needed any help."

"You're a regular Good Samaritan, Ernie. Is that how you see it?"

"Well, yes," he replied, puffing up his chest and sitting up straighter.

"So you won't mind if we go outside and have a look at your car, then?"

Ernie's shoulders relaxed. "Not at all. Look away."

Nate waited a long moment. "Okay, Ernie. You can go. But wait out in front. I'll be out in a minute to have a look at your bumper."

Ernie rose from his seat. His shirt was sticking to his chest. He shot a dark look at Nate and then turned and walked out the door, slamming it behind him.

Nate sighed and placed Ernie's documents in a folder, laying the photo of the dead man on top. He buzzed the intercom for Bradley. The door flew open, and Bradley stood on the threshold. Nate was sure the deputy had been listening at the door to glean whatever information he could.

"Go follow Ernie outside and check out his car. See if you see anything that might look like damage to the front."

"Okay, Chief. But I gotta tell . . ."

"Have they sent over that impression yet? The one of the footprint we found?"

"Uh . . . no, not yet." Bradley sneezed violently.

Nate smiled to himself. "Well, get on the horn and tell them to hurry it up, and then . . ."

"Chief, I gotta tell you . . ." Bradley cringed, already imagining his boss's reaction. He sneezed again. "What's that smell?"

"Ernie took a bath in his aftershave I guess. What are you tryin' to say?"

Bradley sneezed once more and wiped his nose. "They just called from Lincoln Falls . . ." Bradley gulped.

"And?" Nate replied testily.

"The van's been stolen." There, he had said it. He squeezed his eyes shut.

"Whaaat?" Nate bellowed. "It's been what?" he shouted.

Bradley was sure Nate's voice could be heard all the way out on Green Street. "They dusted it for fingerprints, but then they got busy and had to move it to that impound lot a few blocks away. It's privately run; they have a contract for storage with the station. The guard fell asleep, didn't hear a thing, and some kids broke in, they think, and drove it right through the chain-link fence."

Nate rested his head on his hand. "I don't believe this." He shook his head from side to side. "Kids, my . . ." He rose from his chair, almost knocking it to the floor. "Go check out Ernie's car. I'm going over there."

"Where?"

"Lincoln Falls. I'm gonna give those idiots a piece of my mind." Nate stormed out and headed for the back door and his cruiser.

Chapter 24

LUCKY BUSIED HERSELF clearing away dishes and cups from the counter after the morning rush. As far as she could tell, the large number of customers consisted of farmers and locals stopping in for breakfast before setting up their stalls at the Harvest Festival.

She had woken with a low-grade headache after tossing and turning half the night. Elias hadn't stopped in at the Spoonful once, either for lunch or at closing time, as he often did. She counted on her fingers. Three days had gone by since their meeting at the Pub. Since then there had been no blinking light on the answering machine when she returned home. Other than the time she had invited him to Sophie and Sage's apartment, she hadn't spoken to him, nor had he called the Spoonful to talk to her. He was either angry or ashamed or guilty. Maybe he no longer cared. The possibilities spun around in her head.

Sophie's news had completely confused and devastated her. She didn't know what to think. On the one hand, Elias had made a point of saying that nothing in his past affected their relationship, but yet his routine had already varied. That night at the Pub she hadn't felt the same energy or humor or passion from him that she had always felt in their relationship. Was he losing interest in her? Or was he just distracted? Or worse yet, was he lying and making a fool of her?

Jack was taking a break, reading his newspaper at a table by the front window. He had had no trouble noticing there was something wrong between her and Elias. Possibly everyone in town already knew. Was she the last person to learn her relationship was over?

The bell at the door rang. She glanced up and saw Nate at the threshold with Joe Conrad in tow.

"Hello, folks," he called. He held up a hand in greeting and headed for the table where Jack sat.

Janie was in the kitchen helping Sage prepare vegetables for a fresh pot of soup. Meg returned to the counter and grabbed the plastic bin full of dirty dishes. "I'll take care of these, Lucky."

"Thanks, Meg." Lucky pulled out a tray and poured four cups of coffee, one for each of the men and one for herself.

Jack looked up expectantly. His eyes brightened at the prospect of chatting with Nate. "You're early today, Nate. It's not even three bells."

"Started early. Didn't have a chance to get breakfast."

Lucky set the tray on an adjacent table and served the coffee. "I'll have Janie get some muffins for you."

"Lucky told me about the excitement at the festival yesterday," Jack said. "What's the story with the guy who tried to run away?"

"Not much. He's just a kid. He's with the group from Cape Breton—the musicians. Ernie hired him to help run the pony rides."

Lucky was instantly alert, remembering Miriam's story of where her family came from.

Jack harrumphed. "He have an ID?"

"Believe it or not, he did. Canadian driver's license, if it's real. I'm checking it out. Couldn't figure out why he ran like that. And he wasn't very cooperative. Said he didn't know anything about the dead man in the van. Didn't own a gun. Whole thing had nothing to do with him. Then Ernie White showed up to get him. Told me I was sticking my nose in where it didn't belong and started threatening to call his lawyer about interfering with his business advantage and a lot of nonsense like that." Nate shrugged. "Had to let the kid go."

"So he's a traveler for sure," Jack stated.

"Well, he's with them, so I guess he is," Nate replied. "They're a real weird bunch. They've set up camp not too far from the Stones. I guess it's one of their places they visit every few years."

"Heard about that. Lucky mentioned she heard it's a sacred place to them."

"Go figure." Nate shook his head. "Always thought those things were left over from the Indians. Bottom line is I'm no further along identifying our guy in the van. And speaking of the van, everything that could go wrong with this investigation has gone wrong. The van's been stolen. The people in Lincoln Falls sent me over a photo of our dead guy though. I printed it out on the color printer to get a better idea. He does kind of look like the police artist's sketch from that robbery years ago—shape of the face and the eyebrows," Nate said, pulling a folded piece of paper from his jacket. "But I couldn't swear this is the same guy based on that sketch."

"Can I see?" Lucky asked.

"Sure, as long as it won't bother you. There's some facial damage, and his complexion isn't exactly what it should be," Nate replied with a grimace. He passed the photo to her.

Jack peered over her shoulder as she unfolded it. She stopped breathing. She hoped her face didn't reveal the shock she felt. She was looking at the same man she had seen on stage at the festival. Except the man in this photo was obviously not among the living. But how could that be? This was more than a similarity that might exist within a family. It was as if the man who played the violin at the festival, the man who had been watching the Spoonful, the man that Miriam was sure was Janie's father had a twin. That had to be the explanation. But which twin was still alive? She glanced at Jack. His face betrayed no recognition. Of course Jack wouldn't recognize him. The man watching the restaurant had stood in the shadow of an awning. He had turned away quickly once he realized he was being observed. Jack had never had a good look at him. Only she, Sophie or Janie might recognize that the dead man was a carbon copy of the man they had all seen on stage at the festival. Nate must not have had a chance to speak to the musicians. If he had, he would know these two men had the same face. She glanced over her shoulder. Janie was safely away from the table, still in the kitchen with Sage. Lucky quickly folded the paper up and passed it back to Nate.

"What about that driver's license?" Jack asked. "Did that check out?"

"Nope. The man on that license died years ago, and the address doesn't exist. It's a vacant lot in Bangor. The building was torn down seven years ago. They've taken fingerprints over at Lincoln Falls, so maybe he'll show up in a database—here or across the border."

"What about you, Joe? You still think the dead guy might be the one you were looking for?" Jack asked.

Joe nodded. "I've got nothing to prove it. But I think he could be. You saw the photo, and it fits the witness account—very similar to that police artist's sketch. The woman who was at the traffic light could have been one more fatality, but she was able to hit the brakes and the van swerved around her. She got a quick glimpse of the man driving as he pulled off his ski mask. He looked right at her for a second or so. But you know how undependable eyewitness accounts can be.

People are in shock. The brain does strange things. Information can get processed wrong. But she's the only witness they had. She seemed pretty levelheaded once she calmed down. So, for all we know, this is an accurate sketch, and Nate says it sure does look like the guy found on the road."

"If he was a traveler, how could he have gotten a job where he'd have to have a background check or be bonded by a company?" Lucky asked.

"Well, don't forget. He didn't work for the company. He just wore one of their uniforms. It was the other guy who actually worked for the armored truck company." Joe continued, "You'd be amazed how creative criminals can be— the smart ones. The inside guy at the facility, the one who turned off the alarm, eventually we matched him and found out who he really was—Jim Devlin, Jimmy Devlin to his friends." Joe laughed ruefully. "Devlin claimed to be a victim at first. But the more the police started to look at him, the more they were leaning on him as the man who set up the robbery. Maybe this poor fool driving the truck never thought it would come to a murder charge. Maybe he took off with the money and was too scared to go back or contact Devlin. Devlin stuck around for a while, claiming complete innocence, but the more the police—and I—started checking him out, well, that's when he got nervous and took off."

"And no one could ever track him?" Lucky asked.

"He was good. Probably had another ID already set up in case anything went wrong. Maybe he had a few of them, for all I know." Joe took a sip of his coffee. "Maybe I'm crazy, but it's bugged me all these years that the money was never recovered and my company had to pay out. More than that, really, is that some poor guy with a wife and kids had to die for no good reason."

Everyone around the table fell silent. Janie broke the silence when she arrived with her tray. "Are blueberry muffins and jam okay?" she asked.

Nate looked up. "That's great, Janie. Thanks."

Janie attempted to pass the dish across the table but hesitated. Her hand started to shake. She was looking out the window. Lucky grabbed the dish before it fell and smashed on the table. She followed Janie's line of sight. He was back again. The same man stood across the street staring at the front window, looking straight at Janie.

Nate turned his head to look. "Who's that?"

Joe peered out the window to have a look. He stared and then turned slowly and looked carefully at Janie.

Lucky rose and walked toward the window. The man was in shadow. There was a startling resemblance between Janie and this man. The same coppery red hair, the same long face and high cheekbones, but the resemblance was more than just superficial. Lucky couldn't quite put her finger on it, but she thought it was something about the body language, the tall lanky frame, the way Janie moved. Genes were amazing. Two people could walk and move in a similar fashion because of some shared chromosomes, even though they had never met. Lucky was concerned Joe might have grasped the significance of the man who watched the restaurant and Janie's nervousness. She hoped Janie's secrets would remain safe.

"I think I'm gonna have a word with that guy." Jack pushed back his chair and stood. He peered through the glass panes at the front door before finally stepping outside and heading across the street. Lucky watched the scene play out from the doorway. If Jack was in any trouble, she could reach him very quickly. Nate stood and joined her in the doorway. When the man realized Jack was heading his way, he turned suddenly and walked quickly down Broadway. Jack shook his head and returned to the restaurant.

Janie was rooted to the spot; her face had flushed a deep red. She turned and ran back to the kitchen.

"Who was that?" Joe asked of no one in particular.

Nate shrugged. "Couldn't get a good look at him. He took off too fast."

Lucky's first instinct was to protect Janie. For some

reason she couldn't identify, she didn't want Joe Conrad to get a better look at the man. If Joe realized the man who stood across the street was a twin to the man in Nate's photo, Janie could discover her relations were suspected of or involved in a crime. She didn't need to learn that, at least not now. What sort of embarrassment could that cause for her or Miriam? On the other hand, Lucky knew she should share this information with Nate.

"It's nothing," Lucky replied, returning to her seat. She decided to change the subject. "Did you have a chance to talk to the rest of the people out at the festival, yesterday, Nate?"

"No. That kid who tried to run away—that took up the rest of my afternoon. I plan to go back out there today and question those musicians."

Lucky was relieved. Nate would figure things out soon enough without her help. She took a last sip of coffee and gathered up the empty plates. She headed for the kitchen to unload the dishes. Janie was sitting on a stool, covering her face with her hands.

"Janie . . . ?" Lucky placed a hand on her shoulder.

The girl took a deep shaky breath. "I'll be okay." She looked up at Lucky. "He knows who I am. He knows. Why is he bothering me? Why won't he leave me alone?"

Sage was completely in the dark as to the cause of Janie's distress. "I'll just get a few things from the storeroom," he said and diplomatically left the kitchen.

"I don't know. But I imagine he'd just like to meet you." Lucky only hoped that was true, assuming this man really was Janie's father. She was grateful Janie hadn't seen the photo of the dead man that Nate had shared. The real question was which man was still alive? Eamon MacDougal, as Miriam thought? Or his twin? And if the man who walked the streets of Snowflake wasn't Eamon MacDougal, then what business did he have stalking Janie?

Janie shuddered. "Well, I don't want to meet him. I just

want him to leave me alone. Can you let me know when he's gone?"

Lucky sighed. "He is gone. Try not to let this upset you, Janie. It will get better." Lucky hesitated, wanting to try to reach the girl, hoping that she'd listen, or at least listen to her mother. When no further response from Janie came, Lucky gave up and returned to the main room.

Jack was waiting for Lucky. "Everything all right?"

Lucky nodded.

"What was that all about, Jack?" Nate asked.

"No idea." Jack shrugged as he resumed his seat. "We've just seen this guy around once or twice. He watches the restaurant like he wants to come in, but then he just walks away."

Lucky was relieved Jack didn't tell Nate the whole story. Nate could keep his mouth shut, but it certainly was none of Joe Conrad's business.

Nate took a last bite of his muffin. "Lucky—Jack—you let me know if anybody's bothering you or if this guy comes back again. I'll be a lot happier when the festival's over and all these strangers are gone." Nate's phone started to ring. "Excuse me, folks." He hit a button and stood, moving away from the table. Nate mumbled a few words into the phone. Then he shouted, "*What?* You are kidding me!"

Everyone at the table looked up, surprised by Nate's outburst.

"What do you mean you didn't get to him? You're telling me you didn't even *start* the autopsy?" He was fuming. "Don't give me busy! I'll tell you who's busy. I'm busy." Then a long silence as Nate listened to the voice at the other end of the call. "Damn," he said. "I'll be over there in half an hour." Nate clicked off.

"Something wrong, Nate?" Jack asked.

Nate's face darkened. He turned back to them. "Our body's been stolen."

Chapter 25

MIRIAM HAULED THE vacuum cleaner out of the hallway closet and set about methodically going over all the floors in each room, the living room, hallway and dining room. She hoped the noise and activity would calm her frayed nerves. She angrily pushed at furniture with the hose as she moved through each room. When she finished the downstairs, she lugged the electric beast up the stairway and continued on the second floor of the house.

When the vacuuming was done, she pulled a dust cloth from her apron pocket and cleaned all the surfaces in each bedroom, the guest room, Janie's room and finally her own bedroom. When she came to her bureau, she hesitated over the jewelry box that sat atop the dresser.

Her heart began to race. She was exhausted. Her hands were shaking. Unable to sleep well the night before, she had woken every hour as the mantel clock chimed below her in the living room. She had mumbled prayers that Janie would return soon. Then she'd tossed and turned, burying her face in the pillow, trying not to cry. Every morning since the argument, she had woken and prayed again that Janie would return, that her daughter would give her the chance to explain, that Janie would forgive her for not telling the truth years before.

What had kept her from doing so? Miriam sat heavily on the edge of the bed. She reached out and touched the bedspread, the side where Doug had rested for so many years. She imagined him asleep there now, imagined touching him, feeling his arms around her. She missed him terribly. If only he were here now, he would know what to do. He would have been able to talk to Janie. The girl would have listened to him.

Doug had been Miriam's strength, her rock for so many years. While she, weak and frightened, hadn't been able to tell the simple truth to the person she loved most in the world. Was she terrified of being judged? Yet she had done nothing wrong. Her only error was in loving the wrong man with all her heart. And she had been so wrong about Eamon. The real question was, why now? Why was he here, and why was he telegraphing that he knew where she lived? Was that why was he watching Janie? Did he know she was his daughter?

Part of her longed to see his face. The part of her she had buried years before in that wood. Another part of her wanted to strike out at him, to watch him fall to his knees and suffer as she had suffered. How dare he think he could arrive on her doorstep and make any claim, least of all a claim on her daughter, the person she would die to protect? What were his intentions? Did he plan to steal Janie away? To kidnap her? To spirit Janie away as punishment because she herself had turned her back on the family? What did he want?

Her hands were still shaking. She leaned over and curled up in a fetal position on the bed, imagining Doug's arms around her. She had to stay in control. She had to somehow reach Janie, warn her to be careful, warn her daughter that her former family could be capable of anything.

Chapter 26

"HOW DO YOU know for sure, Miriam? How do you know it was Janie's father who left that flower in your mailbox?" Lucky had gone straight to Miriam's house as soon as she was able to take a break from the Spoonful. She hadn't yet said a word to Jack that the man in Nate's photo was a twin of the man she had seen on stage. Each time he stood across the street from the Spoonful, it had been impossible to get a good look at his face. At first it hadn't been obvious he was watching Janie, but it had soon become clear. Even so, he had managed to stay far enough away that neither Lucky nor Jack had been able to get a good look at his face. If she and Sophie hadn't taken Janie to the Harvest Festival and seen the man onstage, Lucky probably wouldn't have noticed his resemblance to the photo of the dead man.

Miriam stood in the center of her kitchen, obsessively wiping her hands on a dish towel. "Of course it's him. It has to be. I know Eamon has a twin brother—identical—but no one else could ever know about the forget-me-nots, certainly not his brother. That was our signal to each other.

We used to pick them in the meadows. Only Eamon would know that."

"Forgive me, Miriam, but how do you know he didn't tell someone else about that? Confide in his brother in a weak moment? Even though it was your secret," Lucky persisted. "They're twins, or at least they were. They must have been close."

Miriam shook her head vehemently. "They weren't. They were as different as night and day, even though they looked exactly the same. No one could tell them apart except for me. I could. I could always look at Eamon's face and know it was him. His heart shone out of his eyes." Miriam sighed. "At least that's what I used to think. Before . . ." She didn't continue the thought.

Lucky knew what she was thinking. *Before he abandoned me.* "How were they different?"

Miriam shrugged and sat heavily in the kitchen chair. At least she had stopped wiping her hands on the dish towel. "Taran was a bad apple. Always getting into trouble. Always causing trouble. Sneaking around. No one ever knew what he was up to."

"Was Taran a musician as well?" Lucky asked.

Miriam looked up quickly. "Yes. That's what they did. The whole family could play several instruments."

Lucky reached across the table and grasped Miriam's hand. "I don't mean to alarm you, but what if the man in the van was Eamon, and the man who's been watching Janie is his brother Taran?"

Miriam gasped. "It couldn't be. I told you—the forget-me-not." Her face fell. "You mean the dead man could be Eamon?"

Lucky didn't respond but waited for Miriam to process this possibility. "What concerns me is which one of them is watching Janie. We have to find out. You have to see him yourself to be sure. Talk to him. I don't think the brother . . . Taran . . . could keep up the pretense if he isn't Eamon."

"I can't, Lucky. I can't see any of those people. You don't understand," Miriam cried. "I've spent my whole life hiding from the clan. I've spent my whole life recovering from my life with them. I can't just waltz up to them and say, 'How are you doing?'"

"What day did you receive this flower in your mailbox?"

"Uh . . ." Miriam thought for a moment. "It was . . ." She calculated the days on her fingers. "Five days ago."

"On Saturday?"

"Yes."

"That's the same day Nate discovered the body on the road."

Miriam gasped, her mind numb with the possibility that Eamon might be dead.

Chapter 27

JANIE DROVE AIMLESSLY up and down the streets of Snowflake. She couldn't bear another night of hanging around Lucky's apartment or talking to Meg or Rosemary on the phone and not being able to tell them what she was upset about. All they had to say was that she should go home and make amends with her mother. They didn't understand. How could they? They knew who their parents were, where they came from, who went before them. Nobody was telling them they were the illegitimate children of gypsies. She checked her gas gauge, half full. At least she wouldn't have to stop anywhere for fuel. She realized she was driving in ever-widening circles.

She hated to admit it to herself, but she missed her house and her mother's cooking and her room with all her favorite CDs and books. If this hadn't happened, that's exactly where she'd be. Or maybe she'd be with Meg, and they'd be at the festival . . . why did she have to see that man there yesterday? And could he really be her father? She thought back to the times she had seen him outside the restaurant, in the market, walking across the street, paralleling her path, yesterday onstage playing a violin. He was a musician obviously, but he probably couldn't even read music. Maybe he couldn't even read period. And her mother. Had she come from the same background? She'd never know unless she talked to her mom. If her mom had been a traveler, how did she ever become the middle class woman who worried about redecorating her house and gardening if she had never known a house or a garden as a young girl? But she had no desire to talk to her mother. She didn't know if she'd hear the truth or just more lies. There was no way to be sure. She felt as if the ground had turned to quicksand beneath her feet and she was being sucked down into a murky chasm, unable to breathe.

She continued along the road that led out of town. Without being conscious of driving there, she found herself at the entrance to the parking lot of the festival. She couldn't admit it to herself, but she was curious, morbidly curious. She wanted to get a closer look at the strange man, at *him*. Perhaps by staring at him as he had stared at her, she'd derive some answers—answers about her own origin.

The lot was full, but she was able to find a spot at the end of the parking area, squeezing in between a truck and a subcompact car. She parked and walked toward the entrance. Inside the grounds, a large crowd was gathered at the far end of the field where the band was still playing onstage. All of the farmers had packed up and gone. The only booths still open were those selling handmade goods—jewelry, pottery, kitchenware. Many people milled around the small carousel and the pony corral; they were mostly parents with young children who tugged on their hands, begging for another ride or another run through the corn maze. She spotted Remy near the corral and hoped he didn't see her. She didn't want to talk to anyone.

She pulled the hood of her sweater over her hair and slouched against a tree. There were, she was sure, plenty of people here that she knew—neighbors, old school friends. She hoped to avoid them. She needed to remain invisible, anonymous.

He was onstage, playing a fiddle, but now he accompanied a banjo player and another violinist. The music was up-tempo, like a jig, moving faster and faster. A good-sized audience had gathered to listen to the song. With a final crescendo the music ended abruptly, and a swell of applause filled the air. The band was very popular. They bowed to the audience and were greeted by another round of applause. Smiling, they took a second bow. The lights dimmed, and the musicians turned away, preparing to clear the stage. The crowd, excitedly talking and laughing, began to disperse.

Janie watched as the musicians packed up their instruments and equipment. She heard snatches of conversation from the stage but wasn't able to make out the words. At the edge of the outdoor lighting, she was invisible. As long as she stood in the shadow of a tree trunk, she couldn't be seen. Softly, she moved closer to the next large tree. Her jeans were dark, her sweater a charcoal gray and her hood covered her hair.

Several people still remained in front of the stage. They were busy folding up picnic blankets and preparing to leave. It was quieter now, and the conversations onstage were audible. She realized with a shock the musicians weren't speaking English. But what? Confused, she wondered if they were not just travelers, but foreigners. Her mother would know, but she couldn't ask her now.

Janie watched the tall red-haired man carefully as he moved about the stage, winding cords and helping the others pack up. He stopped to talk to a woman in the upstage area who balanced a stand-up bass against her shoulder. They chatted for a few moments, and then he carried the bass off stage and into a waiting van at the side.

How could this man have a connection to her? Granted they were both tall and slender. They both had auburn red

hair, but was there any other resemblance? Was that
enough for her to accept that this man really was her
father? She thought about the mild-mannered, kind and
silly father she had known. Doug Leonard's hair was
brown and later turned to salt-and-pepper and finally completely gray. He always wore glasses and was fond of singing off-key to her. Janie had loved him with all her heart.
He had been the perfect Dad. She felt a deep sense of guilt,
of disloyalty at even accepting that he might not be her
father. He had been only slightly taller than her mother,
and Janie, at age fourteen, towered over both her parents.
When she was a child, she wondered why her hair wasn't
deep brown, almost black, like her mother's. Why was it
so red, she had asked. She had never liked her hair color.
She wanted dark hair, like her mother, but she had been
told her great-grandmother had red hair like hers. As a
child, she had heard jokes about being stolen by the gypsies. In her case she had been stolen from the gypsies.

She watched as the first van pulled away, followed by a
second older and rusty vehicle. The man and all his com-
panions were gone. Where were they staying while in
Snowflake? The town had no hotels, except for the Resort
at the top of the mountain. And there was only one bed-
and-breakfast. But if they were travelers, would they have
RVs, a campsite somewhere in the woods around the town?
She'd probably never know anything more about this man
than what she'd seen tonight.

She glanced around. The field was empty. Not a soul
remained. Silently she climbed the stairway to the stage.
It held an earthy aroma of warm wood and sawdust. She
stood on the spot where he had stood and looked out over
the vacant grassy field. What would it be like to play an
instrument? To stand on a stage in front of clapping, cheering people? Was it frightening or was it a heady feeling?
Or were the musicians so lost in the swell of notes they
forgot the onlookers?

She shivered in her light sweater. The night had grown colder. Even the stalls that were still open when she arrived were closed. The corral was empty. The horses must have been led to a barn for the night. No one remained. No one she could see at least. She felt a shiver of fear. It was time to go home—home to her temporary digs at Lucky's apartment at least.

She descended the stairs of the stage and walked out through the gate to the parking lot. The lot was empty. Her car stood alone. She dug her car keys out of her jeans, anxious to climb in and turn on the heater. With shivering fingers, she slid her key into the door lock. She sensed movement behind her. She turned quickly. A strong arm grasped her neck, choking her. A rough hood was pulled over her head. She tried to scream, but there was no one to hear.

Chapter 28

LUCKY WAS ABOUT to flip over the sign at the front door when she spotted a figure heading toward the Spoonful. She hesitated. It was Remy. She opened the door for him. "Hi, Remy. Are you looking for Sage?"

"No, I just stopped by to talk to you and Jack for a minute, if you don't mind."

"Not at all." There was something in his tone that told her this wasn't just a social call. "Come on in. Would you like coffee or anything?"

"No. Thanks, I'm fine. I can't stay long. I have to get back soon. I just . . . uh . . . wanted to talk to you both."

"Have a seat." Lucky sat down and leaned on her elbows, giving her full attention to Remy. Jack joined them.

Remy took a deep breath. "Something happened today out at the festival that's really been bothering me. It happened near the corral, that's how come I saw the whole thing." Remy looked at them to gauge their reaction. He had their full attention. "One of the women from the band got in Ernie's face. She was really upset. She's a big woman, and she started pushing Ernie around, attacking him almost, yelling at him."

"What was she saying?" Jack asked.

"Well, they had some words before it got really loud. I think it kinda freaked out some of the people who were near the horses. She started screaming at Ernie, saying, 'What did you do to him, what did you do to him?' She kept getting more and more hysterical. Finally a couple of the guys from the band rushed over and dragged her away."

"What did she mean?" Lucky asked. "What did Ernie do with *who*?"

Remy shook his head. "I don't know who she was talking about. But when it got really loud, Rory walked over. He put his hand behind him, like he was reaching inside the waistband of his trousers, and I saw something there." Remy looked up, a frightened look in his eye. "Lucky, I think he was ready to pull out a gun."

"Jeez," Jack remarked. "Why would he need a gun to run a pony ride for kids?"

"That's what I'm wondering," Remy said. "I don't know what to do, that's why I wanted to talk to you and Jack."

"Have you told Sage?"

Remy shook his head. "I didn't want to. Sage would try to get involved, and I don't want him to feel he has to, especially if it's dangerous. What do you think I should do?"

"I think you should call Nate first thing in the morning. Whoever this woman is, she obviously thinks Ernie's done something to someone. She must know something Nate needs to hear. And as far as Rory carrying a gun, what's that about? Nate needs to know this stuff, Remy."

Remy nodded. "I think you're right. Nate's not my favorite person in the world, not after he arrested Sage the way he did last year, but I'll call him." Remy took a deep breath. "I'll tell you, I'm ready to call the owners and pull those horses out of there and bring 'em home. I don't like what's happening at the festival one bit."

"I'm glad you told us, Remy. It sounds like it could escalate, and the last thing you need is a gun being waved around, especially with little kids and animals nearby."

Remy heaved a sigh. "Don't say anything to Sage, will you? I'll tell him myself eventually after I talk to Nate. I know he worries about me, and I don't want him gettin' involved."

Lucky glanced at Jack. "We won't say anything. But you should tell him anyway as soon as you talk to Nate."

Remy rose from his chair, a troubled look on his face. He stuck his hands in his pockets. "You're right, I know. But I gotta go now. I don't like leaving the horses alone." He turned away and headed for the door. "Thanks, Lucky . . . Jack."

Lucky locked the door behind him and flipped the sign over. She watched Remy till he was out of sight. "What do you think, Jack?"

"I think the more I hear stories about Ernie White, the less I like him. And that's sayin' a lot." He sat down on his stool behind the cash register. "I'll finish counting up. I'll be done in a few minutes, and then we can go home."

Lucky went into the kitchen to make sure everything had been put away. There wasn't much to do except start the dishwasher. Sage had left everything in perfect order. Jack called out to her, "We've got another visitor, my girl."

Lucky's heart skipped a beat. Was it Elias? Perhaps he had decided to stop in, perhaps he wasn't angry. She peered through the hatch. Her heart fell when she saw Horace waving through the glass. Cicero, his adopted dog, was on a leash next to him. She returned to the main room and unlocked the door for him.

"I hope we're not too late for a visit." Cicero's tail was wagging. The dog looked up hopefully.

Lucky forced a smile, not wanting her disappointment to show. "You're not too late. Always good to see you."

"Cicero and I were just taking a walk. Is it okay if he comes in?"

"Sure. No one else is here—just me and Jack." She reached down to pat Cicero's head and was rewarded with a wet kiss on her cheek. "Can I get you some tea?"

"Oh, lovely, yes, herbal please. Thank you." Horace took a seat at a small table and unclipped Cicero's leash. The dog settled happily at his feet. "You two have very serious looks on your faces. Anything wrong?"

"Nah. We're fine, Horace. We were just talking about these travelers and the disappearing body."

"Did you say disappearing?" Horace asked.

"Yes, but keep it under your hat. Nate just found out this morning that the body was stolen from the morgue."

"Interesting," Horace replied. "Very interesting. I heard about the insurance investigator who's chasing a traveler, or thinks he is at any rate." Horace was silent for a few moments and then finally asked, "How often do these travelers come through this area?"

Jack thought a moment. "Maybe every few years. They always stay up by the Stones."

"Fascinating," Horace replied.

Lucky returned with Horace's tea and a hunk of chicken wrapped in a napkin. "You know, when we were kids, there were a lot of stories about the Stones, that they're haunted, that a woman hung herself there and her ghost torments anyone who comes close—all that silly stuff." Cicero rested his head on Lucky's knee. She unwrapped the napkin and the dog neatly devoured the treat.

Jack shut the drawer of the cash register and joined them at the table. "There've always been a lot of stories and legends about the Stones—as far back as I can remember. Even *my* grandfather used to talk about them. He always believed the Indians had nothing to do with them—that the Stones went much further back in time than that."

"Oh yes," Horace replied. "In fact, there are stone structures, megaliths if you will, all over New England—Maine, Massachusetts, New Hampshire, not just Vermont. And in truth not just New England. They've been found as far away as Iowa, New Mexico, places like that."

"Really?" Lucky questioned. "I had no idea. I thought our Stones were unique."

"Unique, yes, but not rare. There are some amazing sites. There's the Woodstock, Vermont, megalith, and the Mystery Hill structure in New Hampshire, the Gungywamp Complex in eastern Connecticut, the . . . uh . . ." Horace thought for a moment. "Let's see, the Upton stone chamber just outside of Boston, and the Wendell Beehive Cave, also in Massachusetts and many more. And then in Ontario there's a protected site that has a great deal of evidence about the voyage of a Bronze Age Scandinavian king named Woden-lithi around 1700 BCE. I think I've read there are eight hundred different sites discovered in New England alone. And that doesn't even begin to take in the rest of America."

"So strange. I grew up here, but I've never given it much thought."

Horace laughed. "Most people don't or don't take any interest. Let's see, the Bronze Age is considered 3000 BCE and late Bronze Age is, I think, 1500 to 1200 BCE. Bear in mind, stones can't be carbon-dated, so I have no idea how the archeologists have arrived at the figure. Perhaps they can date tree roots that have grown through the sites or implements found in them. But here's another interesting thing—most of these sites, if not all, have openings that line up with the solstices or the spring and vernal equinoxes. Maybe they don't anymore because of the precession of equinoxes over thousands of years, but it's thought that the openings of many of these chambers would have lined up perfectly thousands of years ago."

Jack whistled. "I've never even heard that."

"Sadly, they've pretty much been ignored until recent years. It was assumed they were colonial root cellars, but that doesn't make any sense. The colonists wouldn't have stored food that way. There are even written accounts that the early colonists who found strange markings on the stones sent inquiries back to England about them. I doubt they ever got any answers to their questions though. No one could decipher the written language."

"What kind of markings?" Lucky asked.

"Well, that's where it gets truly interesting. There are lots of theories out there, and I'm not really sure what the latest thinking is. My interests lie several centuries beyond that time." Horace chuckled. "But you can be sure most of this stuff is hotly debated. There are books about the markings and the megaliths written by a professor from a very well-known university in Boston. I think at the time they pooh-poohed his theories. I may still have one of those books. I'll have to have a look. If you're interested, I'll dig it up."

"Well, no wonder these travelers might consider the Stones a sacred site, something built by their ancestors thousands of years ago," Lucky said.

"Yes," Horace replied. "Perhaps they know a lot more than the academics. I'd be interested to hear what *they* have to say about the Stones." Horace took a last sip of his tea. "Thanks, folks. I'll be on my way. I'm sure I've bored you silly by now."

"Not at all, it was fascinating, Horace." Lucky rose and walked Horace to the door.

Horace said good night and pocketed Cicero's leash. Lucky watched as the dog followed him dutifully to the car.

"Good night. Drive safe," she called out as she locked the door behind their guests. Lucky returned to the table and stacked the cups and saucers.

"Jack, I think we should talk to them ourselves."

"What? Who?"

"These people. The travelers."

"I'm not sure that's such a good idea."

"Why not? They're just people. I saw them today at the festival. They're wonderful musicians. They're not baby killers. There's something else, Jack. I couldn't say anything before because . . . because Nate was here with Joe Conrad and I didn't want to blow Janie's cover. And I know Nate will figure it out instantly as soon as he gets a chance to meet the musicians from the festival."

"What's that?"

"The photo they e-mailed to Nate from Lincoln Falls? The photo of the dead man? He's a twin of the man who's been watching the restaurant."

"What?" Jack looked stunned. "A twin? How can you be sure?"

"Because I got a good look at him at the festival. He was on stage, he stepped forward, and his face was very memorable. It's the same face as the dead man, and Miriam confirmed that Eamon MacDougal had a twin brother."

"What do you know!" Jack said. "He took off so fast when he saw me coming across the street, I couldn't swear I'd be able to identify him if I did see him again. But why didn't you tell Nate right away?"

"I don't know. If it had only been Nate sitting there, I would have. That's why I asked him about talking to the musicians—if he had had a chance to do that. I know as soon as he gets a good look at the violin player, he'll put it together. It was because of Joe. Something made me hold back. I was being protective of Janie. I'm not sure why. I think the whole story about Miriam and Janie and the travelers will probably come out eventually. For now, I'd just like it to be only Nate who might find out—other than us. Sophie knows a little bit. I had to tell her when she saw Janie freak out at the festival, but I just stuck to the main points. And I trust Sophie. She'll keep her mouth shut and not say anything to embarrass Janie."

"I guess you're right. But check with Nate tomorrow and make sure he's figured it out."

"I really want to talk to that man. It doesn't look like Miriam is going to, and it could be important to figure out which brother died. If he really is Janie's father, Janie should meet him. He obviously has an interest in her. But if he's not her father, why has he been following her all over town? Somebody needs to figure out exactly who he is. And is he the traveler Joe's been looking for? I think the thing to do is to go up there to their campsite."

"When?"

"Now."

"Now?" Jack jumped. "It's late. It's dark. You don't even know for sure where they are. Why don't you wait till tomorrow?"

"We'll be busy here, and besides they're working at the festival during the day. I have a good idea where they're camped from what Miriam has told me. They're near the Stones; it must be that road that leads to the big clearing at the top of the Pilgrim Trail. If I go up there tonight, I can be sure they'll be home—home at their campsite at least."

"Lucky, I can't tell you what to do, but I don't like the idea of you traipsing up there all by yourself. If you're gonna be stubborn, then I'm going with you." Jack pushed his chair back. "Go get your jacket. It's colder than a witch's you-know-what tonight."

Chapter 29

LUCKY DROVE SLOWLY along the Old Colonial Road. Normally she would have driven much faster, but she knew Jack never liked it when she did. He was a much better driver than a passenger. He had a tendency to reach out to the dashboard or stomp his foot, unconsciously reaching for a brake pedal when he was nervous about her speed. She was relieved he hadn't objected more strongly to her desire to talk to the travelers and even more relieved he insisted on coming with her. What looked like a good idea an hour ago at the Spoonful, now seemed questionable. Without Jack it would be a lonely odyssey indeed.

The road narrowed. Only a thin sliver of moon showed above the treetops. She knew nothing about these strangers. Would they be hostile? Or friendly? Would they threaten her or try to drive her away? There was only one way to find out. Talking to the man Miriam believed was Janie's father seemed the only course of action left. Miriam hadn't been able to bridge the gap with her daughter, and Janie had become even more stubborn in her attitude.

Lucky hoped against hope that talking to this man would relieve her anxiety and give her some insight to help Janie reconnect with her mother.

Miriam believed that Eamon had abandoned her. She had run away from her family, but Eamon had failed to follow, leaving her to fend for herself. Miriam admitted that she herself wasn't even aware she was pregnant. It followed that Eamon wouldn't have known either. If so, how did he find out about Janie? How had he even found Miriam? And why now of all times? She wished she had a few answers to her questions. Perhaps this man, whoever he was, could provide some.

Lucky slowed. She knew the turn was coming up, but the road was so dark, she wasn't sure she'd be able to see it.

Jack leaned forward. "Slow down. The turn off is coming up real soon." Jack peered at the road. "Ah, here it is."

The headlights swept over a stand of birch trees growing up to the edge of the road. An owl hooted in the distance, and a chill wind blew through the treetops. This road was narrower, sometimes curving and sometimes turning back upon itself as it climbed the hill. For all she knew, they could arrive at the Stones and not find the travelers' campsite. It was only a guess that this was where they were camped. Near the top of the hill the road ended, and a dirt path wide enough for a large vehicle ran in two directions, at right angles to the road they had climbed.

Lucky stopped the car. "What do you think Jack?"

"The Stones are to the right. I don't think they'd camp there, but they'll want to be near it. Let's go left."

"Okay. You're the boss."

"I doubt that," Jack said. Lucky looked at him quickly. She could see by the dash light he was smiling. Lucky drove farther along the road for a few more minutes.

"Slow down here." Jack leaned forward in his seat. "Stop the car and turn off the lights. We don't want to scare them."

Lucky crawled to a stop, hoping her brakes wouldn't squeal, and flicked off the headlights. The night closed in around them.

"We should walk the rest of the way."

Lucky glanced at Jack. She could barely make out his features in the darkness. She rolled down her window. Above the silence of the woods a strain of sound came. She turned to Jack. "Did you hear that?"

Jack nodded. "We're close. I'll get the flashlights." He reached into the glove compartment and handed one to her.

They climbed out of the car and closed the doors as quietly as they could. Aiming the beam of the flashlight at the dirt road, they followed it to the top of the hill where it narrowed even more. Jack took the lead, and they continued along the path. A deep reverberating sound filtered through the trees then, voices harmonizing without words. The music had a mournful feel. Lucky and Jack stopped before the last turn that would lead them into the large clearing.

Lucky whispered in Jack's ear. "What are they doing? Is that a bagpipe I heard?"

"Yes. I'd guess it's a wake, a wake for the dead man."

"If it really is some kind of a requiem, why haven't they talked to Nate? Why didn't they claim the body legally?"

Jack shook his head. "It's hard for you to understand. They can't. These people do their best to avoid the police. They wouldn't want to be involved in what we consider normal society. They'd just take care of their own."

"You think they still have his body?"

"Oh no," Jack murmured. "He'd be shrouded and buried already, someplace that'd be known only to them."

"At the Stones?"

Jack shook his head. "I doubt it. Not if they consider that some sort of sacred place belonging to ancestors. But it's best not to mention it."

"Maybe we should wait until they're done singing."

"No need."

"What do you mean?"

"We need to step out and introduce ourselves. They know we're here."

"What? Why do you say that?"

"The music's changed."

Lucky listened. The next sound she heard was the ratcheting of a shotgun. A large man stood behind them on the dirt path, a long-barreled gun in his hands.

Chapter 30

"KEEP WALKING AND you won't get hurt." The man spoke in a gravelly voice with a lilting rhythm.

Lucky stopped breathing. She grasped Jack's arm, immediately regretting her decision to come here, regretting that she had exposed Jack to this. He was strong, but he was elderly.

Lucky shone her flashlight at the man's face. He was at least fifty years old and heavyset with a square broad face. He wore dark rough work pants and only a flannel shirt in spite of the chill night. He didn't turn away from the light.

"Come on, Jack," she whispered.

They turned away from the man with the shotgun and walked the rest of the way into the clearing. "In for a penny, in for a pound," Jack muttered.

At least twenty people stood in a circle watching them carefully as they approached. The music had stopped. Men, women and children, all ages, all sizes, their faces lit by the flames of their campfire, stood in silence, watching their progress. Lanterns were placed all around the clearing, creating bright spots and elongated shadows. Lucky noticed the woman she had seen playing the large bass at the festival. If someone had been playing a bagpipe, it wasn't in evidence now. Three large RVs and two vans formed a semicircle around the site. No one spoke a word as they approached. Lucky glanced back. The shotgun was still aimed at them. When she and Jack neared the fire, a shadow at the rear moved and came forward. It was the man who had been watching the restaurant for days, the violin player from the festival.

"What business do you have here?" he asked.

Lucky had no doubt he was well aware who they were. "We didn't mean to interrupt. We only wanted to talk to you."

"Did you bring the police?"

"No." Lucky waited while the stranger mulled over the possibilities. "We only wanted to talk to you about Janie."

His face softened. He whispered the name. "Janie. Jane. Is that her name?"

"Yes." Lucky nodded.

"Please. We don't mean to be rude. Come forward." He gestured to a young man who then carried three rough wooden stools close to the fire.

Lucky turned and saw that the man in the flannel shirt had lowered his shotgun. She sat close to the campfire and warmed her hands. For a moment she was ten years old again, ice-skating at the pond, skating until she was chilled to the bone, her feet stiff with cold, her toes numb. She'd rest by the fire until sensation returned and head back to the ice to do it all over again.

"The music was beautiful. I thought I heard a bagpipe playing."

Eamon nodded. "A *piobaireachd*—a lament." He stared at Lucky intently. "I never meant to frighten her."

Lucky was sure this man was Janie's father. It was the shift in his expression, the way he softly spoke the name.

"Are you really Eamon?"

"I am."

"And the man they found at the accident on the road?" Lucky was curious how he would respond.

Something flashed in his eyes. He glanced around at the group of people who stood back, but were obviously curious. "I think you already know the answer to that. He never died from that accident. He was shot."

"We heard," Jack spoke.

Eamon looked at him, studying the old man's face. "And do you know who did that to him?"

Jack shook his head. "No. That's what the police want to know. They're fairly sure he's one of your group, but they can't prove it. And now . . ." Jack trailed off, not wanting to put Eamon on the spot about stealing the body.

Lucky needed to bring the conversation back to Janie. "Your daughter knows who you are."

"She does? How?"

"Her mother told her."

"Morag?"

Lucky remembered that Miriam had confided her birth name. "Yes. She's called Miriam now."

Eamon stared into the fire for a long time. He finally spoke. "I had no idea. No idea at all about the child . . . Jane." Again, he whispered the name as if afraid to speak it aloud.

Lucky longed to ask him why he would abandon a woman he supposedly loved, to leave her on her own with less than nothing to survive on, but she was afraid to break the shaky welcome they had gained. Jack sat silently, saying nothing and studying Eamon's face.

"You were there that day." He turned toward Lucky. "I saw you at the festival. You were with the police."

"That was Nate. He's the Chief of Police. He's a friend, a good friend of my grandfather's," she said, indicating Jack.

"Are they still holding Daniel?"

"Daniel? Is that the man who ran away from the pony corral?"

Eamon nodded. "My nephew."

"No. They're not. Nate didn't arrest him. He only wanted to ask him some questions."

"If the police aren't holding Daniel, then why hasn't he come back to us?"

Lucky was taken aback. "Nate told us Ernie White, the man who runs the festival, bailed him out. Well, not bailed him out, because he really wasn't under arrest, but picked him up from the police station," Lucky offered.

"Daniel would never have gone with him. He's afraid of the man." Eamon exchanged a cryptic look with the man who held the shotgun. "We don't know where he is. He hasn't come back here, and he hasn't shown up at the festival."

"Do you want us to talk to Nate about him? Maybe someone in town has seen him."

Eamon shook his head. "No." He offered no other explanation. "We'll find him ourselves."

He turned back to Lucky. "What is she like?" he asked.

Lucky smiled, knowing he referred to Janie. "She's a dear. She's full of energy, high-strung I guess you'd say, but a really kind person. She finished high school last year. She's well liked by everyone and she has two close girlfriends. No boyfriend as yet, at least none that I know of. She's . . . she was very close to her mother always . . . well, until this came to light. She's vulnerable right now. She's just out of her teenage years, and she's learned her parents have lied to her—the parents she knows at least. She's staying with me right now because she's angry at her mother and refuses to talk to her. Her father, I mean her mother's husband, died just a few months ago. Janie was very close to him, so now, I guess you'd say, she's in a state of shock," Lucky continued. "We came here tonight because . . . well, I'm hoping perhaps you could talk to her, explain what happened, help her understand. I've talked to Miriam, but I don't feel I have the right to say much to Janie. It's really her mother's place or yours . . ." Lucky trailed off.

"I will. I've been afraid, but I will do that. I'm sure Jane has had a better life than any I could have given her. Morag kept her secrets. She had her reasons; I can't argue with that. But blood is blood. I never knew about her, and if she's my daughter and I have no doubt she is, then I at least have the right to talk to her, to hear her voice, that's all I ask. And maybe explain some things to her—that's if she'll talk to me."

"Good. That's all I wanted to say. Something has to break this impasse."

Eamon took a deep breath as though in dread of approaching his daughter, fearful of the wounds she could inflict upon him. "You should go now. Ronan will take you back." He gestured to the man who stood near. The shotgun had disappeared.

"Good night. And thanks for talking to us."

"Thanks to you." Eamon stood.

The man called Ronan walked with them down the rise to Lucky's car. He opened the driver's door for Lucky without saying a word. Lucky waited until Jack had his seat belt in place before she started the engine. The road was so narrow, she was forced to back down the hill until they came to the paved road that led them back to the turn off and the Old Colonial Road.

Once they had gone a mile or so and were nearing the town, Lucky breathed a sigh of relief. She reached over to squeeze Jack's hand. "I'm glad you wanted to come with me, Jack. I wouldn't have liked to tackle those people alone."

"They're all right. They're just . . . what's the word for a throwback in time?"

"An anachronism."

"Yes, that's the word I couldn't think of. But they see themselves as free."

"Are they free? Really? Always looking over their shoulders? Afraid of the authorities? Having to skulk over borders? Maybe the best way to be free is to conform, to be just another number on the government's records. Think how hard just their daily routine must be."

"There's that," Jack replied. He was silent a moment as Lucky took the curves in the road back to town. "It's sad though. The world is determined to squeeze them out. We're all numbered and accounted for, with spy satellites beeping out in space that can track us in our homes and pretty soon televisions that'll work both ways. No one will have any privacy anymore. It's a frightening new world for somebody my age, and these people are the last ones to resist. The last of the free spirits."

Chapter 31

LUCKY STUMBLED OUT to the kitchen the following morning. She felt as if she hadn't slept at all. Her neck was stiff from a night of dreaming about frightening people, their faces lit by a campfire. A result, no doubt, of her visit to the travelers with Jack the night before. She filled the kettle with water and put it on the burner to heat. She glanced at the kitchen sink. Janie must have had another kitchen adventure. A pile of dirty dishes filled the sink. The girl didn't seem to be able to boil water without using every pot and pan in the house. Lucky had tiptoed in the night before and made a point of not even looking in the kitchen. She had been too exhausted to deal with another mess.

She sighed. She could put her foot down and insist that Janie do a better job of clearing up her messes, or she could leave the girl alone in her misery. Lucky opted for the latter. She wasn't sure what state Janie was in, but she didn't want to cause an upset that would make Janie flee into the night. She needed Janie at the restaurant and needed to know Janie was safe. She turned on the faucets, dribbled dish soap and let the basin fill up with soapy water.

When the kettle whistled, she turned off the stove and scooped coffee into a filter. Should she make two cups and wake Janie up? Lucky checked the clock. Seven forty-five. It was time to wake her. She called Janie's name as she walked down the hall to the living room. Clothes were strewn over chairs, several pairs of shoes were thrown under a table. Janie's backpack was lying on the floor, its contents spilled. A pile of blankets covered the sofa. Janie was buried somewhere underneath.

"Janie," Lucky called.

"Janie?" She waited. No response.

The hairs on the back of Lucky's neck rose. The room was too still. She walked slowly to the sofa and pulled the covers back. The couch was empty. No Janie.

Lucky's stomach clenched in a knot. Where was she? Had she gone out very early? It was late when she and Jack had returned to town after their talk with the travelers, and she had been exhausted. The lights were out in the living room, and she had assumed Janie was already asleep. What if she hadn't been asleep? What if she hadn't come back to the apartment last night? Where could she be?

Lucky tried to quell the rising panic and tell herself that everything was fine. Janie must have woken early and headed to the Spoonful. Lucky pushed the thought out of her mind that something might have happened to her. If it had, then she, Lucky, was responsible. Janie, though technically not a minor, was in her care. How could she ever explain another disappearance to Miriam?

She hurried back to the kitchen and grabbed the phone. Dialing the number of the Spoonful with one hand, she poured the still hot water through the filter. She was in desperate need of caffeine. She had to think.

Sage answered on the second ring. "Sage, it's me. Is Janie there with you?"

"No. She's not due here for a while anyway, is she?"

"You're right. I was just hoping . . ."

"Is something wrong?"

"No. At least I hope not. When I woke up this morning, she was gone."

"She might have gone out to do an errand, or maybe she went to Meg's."

"I'm kind of nervous because I got in late last night, and stupidly, I didn't think to check on her. I just assumed she was already asleep. Can you do me a favor? Can you call Meg and see if she's at her house, but don't say I'm worried? Find an excuse to call."

"Sure. I can do that. But don't worry; I'm sure there's an explanation."

"I hope so," Lucky replied as she hung up the phone. She poured cream into her coffee and stirred it, downing three large gulps. She dialed Miriam's number, groaning inwardly.

"No, she's not here." Miriam's voice rose in pitch as though Lucky's panic was contagious. "When did you see her last?"

"Um, yesterday evening. She left the Spoonful. Jack and I stayed behind. As far as I know, she was heading back here."

"And you didn't see her when you came in."

"Actually, Jack and I . . ." Lucky trailed off, unwilling to explain her visit to the travelers' campsite to Miriam. "We, uh, we had something to take care of, so I didn't get back until very late. I just assumed she was already asleep."

"You didn't check on her?" Miriam's voice was sharp. There was an accusatory tone to her question.

Lucky cringed. "No. I'm sorry. I didn't."

"Oh, no." Miriam sounded close to tears. "Where could she have gone now?"

"Sage is checking at Meg's house, and I'll stop by next door at the Clinic in a few minutes. Maybe Rosemary has seen her. Don't panic, Miriam. I'm sure there's an explanation."

"You don't understand how hard this is for me, Lucky. Janie's always been so . . . dependable, good about telling me where she is so I won't worry. She's not your normal teenager." Miriam hesitated. "Did she leave you a note or anything?"

"Not that I saw." Lucky neglected to mention that the living room looked more like the Russian army, not a normal teenager, had camped there for a week. "But I'll check all around and make sure I didn't miss anything. I'll call you right away as soon as I locate her. Please try not to worry."

Lucky hung up and gulped down the rest of the coffee. She dumped the mug into the soapy pile in the sink and showered and dressed as quickly as she knew how. She brushed her hair, not bothering with makeup, and grabbed her purse. She hurried down the stairs and ran next door to the Snowflake Clinic. The front door was unlocked, and Rosemary was on duty at the reception desk. She looked up in surprise. "Lucky! Nice to see you." She glanced down at the appointment book. "Did you have an appointment today?"

"Oh no. I'm on my way to the Spoonful. But I was wondering, have you seen Janie? This morning or last night?"

"No. In fact, I've called her, and she hasn't returned any of my calls. Is something wrong?"

Lucky wasn't sure how much or how little Rosemary knew. She didn't want to give away any of Janie's secrets. "No. Nothing's wrong. We were supposed to meet, and she's not here. Maybe she misunderstood. Maybe she's at the Spoonful already."

"That must be it," Rosemary replied.

Now that she was actually here at the Clinic and no one seemed to be waiting for an appointment, it might be a good time to try to see Elias. Truth be told, she was embarrassed about her reaction at the Pub earlier in the week, and wished she had handled it better. Did she have a right to be put out that Elias had never mentioned a prior relationship to her? Maybe. Or maybe it was as he said—no longer important. Was she threatened by his hiring of a former lover? Well, yes. It certainly didn't make her feel very comfortable. Did the fact that he hadn't called but had been seen having dinner with Paula at the Lodge bother her? Absolutely. But what really galled her was the energy she had felt when she had entered his office. An atmosphere of intimacy, an overfamiliarity inappropriate to a working situation and a direct impression that Paula was out to seduce him.

So far she only had Elias's words to hang on to. Elias was right; she had acted like a jealous lover. More than anything, though, she wanted him to confirm or deny the rumors that Sophie said were flying around town.

"Is Elias in yet? There's something I've been meaning to talk to him about."

"Oh, sure. I think he's in his office. Only one patient's arrived so far. Go right ahead." Rosemary turned back to her computer screen.

"Thanks." Lucky pushed through the waiting room door and walked down the corridor. She tapped on Elias's office door and stepped in.

Elias stood against the light from the window. He was leaning forward, his head bent toward Paula, whose face was inches away. Lucky's heart stopped beating. Was he about to kiss her? Elias turned and looked over quickly at Lucky standing in the doorway. He straightened. Paula's cheeks were flushed. Her eyes hardened when she saw who stood in the doorway.

Already upset about the gossip Sophie had conveyed, Lucky was stunned. Just what was going on?

"Lucky!" Elias spoke first. "I didn't know you were coming in."

Lucky remained silent, staring at Elias. She was sure her cheeks were flaming red.

"Uh . . . Paula had something in her eye . . . uh . . ."

"I wanted to ask you something."

"Oh." Elias cleared his throat. "What was it you wanted?"

Before Lucky could answer, the intercom on the desk buzzed. Rosemary was letting Elias know a patient had arrived.

"Excuse me a second." He moved toward the desk and grabbed the phone. "Yes?" He seemed flustered. "Room 3? Okay. I'll be right there. Thanks."

He turned back to Lucky. "Sorry. My patient just arrived. Can I call you later?"

"Of course," Lucky replied, doing her best to keep any hint of anger from her voice.

With a nod to both women, he left the room.

Paula was silent. She remained by the window. She stared at Lucky as though a cockroach had just landed on her plate. There was no mistaking her animosity. "Elias told me," she stated flatly.

Lucky hesitated. "Excuse me?"

"He told me how upset you were about my being hired."

Lucky knew without a doubt that another flush was creeping up her cheeks. How could he? What did he do, run directly to Paula and convey everything she had said to him? She felt humiliated. How could he do that? Worst of all, she wasn't in a position to deny it.

She took a deep breath and counted to three. Taking the high road was the best course of action. "I'm sure everything will work out just fine. I certainly wish you the best in Snowflake." *Or better yet, fall off a steep cliff*, she thought.

"I know you'll come to understand how close Elias and I have *always* been. One can't simply ignore those feelings, don't you agree?" She smiled slowly.

Lucky felt as if her face had frozen. What exactly was

Paula saying? That something had already happened, that it was just too bad if it caused a rift between Lucky and Elias.

"I know that it must hurt you, and I'm sorry if that's the case. But I think it's best to be honest, don't you?"

Lucky wanted nothing more than to put her fist into Paula's face and wipe that smirk off of it forever. Just like she had done to Jimmy Pratt in grade school. It took every ounce of dignity and restraint she had left not to do just that. As if Paula could read Lucky's mind, she raised an eyebrow and waited, a superior expression on her face. Perhaps she would welcome the attack, proving once and for all to Elias how unsuitable for him Lucky really was.

"Absolutely," Lucky replied. "Honesty is always the best policy." If there had been any lingering doubt in Lucky's mind about Paula's agenda, there wasn't any longer. She was determined to seduce Elias and drive Lucky out of the picture. The real question was where Elias stood in this milieu.

Lucky turned away and shut the office door behind her, managing not to slam it in her fury. She hurried down the hall, through the waiting room and out to the sidewalk, not looking in Rosemary's direction.

Chapter 32

TORN BETWEEN HUMILIATION and a furious anger, Lucky stomped through the back door of the Spoonful, slamming the door behind her. What was Elias trying to say? That something was in Paula's eye? What nonsense! She couldn't bear to think what she had interrupted. If she did, she'd burst into tears. The rumors must be true. She was such a fool! She had fallen in love with Elias. And in her defense Elias had done everything but get down on one knee and actually propose. He hadn't said those words, but he had done and said everything that could lead up to that moment. She had been the one who was hesitant, fearful, afraid of losing independence, not sure if she was on solid ground since the death of her parents. She wanted to enjoy the romance, but she wasn't in a hurry to rush into a permanent commitment. In spite of all that, she was crazy about the man. She felt as if a serrated blade had been plunged into her chest. If only she hadn't been so cautious. Elias was ready for that kind of change in his life. He had been alone for a long time and was more than ready. If only she hadn't been such a scaredy-cat, then perhaps Paula could not have come between them. But what if that wasn't the case? What if Elias had harbored feelings for his former love all along, but didn't know it? Lucky cringed when she pictured herself stomping into his office. She, with her hair stuck on her head, no makeup and old jeans. Paula, elegant in an expensive outfit, her hair shaped perfectly, makeup subtle but enhancing. Lucky felt like the proverbial bull in a china shop. She could imagine the comparison between her and Paula. No wonder Elias was smitten and ignoring Lucky.

She slipped into the office and shut the door, taking deep breaths to stop the tears. Sophie was right to tell her what was happening behind her back. Only a good friend would take the chance of being the bearer of unpleasant tidings. Lucky pulled a tissue from the box on the desk and wiped her eyes and blew her nose, finally regaining some level of calm. She had to pull it together. Another long day was starting, and she still didn't know where Janie was.

She heard voices in the corridor. First Sage and then, unmistakably, Meg's voice. Lucky slipped her jacket over the chair and stuck her purse under the desk. She walked out to the hallway, pulled a fresh apron from the closet and headed to the kitchen.

"There you are," Sage said. "I thought I heard the door slam in the back."

Meg stood by the worktable. She spoke breathlessly. "I heard you were looking for Janie. Sage told me. But I haven't seen her since yesterday. Have you called her mom?"

"Yes," Lucky replied. "I just got off the phone with her. I'm concerned, but I'm sure there's an explanation."

"She's scheduled to start at nine this morning. She'll show up."

Lucky nodded. She didn't trust herself to speak. The way this day was going, she was certain of nothing. She glanced at Sage. He was quiet, but she was sure he saw through her controlled demeanor.

Nine o'clock came and went, and there was still no sign of Janie. Meg was rushing back and forth, doing her best to fill the breach. The morning regulars, Hank and Barry, had come and gone, and now the restaurant was crowded with later arrivals. Lucky glanced over the counter and around the restaurant. It seemed everyone had descended on the Spoonful at once. Now several people were preparing to leave. In another half an hour, things would settle down. She'd check in with Miriam at the first opportunity.

Lucky looked up as Ernie White and the big man who must be Rory came through the front door. Jack glanced over quickly and then ignored the new arrivals, intent on making change for exiting customers. Ernie headed straight for the counter, his companion followed.

"Hello, Lucky," Ernie said. The other man grabbed a menu and didn't look up.

"Ernie. What can I get you?"

"How 'bout coffee to start?"

"You got it." Lucky returned with two cups of steaming hot coffee and placed them on the counter.

"Lucky, this is Rory. He's working for me out at the festival."

Lucky smiled. "Nice to meet you."

"We're not all ruffians out there," Ernie said. "Lots of nice people have a stall going. You'd enjoy it. I know you would."

"We've been over all this before, Ernie. You know how Jack feels."

"I do. I do. But Jack's old hat. You're young. You can understand how businesses have to market themselves these days. I'm sure you could overrule him if you made up your mind."

Lucky was losing patience with the man. She did her

best to bite her tongue. "Thanks, Ernie. But no thanks. We have all we can handle here as it is. You can surely see that."

Ernie nodded and watched her carefully. "I saw you talking to Nate the other day."

Lucky had the feeling Ernie was broaching the subject he intended all along. "Yes." She wasn't sure where this was leading. She only wished they'd place their orders and be done with the politicking. She was suffering from a low level of anxiety about Janie and wanted a chance to call Miriam back. Lucky was hoping against hope that Janie might have returned home.

She turned to Ernie's companion. "We have a really great pumpkin rice soup with a half sandwich of turkey and dried cranberries on rosemary bread, if you'd like to try that."

"Sure," the man called Rory replied. "That sounds good."

"Same for me," Ernie chimed in.

Lucky placed the order slip on the hatch. One by one most of their customers were leaving. There wasn't much to do at the moment except whisk away a few dishes. There was no way to escape Ernie's clutches.

Ernie picked up where he had left off. "I told Nate in no uncertain terms I didn't want him coming around whenever he felt like it and disrupting all my operations out there. Throws everything off schedule. And telling that dork of a deputy to chase down the kid certainly doesn't help my business. I had to hire another guy to work the pony rides. I gave Nate a piece of my mind. I told him he better have a damn good reason to be sniffing around the festival. There's no funny business there. Everything's aboveboard."

Lucky recalled the travelers' concern of the night before. If Ernie had stopped by the police station to rescue Daniel from Nate's clutches, where was the young man? She was on the verge of asking if Daniel had returned to the festival when she spotted Nate outside the front door. She breathed a sigh of relief. Now she might have a chance to talk to Nate privately about Janie.

Nate came through the door and approached the counter. Ernie had built up a swell of anger. He was on a roll and was not to be silenced.

"And if I see Nate Edgerton again, I'm gonna tell him straight out . . ."

"What's that Ernie?" Nate laid a hand on the man's shoulder. "What are you gonna tell me?"

Ernie jumped. His face darkened. "Uh . . ." He gestured to Lucky. "I was just tellin' this young lady here that I run a real clean operation. Everybody's happy who's workin' at the festival."

"Good to hear." Nate took a stool next to him. "I'll have a cup of coffee, Lucky, and a bowl of chili if you've got that today."

"Sure, Nate." Lucky was relieved she wouldn't be held hostage to Ernie's ramblings any longer. She poured Nate a cup of coffee and placed his order. "I'll bring you one of those pumpkin rolls too."

She returned with Ernie's and Rory's orders. Ernie had fallen silent, as had his sidekick. They were doing their best to ignore Nate's presence.

Three more people came through the door. Lucky glanced over at Meg. She was doing an excellent job but was beginning to look a little harried.

Where could Janie have gone? This was so unlike her. Even upset as she had been all week, she hadn't missed a day of work. Janie had always been conscientious. Lucky hoped Ernie and his sidekick would leave soon so she could have Nate's full attention. Or maybe he was here because Miriam had already called him about Janie?

The new arrivals found tables, and Lucky noticed that Joe Conrad had come in behind them. Her heart sank. She wouldn't have a minute to talk to Nate now unless she dragged him into the office. Joe looked around the restaurant and finally spotted Nate at the counter. He headed straight for the stool next to Nate, greeting Jack at the cash register.

"Hello, Lucky . . . Nate." Joe sat down.

Nate acknowledged Joe's presence with a nod. "Oh, by the way, Isaac said to say hello."

Joe's face brightened. "He did?" He smiled widely. "How's he doing?"

"Fine, I guess. Said he hoped to hear from you."

Joe laughed. "Well, he's being polite. He probably breathed a sigh of relief when he didn't have me looking over his shoulder. I'll give him a call though—it'll be nice to catch up."

Ernie and Rory shot a look at Joe and, after a discreet look passed between them, rose without a word and walked over to Jack to pay their bill.

Joe had taken notice of them, and curious, he spun around on the stool, watching as they paid and left the restaurant.

Nate pulled two plastic bags out of his pocket and, reaching over, slipped the cups that Ernie and Rory had used into the evidence bags. He pulled a pen from his pocket and made a mark on each of the bags. "You don't mind if I borrow a couple of the Spoonful's cups, do you, Lucky?"

Lucky stared at him. "Not at all. They're yours. You can keep them. What's going on, Nate?"

Nate shook his head imperceptibly to indicate this was something he wasn't willing to discuss. He turned to Joe. "Something wrong?"

Joe shrugged his shoulders. "No. It's just . . . that guy who just left. You know him?" Joe looked from Lucky to Nate.

"The one in the suit? That's Ernie White. He lives over in Lincoln Falls. He's the man who organized the festival. Why do you ask?"

Joe shook his head. "Sorry. Just something about him . . . looked familiar. Like I know him from somewhere but can't place him."

"You've probably seen him around town or out at the Harvest Festival."

"Yeah," Joe replied. "That must be it." He glanced at the plastic bags on the counter and quickly looked at Nate. "Any news about your stolen body or the van?"

"Nah," Nate said, taking a sip of coffee. "I'm heading over to Lincoln Falls in a little bit. We got a report of an abandoned car on someone's property outside of town. It's been towed, and I'm gonna have it gone over and checked for fingerprints. I could be wrong, but it's the right color and it may be the car that sent the van off the road. The techs can have the paint analyzed, and we'll see if it matches. We don't have a gun, but if it's the right car, I guess we have a murder weapon."

Meg carried a tray of dishes back to the counter. Lucky rinsed them off and loaded them into the bin. "Lucky, I'm gonna take a break as soon as that bunch leaves," Meg said, indicating a large round table in the center of the room. "Is that okay?"

"Sure. That's fine. I can manage the rest." Lucky glanced over Meg's shoulder. Miriam stood on the threshold. Her face showed the strain of the last few days. She looked carefully all around the room, undoubtedly hoping to see Janie at work.

Lucky and Meg exchanged a look. "You haven't heard from her, have you?" Lucky whispered.

Meg's face fell. "No. And that's really odd."

Miriam spotted Nate at the counter and walked directly to him. Nate, sensing that something was wrong, turned to follow Lucky's gaze.

"Bradley told me I'd find you here," Miriam said to Nate. "Can I talk to you?"

"Why, sure, Miriam. What can I do for you?"

Miriam glanced at Joe Conrad. Nate could sense her discomfort.

Lucky moved closer to Nate. "Why don't you use my office?"

Nate shot a look at Lucky. From her expression he could tell she was already aware of Miriam's concern. Something important was brewing. "Let's go." He stood, picking up the two evidence bags, and ushered Miriam through the doorway to the corridor.

Jack telegraphed a silent question as Meg disappeared into the kitchen for her break. Jack had realized something was wrong when Janie didn't turn up.

Lucky turned back to Joe. "What would you like?" Nate's chili was cooling on the hatch, and Nate might be closeted with Miriam for a while. "We have some great chili," she said hopefully.

"Fine. Chili would hit the spot right now."

"You got it." Literally, she thought, placing the bowl on the placemat.

"Are you a mind reader?" Joe laughed.

"It is one of my talents," she replied.

"You know, I have a date with a lovely woman this evening," Joe offered.

Lucky's eyebrows rose. "You do? Why, that's wonderful. Who is the lucky lady, if I may ask?"

Joe smiled. "I'll give you a hint. She runs a ladies' clothing shop right here in Snowflake."

"Oh!" Lucky grinned widely. "Hmmm. Let me guess. Could her name begin with a C and end with a Y?"

"Sure does. I've made a reservation at that fancy restaurant up at the Resort. Do you think she'd like that?" he asked with a trace of nervousness.

"Yes, I do. I'm sure she'd be very pleased. You'll both have a wonderful time. The food is excellent."

"You know, Lucky, I've been a widower for a long time.

This is the first time . . . well, this is all new to me." He grinned sheepishly. "I'm out of practice."

"Cecily's a delightful person. It won't be an awkward date at all." Lucky hoped Marjorie wouldn't interfere with Cecily's high hopes. Marjorie, so reserved and conservative, certainly disapproved of Cecily's going out for the evening with a man who was a stranger in town. Cecily, on the other hand, had such an open heart. She'd be thrilled to be the object of a little male attention.

Meg returned from the kitchen. "I'm back, Lucky."

"Great. Can you cover here for just a minute? And then I'll help you clear the tables?" Lucky asked.

Meg stepped behind the counter. Joe looked at her. "You seem short-staffed today. Where's your other waitress, the tall one?" he asked.

Lucky hesitated, waiting for Meg's reply.

"Oh, she's just taking a few days off," Meg responded.

Lucky breathed a sigh of relief. Meg had covered for Janie. Lucky left the counter and hurried down the corridor. She tapped lightly on the door to announce her presence and pushed it open. Miriam sat across from Nate. She was crying and nervously digging tissues out of her purse.

"Miriam." Lucky placed a hand on her shoulder. "I'm so sorry this is happening. I just didn't think for a minute . . ."

"That's exactly right." Miriam turned to her angrily. "You didn't think! If you had been thinking, you never would have just assumed that Janie was asleep. You should have checked on her. I trusted you. This never should have happened—"

"Easy, Miriam," Nate interrupted her tirade. "It's not fair to go blaming Lucky. Even if she had realized . . ."

"If she had been more responsible, we would have known Janie was missing twelve hours ago."

Lucky pulled her hand away. She felt her face burning.

"Miriam," Nate replied patiently. "We don't know she's

missing. Whatever caused her to run away from home, well, something could have upset her. She could be hiding out at a friend's house—she could be anywhere."

"I want you to find her, Nate. You have to find her. This isn't like her."

"I will, Miriam. I'll do everything I can. First order of business is to find her car, and we'll go from there. But I have to be honest with you. Given the argument with you and the fact that she doesn't want to go home, I'm not inclined to jump to the worst possible scenario. But I'll check for accident reports and all the usual stuff. In the meantime, let's go to the station and do what we need to do officially. Then, you should go home and start making calls. Call everybody you can think of, and let me know if you come up with anything."

Miriam stood. "Fine. I'll do that. But, Nate, just find her. Quickly." Without a backward glance at Lucky, she pushed past and headed down the corridor.

Nate sighed and rose to his feet. "Sorry, Lucky. I know it's not your fault. You didn't sign on for babysitting duties."

"I know I didn't, Nate, but all the same, Miriam's right. I wasn't thinking like the mother of a teenager, I just . . ." Lucky paused. "I'm kicking myself now."

"Well, don't take Miriam's words too harshly. She's on her last nerve right now. I'm sure she'll realize she shouldn't be blaming you."

"I hope so."

Nate turned to go back to the front room. "Look, you might as well cancel that order."

"No problem. Sorry you can't stay for lunch." She followed Nate back to the restaurant. As he passed by the counter, he glanced at Joe's bowl and frowned. "Is that *my* chili?"

Joe looked up. "I don't know. Is it?"

"Sure looked good," Nate replied. "I'll see you folks later. I have some business to take care of." He waved and left the restaurant. Miriam stood on the sidewalk outside waiting for Nate.

Lucky couldn't imagine what Nate could do about Janie's disappearance. Janie was already considered a runaway and in an unstable state. It was more likely she would head for a friend's home. What was unlikely was that she hadn't communicated with her closest girlfriends—Rosemary and Meg—and hadn't left any messages with her job. That was the one fact that made Lucky very nervous. She was sure Miriam was worried sick Janie might have had an accident. But Nate would be able to check accident reports and hospital admissions better than anyone.

"Something going on, Lucky?" Joe asked.

Lucky shook her head. "I have no idea," she replied blandly.

"Is that your waitress's mother, that lady who left with Nate?"

"Uh, why, yes. That's right. How did you know?"

"Hmm. Just figured she was."

Lucky smiled noncommittally and busied herself clearing the counter.

Chapter 33

THE FIRST THING Janie heard was the chirping of birds. The sound was very close. Outside somewhere but close. She struggled to open her eyes, fighting the desire to fall asleep again. Her nose itched, but when she tried to scratch it, she couldn't move her arms. Her wrists were bound behind her back. She managed to force her eyes open, but only a small amount of light filtered through the rough fabric that covered her face and head. She whimpered, remembering the rough hands that had overpowered her in the night. Had she fallen asleep? She had been lifted and shoved into something—the trunk of a car. She could smell exhaust fumes. She had kicked at the inside of the trunk, but nothing had happened. It wouldn't release, and she couldn't do more because her hands had been bound.

The man—she was sure it was a man—he was tall and his hands were large. He had dragged her out of the trunk. She tried to twist away and kick at him, but blinded by the sack over her head, she couldn't do any damage. He easily avoided her attempts to struggle. He lifted her to the ground. A hard metal cylinder was pressed against her temple. Her arm was gripped so tightly, she wanted to cry. Then she was forced forward a few yards and up a short step. She heard the sound of wooden boards creaking beneath their feet.

Her captor pressed her against a wall and pulled something tight around her ankles, then something heavier was wrapped around her waist. She was crying and begging him to let her go, but he made no response. When she tried to scream, the man again held the barrel of the gun against her head. He never spoke. It was his silence that frightened her more than anything. She felt his hand near her face and then the rip of a knife as he cut a tiny hole in the sack that covered her head. She saw a bright light through the opening. A flashlight?

A straw was shoved through the hole and into her mouth. He said one word: "*Drink!*" She tried to wrench her head away, but he pressed the gun to her temple. She struggled to stifle her sobs and sipped the sweet liquid.

"More," he said. She tried to drink again but gagged and began to choke, the liquid running down her chin and onto her sweater.

He shoved the straw back into her mouth. "Drink it all," he growled. She couldn't recognize the voice. Who was he? Why did he take her? What did he want? She continued to sip, being careful to swallow the liquid in her mouth and trying not to breathe at the same time. She was so nervous, she was hyperventilating. She felt dizzy—dizzy from fear and lack of oxygen. Once the straw made a gurgling sound and the liquid was gone, he released the pressure from the side of her head. It had to be a gun. Was he planning to kill her? Her terror made it difficult to breathe.

Heavy footsteps moved away from her. One person only. Then the sound of a door latch and all went dark. She started to scream. She screamed for help until her throat was raw. Then everything started to spin in front of her, and warmth suffused her body. She couldn't remember anymore why it was so important to reach help. She slept.

DIFFUSED LIGHT FILTERED through the rough material covering her face. It must be day. Her limbs felt stiff, and she still couldn't move her arms. When she tried to swallow, her tongue stuck to the roof of her mouth. Where was she? How far had they traveled from the parking lot of the festival? And why would someone want to keep her here? Was it the man who had been playing the fiddle onstage? Her father? Had he done this to her? Even if he knew who she was, why would he do this? Or worse, was it a stranger with a more sinister motive? Was there no rhyme or reason to why she had been taken? Her mother had always warned her, begged her to be careful, to never trust a stranger, not wanting to spell out exactly what could happen to a young girl. Janie sobbed. Why had she run away from home? Why had she gone to the festival? And most important of all, why hadn't she left a note for Lucky? When would Lucky notice that she hadn't returned home last night? Or would she only discover her absence in the morning? And her mother! This would destroy her mother. Why hadn't she been more sensible?

The light was starting to diminish. It was afternoon, not morning. She had slept through the night and most of the day. She was sure she had been drugged by the sticky-sweet drink. She wet her lips. What she wouldn't give for a drink of cool water. She could still taste the residue of the liquid in her mouth. Her stomach growled. When was the last time she had eaten? At Lucky's apartment the night before? No wonder she was starving.

Her brain was fogged. Her body ached. She rested her head against the wall behind her. Then a sound. Footsteps. The crunching of leaves and the click of the door handle. He was back.

Chapter 34

THE STATION WAS locked up and dark. Bradley had gone home. Nate turned on the computer and clicked open his e-mail account. The desk lamp cast a warm pool of light over his green blotter, a blotter covered with weeks of notes, drawings and doodles. He slipped his glasses on and peered at the screen. There it was—the e-mail he had been waiting for, the tape from the security camera at the impound lot. He wanted no interruptions while he watched. At least those guys had managed to do one thing right, he thought. Of course, he had had to raise hell over there to get even this much. But it was the least they could do after dumping his van in another lot and not completing their work.

He clicked on the link and watched the security footage of the guard's enclosure at the entrance to the lot. The cubicle was well lit. Nate stared as the guard opened a newspaper, yawned, read for a while and then tossed it aside. The man pulled a cell phone out of his pocket and stared at it, but didn't put it to his ear. A text? In the meantime, a few shadows passed by on the sidewalk.

Nate scanned the background behind the guard's enclosure carefully, more focused on that area of the screen than on the guard. He could barely make out the shapes of the cars parked within the enclosure. Unfortunately this was the only camera; there were no others inside the lot, and the van had been parked far away near the rear. There was no way the van could be sighted from this direction. He muttered under his breath and cursed the idiots that had decided to shunt his investigation to the side to take care of something they considered more important.

The guard stood up and stretched, then returned to his newspaper. Nate dragged the mouse across and the footage flew by, frame by frame. He spotted movement. He backtracked a little and then hit the arrow for normal play. Someone stood in front of the guard's cubicle with a . . . what was that? A six-pack? The guard responded to the newcomer and stepped out to open the gate, then returned to his enclosure. The man who had just arrived shut the gate behind him.

Nate rewound and watched the same part again. Was that a shadow that passed near the entrance gate? He couldn't tell if there was something there or if his eyes were playing tricks on him. The lighting and quality of the footage was poor. The newcomer entered the guard's enclosure and finally turned around. Nate sucked in his breath—Ernie White. Ernie was visiting the impound lot on the night of the theft.

Ernie took a stool, and the guard returned to his seat. Ernie opened two beers and passed one to the guard. As three quarters of an hour in real time elapsed, the two men polished off three beers each. Then Ernie stood, slapping the guard on the back. He was nodding and talking—must be saying his good-byes. The guard released the gate. Ernie stepped outside, waved and strolled down the sidewalk until he was out of sight.

Nate continued to watch. The guard leaned back in his

chair, put his feet up on the stool and closed his eyes. After a few minutes, his head lolled back and his mouth opened slightly. Nate could almost hear the sound of the guard's snoring. Suddenly, as if hit by an electrical shock, the guard jumped up. He rubbed his eyes and looked all around the enclosure. Then he ran out into the darkened parking lot where the camera couldn't follow. Two minutes later he returned to his post and picked up the phone. Nate could see the guard's mouth moving as he spoke excitedly into the phone.

Son of a . . . I've got you now, Ernie White.

Chapter 35

CECILY'S EYES SPARKLED as she glanced around the Mont Blanc Room. She was thrilled and flattered that Joe had reserved a table at the most exclusive dining room at the Resort. Crystal chandeliers hung from the ceiling, their light reflected in antique mirrors lining the walls. Other than one or two diners, the restaurant was virtually empty. It felt as if they would be having dinner in a palace all their own. A waiter arrived bearing menus while another lit the candelabra at their table.

As soon as the two waiters melted away, Joe leaned across the table. "Do you see anything you like?"

Cecily smiled. "Lots of things. The seared salmon sounds wonderful."

"I was thinking of the same thing. Seared salmon it is, then." Their waiter materialized again, and Joe gave him their order.

Joe smiled across the table at her. "Thank you very much for accepting my dinner invitation. I . . . uh . . . I was a little nervous asking. I was afraid you'd turn me down flat."

"Not at all," Cecily said, wide-eyed. "It's my pleasure. I'm afraid my life is rather routine with the business and all. I really don't get to dine out very much, especially at such an elegant place." She bit her tongue as soon as the words were out of her mouth. She didn't want Joe to think she lived the life of a shut in, but perhaps, now that she thought about it, that's exactly what her life had become.

"Well, my life in retirement has been rather boring, and I'm sad to say, I'm forced to eat out much more than I would like but never with such attractive and charming company."

"Oh." Cecily waved her hand in the air dismissively. "You mustn't flatter." A flush of red tinged her cheeks.

The waiter arrived again and uncorked a bottle of wine. He poured a small amount in a glass, handing it to Joe. Joe swirled the glass and held it close to his nose, then tasted it. He nodded at the waiter who then poured the wine into two crystal goblets.

Joe's face became very serious. "It's not flattery, Cecily, believe me. When I met you the other day, you seemed to light up the room. Yours was the friendliest face I've seen in a very long time." He sighed. "People talk about retirement as if it's some dream come true, but I spend most of my time wondering what to do with the time I have on my hands."

An image came to her of Joe, sitting alone in a long string of restaurants, day after day, night after night. The thought made her terribly sad. She was lonely too, but she was fortunate she had her sister. She had never had to eat alone, at home or in restaurants.

"You probably think I'm a bit mad to still be concerned with such an old case as that robbery, but I guess it keeps me sane." He laughed in a self-deprecating manner. "I like to think it keeps the little gray cells active."

Cecily smiled and sipped her wine. "It must be the mental challenge you miss."

"Yes, that. And being out in the field. I was never very good with sitting in my office and preparing paperwork. Too restless, I guess, especially when I was younger. Law enforcement never appealed to me, but I guess I might have considered it if I hadn't done so well in the insurance industry."

"You must have had a very exciting career." Cecily could feel the effects of the wine already. She wasn't the least bit used to drinking alcohol. In fact, she couldn't remember the last time she had had even one glass of wine.

"Oh." Joe shrugged. "Not really. Most of my work was eliminating baseless claims or uncovering deliberate fraud. It's shocking what lengths some people will go to extort money. Almost as if they feel their insurance company owes them for all the years of premiums they've paid. And of course, all those sorts of claims just drive up the cost for honest people. But they don't see it that way."

"Fascinating." Cecily tried to imagine Joe as a policeman or as a detective. He would look very handsome in a uniform. "I guess in a way you have been in law enforcement."

Joe shrugged again. "I think that's why I liked Nate Edgerton as soon as I met him. He seems like a very competent officer. A real down-to-earth man."

"Oh, yes. He is. Nate's been our Chief of Police for many years."

"You're good friends, then—in such a small village."

"Well, we're friendly of course. His wife, Susanna, is a good friend of mine and my sister as well. She comes into the shop a lot, so we get to chat frequently."

"Ah," Joe replied, pouring more wine for Cecily.

She took another sip. She thought it was a good thing Marjorie wasn't here to see her drinking a second glass of wine. Marjorie probably wouldn't have approved even the first.

"I'm very grateful that Nate has taken me into his confidence as much as he has. Of course," Joe looked across the table, "there are things he's doing that he doesn't feel free to tell me, I'm sure, but he's certainly included me a little bit in his investigation and treated me with respect, even though I'm no longer active."

"I'm sure he's considered your . . . belief . . ." Cecily trailed off.

Joe smiled and shook his head. "My hunch, you mean." He smiled. Cecily noticed a faint hint of dimples in Joe's cheeks. The light from the chandeliers cast a silvery glow over his gray hair. She was definitely feeling a little warm and dizzy from the wine.

"Your hunch." Cecily smiled widely at Joe's self-deprecating remark. "That this body, this poor man they found, could be one of the robbers from years ago."

"Well, it's only a possibility, mind you. But I'm a big believer in trusting my nose, my instincts. For example, this van that was stolen . . . such bad luck for Nate."

"Oh yes. I saw Susanna in the shop just this morning. She told me Nate was apoplectic about it. She worries about him a lot—his health, you know. She doesn't like to see him stress so much."

"I can understand that." He smiled. "My wife used to worry about me a lot too." A wave of sadness passed over his face. "I was a lot older than she. I always thought I'd be the first to go. But I guess life is like that. What you think is going to happen never does, and then life hits you with a curveball. She was the one to go first."

"I'm so sorry for your loss, Joe. You must miss her very much."

Joe nodded in acknowledgment. "It's been a lot of years now, but it still comes to me every now and then, what a hole it's left in my life. I can understand why Nate's wife worries about him. He has a very stressful job, and stress takes its toll. He's not a young man anymore. He has to be careful, and that was a tremendous blow to his investigation."

"Oh, I know!" Cecily breathed. "The technicians

managed to dust for fingerprints, but they never had a
chance to really search the van before it was stolen. That's
why Nate was so upset. Susanna said Nate had a suspicion
there might have been something in that van the murderer
was looking for. That's why he was so fit to be tied."

Joe shook his head. "Terrible." Joe poured another glass
for himself and for Cecily. "Nate's such a hard-working
guy, but he's subject to the inefficiency of another jurisdic-
tion. It's too bad Snowflake doesn't have its own crime lab."

"I don't think our little village is big enough to warrant
something like that. That's why we have to rely on Lincoln
Falls for all those services."

"Well, I think Snowflake is one of the most charming
places I've visited in a long time."

"You do?"

Joe nodded. "In fact, I plan to say for a little while longer." He hesitated and leaned closer. "Don't say anything
to anyone just yet. You're the only one I'm confiding in, but
I'm thinking of selling my house in Bennington. It's too
big and lonesome for me there with my children all grown
up and gone, and my wife too. I just rattle around all day
when I'm home. I'd like to sell that house and look for a
small cottage somewhere in Snowflake."

Cecily could already picture a future dinner date with
Joe, perhaps many such evenings. "Oh," she gushed, "that
would be wonderful. You would love living in Snowflake!"

"I'm sure I would." Joe reached across the table and
gently touched her hand. "In fact, I know I would."

Chapter 36

MIRIAM WAITED NEAR the entrance to the corn maze, now shut down for the night. The smaller children had been taken home, tucked up safely in bed by their parents. All except her child. *Nothing changes when they grow older and bigger*, she thought. *Nothing changes at all*. The same piercing of the heart when harsh words are spoken, when that child rejects a parent's love and concern. She remembered Millie, her husband's mother, teaching her to read. Millie didn't stop with schoolbooks and everyday fiction. She had been a teacher in her younger years and made up her mind that Miriam must be thoroughly educated. They had read Shakespeare together. At first it had been very hard for Miriam to extract meaning from the Bard's English, but after a while the words came much more smoothly along with comprehension of the levels of meaning beneath the words. It was *King Lear* that came to her now. *"How sharper than a serpent's tooth it is to have a thankless child."*

She had carried her burden of guilt for the past eighteen

years, the burden of telling lies to a daughter she loved more than life itself. But what should she have done? Told the truth at some point as that daughter grew? Many times she had been tempted, but she had been fearful her confession might break the bond between her husband and her daughter. A bond she herself cherished and had no desire to injure. And the interminable questions that would eventually come. Where are you from? Who are your parents? Where did you live? How did you live? It wasn't until she had joined normal society, a world in which everyone lived in houses, everyone that counted, that she became ashamed of her own people. She wanted to escape the oppression of a society dominated by men like her father, with rules that would coerce her to marry a man she didn't love and separate her from the man she did—a man who ultimately betrayed her and abandoned her.

She watched him now, onstage, so confident, so happy. A tidal wave of anger threatened to overwhelm her. He had found her. He had left that forget-me-not in an envelope for her to find in her own mailbox. How could he? And how did he know about Janie? He must have seen her somewhere. Followed her. Watched the house. Must have seen who came and went. One glance at Janie and he would know she was his daughter. Had he ever married? she wondered. Had he fathered other children? If so, why torment her now, after all this time? Let him leave this child alone.

Coming here was her last resort. She had spent hours at the police station with Nate, going over everything she could possibly tell him. Everything except the real reason that she and Janie had fought. Whatever happened, she did not want her history to be public knowledge. If only Janie would see reason, would come home to her, they could work it out. Miriam would convince Janie that no one would ever have to know she was conceived out of wedlock, that her parents were travelers, that her father still was.

Eamon must have taken her. What other explanation could there be? Had he become a domineering male as her father had been? Janie would never have done this to her, disappeared without a word to a friend or a phone call to her job. Whatever harsh words had passed between them, Janie loved her, of that she was certain. Janie might be angry, but she had to hope there was a way to work this out.

The last song ended. The crowd had been thinning as the musicians played. A woman held a stand-up bass. She played lightning fast, her bow flying over the strings as the banjo beat a fast tempo. Miriam watched the people onstage closely. With a shock she realized the woman was Eamon and Taran's sister, Deidre. At first she hadn't recognized her, but they had been close as girls, had played together as children. How the years had changed her! It was a hard life staying on the road, being in fear of arrest, not always able to find medical or dental care. Miriam glanced down at her manicured nails, her perfectly cut hair, her expensive clothing, expensive to them at least. What would they think of her if she came forward? If she decided to reveal herself? She imagined the shock she would see in their eyes. But perhaps they already knew she was here in Snowflake. Perhaps Eamon had told them.

She tried to imagine how it would feel meeting them face to face again. Then she quickly dismissed the idea. She had no desire to speak to any of her former family. There was only Janie for her now. Janie was her family, not these strangers who sang in an almost forgotten language, a Gàidhlig she herself had spoken years before.

She had to know if Janie was with them, if Eamon had taken her. Was it possible that, out of curiosity, Janie had gone to see her father? But Miriam couldn't imagine how that could be.

The musicians were packing up their instruments, winding up cords and moving equipment across the stage. Miriam walked around the far side of the pony corral and skirted the edge of the stage, keeping well away so that no one would notice her. She reached the area behind the stage and close to the trees where the vans were parked. She had to pick her moment carefully. Coming here was a very long shot, but she had no other place to search for her daughter. She heard voices calling, and she quickly stepped behind a large tree trunk. She was desperate to find Janie, but first she needed to make sure Janie was not already with them. A woman she didn't recognize descended the short stairway from the backstage area and approached one of the vans. She unlocked the rear doors and pulled them open, then returned to the stage.

Eamon came down the stairs next, carrying an amplifier in one hand. He was still tall and strong, but she had seen streaks of gray in his hair highlighted by the stage lighting. He loaded the amp into the rear of the van and stepped away.

Miriam called his name. He turned, looking all around. She stepped out into the moonlight and waited. He froze, instantly alert. She knew he had recognized her.

He hurried toward her. "Morag!"

Miriam backed away, terrified to allow him to come any closer.

"Morag. I knew you'd come."

Miriam turned away and walked farther into the field. Eamon followed. Her emotions were a jumble. A tornado was ravaging her insides.

"Morag, speak to me. Please," he pleaded.

She felt as if a hand had closed around her throat. She wasn't sure she would be able to speak. She swallowed with difficulty. "My name is Miriam now." She watched him carefully. He continued to stare at her. "How did you find me?" she finally asked.

Eamon took a few steps closer. "It was by accident." His voice was so low she could barely make out the words. "We were driving through town. I saw you coming out of a shop.

I couldn't believe my eyes." He drank in the sight of her. They stood, staring at each other like strangers.

Miriam thought her heart would stop. She was paralyzed. Her heart was racing. "My name is Miriam now." She repeated it, as if it would give her strength. Her voice was cold. How dare he threaten to break through the defenses it had taken her years to build?

Eamon stood in the silvery moonlight, silent. In the distance she could see movement around the vans. Soon they would be looking for him.

"Have you taken her?" Miriam demanded.

Eamon stared at her. He was silent for a moment. "I . . . I don't know what you mean," he said.

"My daughter!" she cried. "Have . . . you . . . taken . . . her?"

"What? No!" he shouted. "What's happened? Where is she?"

"That's what I need to know. For God's sake, Eamon. If you have an ounce of compassion in your heart, tell me the truth." Miriam felt hot tears flowing down her cheeks.

"Oh, Morag!" He moved closer, aching to put his arms around her and comfort her. He felt as if his chest had broken apart. "*Thoir mionnan air mo bheatha.* I swear on my life, Morag. I have not, nor would I. I knew the moment I saw you . . . and her. I knew she was our daughter. I could never harm a hair on her head."

"You were watching her," Miriam said accusingly.

Eamon took a deep breath. "I have. That's the truth." One look at the girl and he knew she was of his blood. His and Morag's. "I wanted . . . I don't know . . . to see her, to hear her voice. It broke my heart, Morag. I never knew. Please forgive me. I never knew."

"That day . . . that you didn't come. I didn't know myself until a few months later." Miriam pulled her jacket closer, protection against the evening chill, protection from *him*. "What difference would it have made if you knew? You abandoned me. What matter that I was pregnant?"

There. She had said it. It was small satisfaction for all the times she had alternately cursed him and loved him in absentia. She had never dreamed the day would come when she would have the chance to face him and accuse him. All the longing and heartbreak she had felt for years threatened to overwhelm her. He had left that flower for her. How could he be so cruel as to tear that wound open again?

"I never did. Miriam." He struggled to use her name. "I *never* abandoned you."

Before she could quell the rush of emotion, she cried, "You never came! I waited. For days I waited. You left me there."

"No. No. It wasn't like that. They kept me at the camp that day. I was like a wild man. I fought them, but there were too many of them. They were so sure you'd come back if they held me prisoner. They never thought . . ."

"That I wouldn't return?" She finished his thought.

He nodded dumbly. "Please believe me, Morag . . . I'm sorry. Miriam. I loved you then, and I love you still. I would never have left you out there on your own. Can't you find it in your heart to forgive me? My life was taken from me as well." Her silence was a stone in his heart. "I searched for you everywhere. Every town, every village. Every time we broke camp. There was never a time I traveled through a place and didn't look for you, didn't ask if anyone had seen someone of your description. They made a terrible mistake. They realized it eventually. Everyone wanted to find you, to bring you back."

"I would never have gone back to them. Never! I would have killed myself before I . . ."

Eamon fell silent. Miriam could see the lines etched into his face, the gray hair at his temples. He was still a fine-looking man, but he had aged. The life had aged him. Perhaps sadness had aged him.

"It's all different now. Not the same family you left. I'm head of the clan now."

"*You?*"

"Yes." He smiled slightly. "The man who would have left it all behind for a life with you." He searched her face. "Have you had a good life? Are you happy?"

She hesitated. "I have had a life at least. A real life."

Eamon stepped closer. Close enough that Miriam could smell the warmth of his skin. Memories were flooding through her mind, as if the door she had closed and locked years before had burst open.

"How long has she known about me?"

"Not until a few days ago. I told her. That's why she won't speak to me."

"She's been with the woman from the restaurant. They came to see me. But you say she's not there now?"

"They went to see you? Where? At your campsite?" Miriam asked.

Eamon nodded in response.

"Something's happened to her, then." Miriam struggled against the panic that threatened to overwhelm her. "I don't believe she's run away again."

"We'll find her. Everyone will help."

"No. Not them. I'll find her." She turned away.

Eamon grasped her arm. "Wait. Please."

Miriam pulled her arm away and stared at him.

"You're as beautiful as the day I first fell in love with you."

Something inside her melted, a part of her that had been cold for a very long time. She felt a sob rise in her chest. She struggled to breathe. "Stay away from me." She turned and ran across the field, toward the parking lot and escape. Eamon called after her, but she didn't turn back.

Chapter 37

ALL THE JACK-O'-LANTERNS around the room were flickering as if tiny spirits lived inside each pumpkin. The room felt alive with unseen energies. Jack had put a CD in the player, and a soft clarinet solo filled the room. Lucky had turned off all the lamps but one and poured two mugs of chamomile tea hoping it would help them relax and give them a few quiet moments before each headed home.

Jack's phone started to ring. He fumbled in his pocket to retrieve it and squinted at the caller ID. "Can't see a thing," he grumbled. He hit the button a moment before the call would have gone to voicemail.

Lucky heard a man's voice on the phone. "It's Nate," Jack whispered.

"Oh!"

"No. Sorry, Nate. Nothing new at our end." Jack paused. "I see. No. I don't like the sound of that either."

Nate's voice was audible but garbled. "Good night." Jack clicked off.

"What's happened?" Lucky asked.

"They found Janie's car this afternoon. They've towed it to the police station. Nate's not trusting the impound lot after what happened to the van."

"Where?"

"In the parking lot of the Harvest Festival."

"Do you think Janie could have gone to her father?" Lucky asked.

"No idea."

"I can't see why she would do that. She had such a negative reaction when she saw him onstage at the festival." Lucky thought for a moment. "Do you think her father could have taken her against her will? There were a lot of people at that encampment. And we know they have guns—shotguns at least."

"That's not as sinister as it sounds. They probably need them for hunting, for food."

"I guess." Lucky sighed. "I just wasn't thrilled to see one aimed at us. I just can't imagine how they live, even if they do hunt wild game in the woods. Where do they get money to buy all the other supplies they'd need for a life on the road? Surely having a short stint at a festival like ours wouldn't pay them that much."

"Those men can do all sorts of odd jobs, day labor, that type of thing. They arouse a lot of suspicion because of some bad apples, but I'd say most of 'em are decent. They're not all out to bilk people."

"What about the guy Joe's been chasing?"

Jack shrugged. "Joe could be right. Who knows? Maybe a traveler was involved in that robbery years ago. And maybe that's the dead man Nate found by the side of the road. We just don't know. It's a lot of maybes. But I can tell Joe's one of those men who are like pit bulls. Persistent. Just can't let go of the one case he couldn't wind up."

"Miriam told me that her family . . . clan, whatever they

call themselves, are from Cape Breton originally. She grew up speaking Gaelic. Their own dialect of Scottish Gaelic. Can you imagine that, Jack?"

"Oh sure. If they'd stayed isolated from other Gaelic speakers for generations, the language would change, grow into something else. They'd have to speak English for sure and undoubtedly French or at least Québécois if they move through Quebec a lot. They'd have to, just to get by. But they maybe can't read or write a word of it."

"And that's another thing. How can they get across the borders if they don't have real identification?"

"They've been traveling this landscape forever. They're not gonna pay any attention to borders or countries. Even now that things are a lot tighter. Years ago it didn't take much more than a driver's license or birth certificate, if that, to cross into Canada or back to the US. Now all that's changed. Our border with Canada is hundreds of miles with numerous crossing paths these people would know about. All the governments in the world couldn't properly stop them." Jack took another sip of his tea. "There used to be towns that straddled the border between here and Canada. A street could start in the US and end up in another country. A plumber in Canada could fix a sink at the other end of town and be in the US."

"I think I read about a place recently," Lucky replied. "Can't remember where. But there's an area that's in the US, and the people of the town believe they should be part of Canada. Or maybe it's the other way around. Canadians that want to be part of the US. Wish I could remember."

"As far as this man Eamon goes . . ." Jack rested his feet on a chair. "I think he was being straight with us. I think he was shocked to figure out he had a daughter, and he just wanted to make some kind of contact with her. And we know it's his twin who was shot. No doubt in my mind they stole the body from the morgue and we stumbled into a wake that night."

"If Joe Conrad's right, Eamon's twin brother, Taran, was the man involved in the robbery. What if he took off with the money and his partner in crime caught up with him?"

"If Joe was chasing a traveler, it's no wonder he never caught the man. And the other guy—the inside man at the armored truck company—may not have been a traveler. Just your ordinary citizen—ordinary criminal I should say. They could've gone their separate ways and had no further contact with each other—till now."

"Which may be why he ended up dead by the side of the road," Lucky replied. "Was his killer looking for the money? Was that why the van was stolen from the impound lot? That's what I'd like to know. For all we know, the travelers could have stolen it. They'd probably consider it their property anyway. It'd be a real feather in Joe's cap if he did manage to identify one of the robbers, especially since the company forced him into retirement."

"I can understand how the guy feels. Nobody who's grown older with years of experience wants to be considered unwanted. My hat's off to the man."

A movement at the front door caught Lucky's attention. Horace was standing outside, a plaid scarf wrapped around his neck. He carried a book tucked under his arm and a shopping bag with handles. Cicero, next to him, was wagging his tail. Lucky jumped up to let him in.

"I hope I didn't stop by too late this evening," Horace said.

"Not at all," Jack replied. "Come on in." He reached over to rub Cicero's head.

"I found this in my library, and I was just so excited, I had to bring it over so you could both have a look. I knew I had it somewhere, just couldn't remember where. I am turning into the proverbial absent-minded professor." Horace placed the heavy book reverentially on the table. "But first of all, to a very important order of business." He reached into the shopping bag and lifted a carved pumpkin out. His jack-o'-lantern had protruding ears, a mouth that sported crooked teeth and a carrot for a nose.

"Oh, that's really a good one, Horace. I like it," Lucky said.

Jack stared. "Looks a little bit like Guy Bessette," Jack said, referring to Guy's unfortunate crooked smile.

Lucky hit Jack playfully on the shoulder. "Stop that."

"Oh! You think so?" Horace asked. "I didn't mean that at all. Maybe I should carve those teeth differently. I certainly wouldn't want to hurt Guy's feelings." Horace looked from one to the other.

"It's fine, Horace. Don't worry. I'll give your pumpkin a number." Lucky placed the pumpkin on the long display table. She rummaged through a drawer behind the counter and retrieved a small bundle of cardstock. She wrote the next number with a black marker and slipped it into a holder in front of Horace's pumpkin.

"You have some pretty impressive entries there. Don't know if mine will be in the running, but I'm happy to compete."

"No worries. It's just for fun," Lucky said. "Would you like some tea?"

"No thanks, not tonight. I can't stay long."

"What's this book?" she asked, returning to the table.

"Well, you remember I was telling you about the professor who had a theory about the carvings on the megalithic stones. At the time, he was laughed at, but now a lot of academics are coming around to his way of thinking.

"Here's a picture of one carving." Horace opened the book to a full-page illustration and turned the book so they could see.

Jack peered at the markings. "Can't see how anybody would make sense of these."

"They look like funny stick figures," Lucky said.

"That's exactly it. It's Ogam, a form of stick writing," Horace said. "That professor I mentioned had a look at the

Bourne Stone in Massachusetts and claimed the markings were a variation of the Punic alphabet found in ancient Spain. He called it Iberic and translated the script as recording a land claim in Massachusetts by Hanno, a prince of Carthage, if you can believe that. That would have been centuries later than the Bronze Age though."

Horace was warming to his subject. "You have to realize that at the beginning of the twentieth century, experts were of the opinion that no Europeans had ever landed in America until Columbus arrived. American scholars actually went to Europe to study Bronze Age sites and completely ignored the megaliths in the Americas. The markings are ascribed to Ogam, an early form of pre-Gaelic, and that writing has been found all over North America. It's important because now it's impossible to ignore that a written language existed in prehistoric America. What's strange about Ogam is the way the language is organized—you know, with vowels and consonants. Ogam had, I'm not sure, either fifteen or seventeen consonants and five vowels. The only other language constructed like that is Basque, so of course, linguists believe there's a connection. And to make matters stranger, Ogam is suspected to have originated in West Africa."

"I thought you said it was early Gaelic?" Jack asked.

"No. What we call Gaelic didn't exist then. Some scholars believe Ogam came to Ireland from North Africa with the missionaries who were preaching early Christianity. And then, some linguists believe that it may have originally reached North Africa from invaders from the North Sea and Baltic civilizations centuries before, so Ogam might really be an early form of a Norse language. The other alphabet found right along with Ogam on some of these stones is Tifinag. Tifinag is the writing that the Tuaregs, a race of Berbers that live in the Atlas Mountains of North Africa, use."

"It's hard to believe prehistoric peoples were able to

travel across the North Atlantic and land in the new world," Lucky remarked.

"The Celts and the Carthaginians were very skilled seafaring people, as were the Scandinavians. You have to remember that during the years of what we call the Bronze Age, earth's climate was quite different. It was much warmer, and it would have allowed easy navigation on westward flowing currents and winds. The North Atlantic route to New England would have been a lot easier than it would be today, three thousand or five thousand years later," Horace continued. "You may not know this, but the structure we have here, outside of Snowflake, has an opening that would have faced the rising sun at the summer solstice. The Celts were pagans, and they celebrated Beltane and the solstices. Today, modern-day pagans celebrate Beltane on the first of May, and"—Horace smiled—"they'll be celebrating Samhain at this time of year, the day when the spirits of the dead can walk in our world and make themselves known. Our Halloween is a hangover from pagan days. Isn't that delightful?"

"Beltane, did you say? That was the beginning of spring?" Lucky asked.

"Yes. Beltane is a time of great celebration—the fires of Bel. That's another thing about our professor. He claimed to have found a dedication to Baal, the Phoenician sun god. Students of ancient mythology have long suspected that the Celtic sun god Bel, for whom Beltane is named, and the Phoenician god Baal were one and the same. Both cultures worshipped the sun. Academics can be very stuffy indeed and resistant to new ideas, so you can imagine they didn't like their cherished theories turned upside down. No longer, though. It's irrefutable that many different peoples were coming across the ocean and landing in the Americas even though the details may be lost in the mists of time."

"This is utterly fascinating," Lucky said.

"Funny how you can live in a place your whole life and never know much about the things right under your nose," Jack said. "I do know the travelers I've seen over the years believe they have a connection to the Stones. Maybe it's superstition, or maybe it's ancient knowledge."

"Well, now that I've bored you sufficiently with my pedantic interests, I'll be on my way." Horace smiled.

"It was anything but boring. It was mindboggling. New England has thousands of years of secrets."

Horace wrapped his scarf around his neck. "Good night," he said, tucking the book under his arm. Cicero, wagging his tail, waited by the door.

"Hang on," Lucky said. She hurried to the kitchen and pulled a hunk of chicken from the refrigerator. She returned to the front door and leaned down. "We can't let Cicero leave without his treat, now, can we?"

Cicero inhaled the chicken and rewarded Lucky with a very wet kiss. Laughing, she wiped her cheek and locked the door behind Horace and Cicero as they left.

She picked up the mugs and cleared the table. Slipping behind the counter, she placed the mugs on the hatch. She was so tired she didn't have the energy to even rinse them out in the kitchen. She'd deal with it tomorrow.

"Jack, I . . ." Lucky stopped in midsentence. A sharp rap came from the back door. She exchanged a look with Jack.

"Could that be Janie?" Lucky asked hopefully.

Jack heaved himself out of his comfortable position. "Let's go find out."

Jack followed her down the corridor to the back door. He flicked on a switch that would illuminate their back stairway. Lucky opened the door, hoping against hope that Janie had turned up. But it wasn't Janie who stood on their doorstep. It was Eamon.

Chapter 38

EAMON'S FACE LOOKED drawn under the overhead light. "I didn't know where else to go."

Lucky felt a chill run up her spine.

"Let him in," Jack said.

She stepped back to allow Eamon entry.

"Let's go into the office," Jack suggested.

Eamon followed them down the corridor. They entered the small room. Jack took the large cracked leather chair behind the desk. Lucky offered one of the two chairs in front of the desk to Eamon. He sat and tried to gather his thoughts. He ran a hand through his hair before speaking.

"Morag . . . Miriam came to see me tonight." He glanced at Lucky and Jack to gauge their reaction. "That's how I found out. She told me no one knows where Janie is. But then, when I went back to the van tonight to pack up my equipment, I found this stuck under the windshield wiper." He retrieved a folded piece of paper from his pocket and passed it to Lucky.

She unfolded it with trembling fingers. It was a typed

message on a cheap piece of plain white paper, probably printed from a computer. It said, "*I have your daughter. If you want to see her alive, bring me the money. No police if you want to see her again. I'll be in contact.*"

Lucky's eyes were wide. Jack was patting his shirt pocket looking for his glasses. Lucky read the note aloud to him.

"Does Miriam know about this?"

Eamon shook his head. "She was already gone when I found it."

"Any idea who might have left this for you?"

Eamon looked distraught. "None. And the worst of it is, I don't know how long it's been there. It could have been there all day, and I never noticed. Morag tells me Janie didn't come back to your place last night, is that right?"

Lucky nodded. "This changes everything. Someone has taken her. And it had to have happened last night."

"The light was so dim, I almost didn't see it. I started to crumple it and throw it away. I thought it was some kind of flyer, some kind of advertisement. I came to you folks because I don't know what else to do. You're both close to her. I thought you might have some ideas."

"Her mother's gone to the police—this morning, in fact, so Nate's been alerted. He's checking accident reports and such, but this puts a whole different spin on things. She's not a runaway. She's been abducted. We have to let him know."

"No," Eamon almost shouted. "No police."

"But . . ." Lucky interrupted.

"No police. If they think I went to the cops, they might kill her."

"And the money? What money is that note referring to?" Lucky asked.

"My brother . . . I've always been afraid he had done some illegal things. I tried to get him to tell me, but he never would. We always fought about it."

Jack looked at Lucky. "So Joe was right."

"Joe?" Eamon asked.

"We've got a retired insurance investigator in town right now. He claims it was a traveler who committed that robbery over in Bennington seven years ago. What do you know about that?"

"Seven years ago?" Eamon rubbed his forehead. "Nothing. I had nothing to do with that. But I had my suspicions about Taran. Nothing definite, mind you, just wondered where his money was coming from. Taran was always in some kind of trouble. He used to take off every so often. No one ever knew what he was up to, but at least he never brought the police to us. A few years ago, he bought us some land in Nova Scotia. Put it in a relative's name, but it's ours if we ever need it. It means a lot to all of us. The life . . . being on the road. It's not good. It's better to have roots, to have a place. I'm grateful to him for that," Eamon continued. "But Taran never seemed to be worried about finding work or about money. Whenever we needed cash, he was always the one to come up with it. I wanted to know the truth, but I didn't get anywhere with him."

"Somebody killed him for it," Lucky added. "And now whoever it is thinks you know where the money is hidden, and they could kill Janie if you don't find it."

"I don't know what to do," Eamon said. "My brother . . . wasn't a good husband or a good father. He used to beat his wife and the boy when he was drinking. We threatened to shun him, kick him out of the clan, but when he'd sober up, he'd be his old self."

"And has Daniel returned?" Lucky asked.

"No." Eamon shook his head. "Daniel's a good kid, just scared of his own shadow. He thought he was being arrested, that's why he ran."

Lucky didn't voice her suspicions, but it occurred to her that Daniel might have something to be guilty about. Was it possible he had killed his own father?

"We still don't know where he is," Eamon continued.

"Well, whoever's taken Janie obviously thinks you're involved or at least that you know something about where the cash is hidden. And it's obvious you're his brother," Lucky continued. "So let's assume it *was* Taran involved in that robbery and there's a secret stash somewhere around here, where would you look?" Lucky asked.

"He could have had many hiding places. We travel all the time. The only thing is . . ." Eamon hesitated, lost in thought. "This time we had plans to head for a town in New Hampshire, but Taran insisted we come here to Snowflake. We were offered a better paying gig over there, but he said he wouldn't go. He wanted to come here now."

Lucky and Jack fell silent, not wanting to interrupt Eamon's memory. "Taran once said to me . . . and I didn't pay much attention at the time . . . he had been drinking heavily. He told me if anything ever happened to him, I should go to the Stones in Snowflake and have a look around."

"The *Stones*?" Lucky said. "You think he could have hidden something there?"

"Like I said, Taran had been drinking, and he wasn't making much sense at the time. I thought it was just drunken nonsense. I had forgotten all about it till now. Look . . ." he said. "If there is anything there, I want nothing to do with it. I just want my daughter safely back. And then I want to find the man who shot my brother."

Lucky and Jack exchanged a look. She spoke first. "Let's go, then. We need to find that money if it exists. But . . ." She hesitated. "If there's nothing at the Stones, then we go the police—tonight. We don't waste a minute. Do you agree?"

Eamon took a deep breath. "I agree. If we find nothing at the Stones, I'll go to the police."

Chapter 39

JANIE FELT A tug on her arms as the man reached down to check the binding. It was tight. Her hands were numb from lack of movement. His shoes scuffed against the wooden floor. She sniffed. Cologne. A man's cologne. She didn't recognize it, but now all her senses were on alert. If she ever managed to escape, it's the one thing she could identify. The few words he had spoken wouldn't give her enough to recognize him again—at least she didn't think so.

She felt his hand on her head. He pulled the rough cloth tightly against her face and slid a straw into the opening, poking it at her mouth. She held her lips tight, unwilling to drink. She had to stay awake. She had to find a way to escape. He pulled away. He knew she was resisting. She felt the barrel of the gun against her head. "Drink," he ordered. She shook her head from side to side and tried to wrench her head away.

He grasped her neck with one hand and squeezed. She could hear the blood rushing through her ears. She couldn't

breathe. She kicked and struggled to pull away, but he was
too strong. Everything was growing dark. Suddenly, he let
go of her neck. She gasped for air. Her heart was pounding
wildly. "Drink," he said again, "or you're dead." He pushed
the straw against her mouth. She sobbed once and drank
the sweet liquid.

SHE WOKE WITH a start. She could still feel the pressure
on her throat. She gasped in fear. It was pitch black. Night
again. Was it the night of the same day? There was no way
to tell. The rope that held her to the frame of the building
had loosened from her struggle. She was able to pull away
from the wall a few inches. She sat up as straight as possible. If only she could pull the hood from her head, she
could see where she was. She might find something that
could help her escape.

Her legs were stretched out in front of her. Her ankles
were bound together, but she could move her legs back and
forth. She swung her legs as far to the right as she could
and felt something soft. Tarps? There was a smell of oil,
like machine oil. Was she in a storage shed? A farmer's
shed? She carefully moved her legs in the other direction
and felt metal against her thigh. She was close to some kind
of machine or equipment. She scooted to her left as far as
she could and twisted away, feeling behind her with her
fingertips. She felt the smooth surface of a blade. It was
narrow, like an old lawnmower. The rope still bound her
to the wall of the structure, but now she was positive she
was in a storage shed and this must be a lawnmower next
to her. If she could keep the blade still, she could work it
against the thin plastic that bound her wrists.

She stretched and felt a muscle cramp in her midsection.
She stopped and took a deep breath, willing the cramp to
relax. Then she tried again. She felt the edge of the blade
with her fingers and positioned her hands so the blade was

against the binding. Slowly, she moved her hands back and forth, hoping to make a dent in the hard material. The blade spun away. She felt a trickle of something warm. Blood. She had nicked her hand. She waited until the blades were still. Then she tried again, very slowly and carefully sawing the plastic strip against the edge of the blade. Whoever owned this mower had taken good care of it. The workings were oiled, and the blades were sharp. She moved her hands back and forth, willing herself to be patient. This could work. Finally, she felt the binding release and fall away. She breathed deeply and inched away from the blades.

Once her hands were freed, removing the sack over her head was easy work. It was tied around her neck with a strip of cloth. Her fingers were stiff, but she easily undid the knots. She pulled the filthy fabric off her head and opened her eyes as wide as she could. It was dark. She listened carefully for any sound that might indicate her captor was returning. She heard nothing.

She had to hurry. She had to escape before he returned. She twisted around, feeling the rope around her midsection. She reached up behind her. It was looped through a large eyehook in the wall. She felt the entire length of rope until she found the knot. It was hard working with her hands above her head. Numbness threatened her fingers. She must remain steady, patient. If she could do that, she'd be able to escape. She found the main knot and, taking deep breaths to keep herself alert, worked at the knot until it gave way. Quickly, she unwrapped it from her body and threw it to the side.

Pushing herself carefully off the floor, she stood. Blood rushed to her legs. Dizziness threatened to overwhelm her. Should she take the time to try to get the binding from her ankles? Or would he return before she could release her legs? A sound outside the building alerted her. Was he coming back? She listened again, terrified to even take a breath. A scurrying sound. Some small animal in the field. She breathed a sigh of relief and sat heavily on the floor. She tried to line up the blade of the lawnmower with the binding around her ankles. One of her sneakers was still on her left foot; the other foot was bare. She felt carefully with her bare foot. She leaned on her hands and positioned her feet against the blade, again moving back and forth gently against the plastic binding. This would take a while even if she was able to keep the blade from spinning around.

A noise. A car's engine in the distance. She held very still. Her heart started to race wildly. A sudden panic took hold. She shouldn't wait. She scrambled to her feet and, shuffling across the floor, moved slowly, hoping she wouldn't faint. With her bare foot she felt splinters in the old wooden floor. Reaching out, she held her hands in front of her as she moved. She only hoped she was going in the direction of the door. She thought she was. She remembered the sound of the door latch and was sure it was in this direction. If only there were a window, something that would allow moonlight to filter through. She reached the opposite side of the room and felt all around with her hands. There must be a door here. There had to be. She only felt a flat surface. Desperately she moved to her left a few inches. Her fingers touched raised wood—a doorjamb. She moved again, shuffling her bound feet. She found the knob. She turned it and pulled it inward. The fresh night air caressed her face. The smell of earth and damp leaves. The outside. She had no idea where she was, but she was sure the cornfield was ahead of her. She could hear the shushing sound as wind washed over the stalks. Was she on the other side of the field from the Harvest Festival? She almost cried with relief. She managed to sit on the threshold and felt the wooden step below her. She pushed herself off the threshold and stood on the ground. If she could somehow get across the cornfield, she could reach help.

She couldn't walk, but she could take small jumps and shuffle slowly. The corn stalks would hide her. She had gone several yards into the field when she heard the sound of an engine. A car was nearby on the road. Was he coming back? Panicking, she tried to move faster. She felt dizzy. The drug he had forced her to drink hadn't completely worn off. She wanted to move faster, but the ground was uneven. Too late she realized she was losing her balance. She was falling. She reached out to break her fall. Something sharp hit the side of her head and everything went black.

Chapter 40

NO ONE SPOKE a word as Lucky drove through the night, her headlights flashing against tree trunks as she navigated turns. She followed the Old Colonial Road out of town for several miles and finally reached the turnoff the locals called the Pilgrim's Trail. She and Jack had bundled up in warm jackets and taken three emergency flashlights and a battery-powered lantern from the storage closet at the Spoonful.

Lucky wondered if they had embarked on a fool's errand. This was only a guess on Eamon's part. He might have been correct when he thought Taran was spouting nonsense about the Stones, but since no one had a better idea, it was worth a try.

She prayed Janie was safe. Even if they located Taran's cache, they had no guarantee Janie was still alive or would be released unharmed when the kidnapper regained what he thought of as his rightful share. Was the theft of the van from the impound lot an effort to locate hidden cash? If Eamon truly had no knowledge, then it was Taran's partner in crime who had stolen it. But where else could Taran have hidden a large bundle? The travelers lived in such close quarters, it must have been impossible to keep a large amount of cash with him.

"Is this the way?" Eamon asked from the backseat.

"It is. This road is the long way there, and we'll have to hike a bit. I thought it would be better than going near your camp."

She saw Eamon nod in her rearview mirror.

As teenagers, she and her friends would sometimes visit the Stones. There were legends galore about the structure—that a woman had hung herself there; that during a full moon the ground would ooze and pull visitors underground, never to be seen again. Some of the boys claimed they heard weird cries in the night. Invariably one of them would tell ghost stories until the girls, laughing nervously, screamed for him to stop. One boy, she remembered, had been teased mercilessly. The others had picked on him until he agreed to spend a night alone at the Stones. In the light of day, it seemed ludicrous to believe in hauntings, but in the dark in the woods the energy that surrounded those rocks was palpable. That boy hadn't returned the following day, and his parents, worried sick, had learned what he had done. They found him in the clearing where the Stones stood just before dawn. He was terrified out of his mind. He would never say what had frightened him so much. Even the boys who had teased him let him be. As for herself, she had always felt a sinister presence around the ancient stone structure, as though the malevolent ghosts of long ago people haunted the place.

Lucky put the car in low gear and proceeded slowly up the dirt trail, finally reaching an overgrown area where she could drive no farther. "It's not far from here. We'll have to walk the rest of the way," she said.

"Be careful." Jack turned around to address Eamon. "Stay as close as you can to the old path. There are some old artesian wells in this area. The ground might not be stable."

They climbed out of the car. Lucky heard scurrying in the underbrush. The moon was waxing but still in the first quarter. This would be a difficult search. She handed the flashlights to Jack and Eamon. "Let's all stay close."

She turned and detoured around the overgrown bushes, finding the well-worn path up the hill. Lucky led the way with Eamon taking up the rear. They climbed single file, going slowly in deference to Jack, each of them shining light on the path ahead and pushing branches out of their way. No one, not even teenagers, Lucky realized, had taken this route to the Stones for a very long time.

She was the first to reach the clearing. A silent, unearthly edifice faced them, exactly as she remembered it from years before—a mystery structure from a forgotten time. What people had built these? And marked them with strange symbols of a forgotten language? Huge flat stones piled upon each other created the outer walls of the structure. A layer of moss, grasses and ivy covered the outer roof. Lucky shone her flashlight at the entrance, a black maw to a frightening enclosure. The opening to the underground chamber was only six feet in height, but inside, the ceiling, also created from huge stones, stood ten feet from the rock flooring.

They stood in silence, staring at the opening. All three flashlights were aimed at the rectangular entrance. The night had grown cold enough that their breath was visible in the air. The wind was stronger here at the top of the hill, creating an eerie moaning sound as it swept over the nooks and crannies of the rocks.

"Where do we look?" Lucky asked.

Eamon paced around the structure more than half buried under the encroaching hillside. One wall, a partial wall and an opening were all that were visible. He shone his light over what he could see of the outside surface. He turned to them. "This vegetation hasn't been disturbed, at least not for a long, long time. We have to search inside."

Lucky shuddered, frightened of going into the earth on a night like this.

Eamon must have noticed her reaction. "I'll go first," he said.

Jack and Lucky waited until the light of his torch had disappeared. They followed him through the outer door along a path that sloped downward into the chamber. The room they stood in was rectangular in shape. Lucky guessed it was ten feet wide and fifteen feet long, half buried into the hillside.

"Where do we start?" Jack asked.

"Let's go over the foundation stones. Look for any signs of digging or disturbance. If anything was buried here within the last few years, we might be able to see it. Look for any indication a stone was moved," Eamon continued. "Let's do this together. With three sources of light and all of us focusing, we stand a better chance of not missing anything."

Eamon moved to the far corner, and Jack and Lucky stood on either side of him as they methodically went over every square foot of the chamber. None of them noted any misaligned stones or disturbed earth. A half hour later they continued on to the sloping pathway of the chamber, examining it to no avail. Discouraged, they returned to the lower chamber.

Lucky turned on the lantern and placed it on the stone floor. She shone her flashlight at the ceiling of the structure. "This place is amazing. I never fully appreciated this when I was a kid."

Jack looked at her sharply. "And what were you doing here?"

Lucky smiled sheepishly. "Nothing much, just fooling around with the other kids."

"Good thing your parents didn't find out. You'd a been grounded for life."

Eamon shone his light at the opening to the world

above. "These were constructed to allow the light of the rising sun to shine upon a particular spot at a certain time of year."

"You mean the spring equinox?" Lucky asked.

Eamon smiled. "We celebrate Beltane, the beginning of summer, on the first day of May."

"So if the rising sun comes through that opening on a certain day, then . . ." Lucky turned in a half circle away from the opening and shone the light on a large square stone, slightly different in size and shape from the others surrounding it.

"That symbolism would appeal to Taran," Eamon said, moving toward the square stone. He studied it, running his finger around the circumference of the rock. "I do think this has been moved in the recent past. Look at this." He pointed his flashlight to illuminate fresh scrape marks on the stone below.

Jack and Lucky moved closer and aimed their flashlights at the rock that Eamon struggled to dislodge. His face became red with the effort.

"My fingers are smaller. If you can move it just a little, I can reach into the groove and pull," Lucky said. "Jack, can you hold both flashlights so we can see what we're doing?"

Jack nodded, and with a flashlight in each hand, he shone the light against the rock as Lucky and Eamon struggled. They heard a grinding sound, and suddenly the rock came away so quickly, it almost fell. It was only a few inches in thickness. Behind it was a small cavern. Eamon picked up his flashlight and aimed it into the opening. They all saw a flash, a glint of something metallic.

"Here goes," Eamon said. He reached inside and, grasping the object, dragged out a dark green box of sturdy metal, perhaps two feet in length and eight inches in height. He stared at the container for several seconds and took a deep breath. Lucky and Jack were silent, hoping that whatever they found would free Janie. Lifting the heavy box out of the opening, Eamon placed it on the stone floor.

Lucky trained her flashlight on the box, as did Jack. The light reflected eerily off the metal where the paint had worn away, and danced around the walls of the chamber. The box was secured with a small hasp. Eamon tugged, and the lid came open with a screech, revealing stacks of bills held together with paper bands.

He picked up one of the bundles and flipped through the stacks, counting under his breath. "One of these is maybe ten thousand dollars, so we have about two hundred thousand here. That's just a guess. I can't be sure unless we're inclined to count it. This is what our kidnapper is after."

"But didn't Joe tell us the robbery netted more than $800,000?" Jack asked.

"I wouldn't know about the robbery, but I do know Taran bought land in Nova Scotia a few years ago. I have no idea what that cost him. And if he's been living off of this for the past seven years . . . maybe this is all that's left. Maybe this is the only cache."

"So what do we do now?" Lucky asked.

"We take this with us and wait to be contacted. I do not want to go to the police. I'm too worried they'll interfere and mess it up, and Janie could get hurt in the meantime. All I want to do is hand this over and get my daughter back."

"I think we should put this stone back where it came from," Jack said.

"You're right." Eamon bent down and lifted the rock, lining it up with the opening from which it had been taken. Jack stepped forward and helped Eamon push it back into place.

"My brother brought this upon us. God rest his soul." Eamon brushed off his hands and lifted the container.

"What do we do now?" Lucky asked.

"No choice but to wait for some contact."

"Maybe we should bring it back to the Spoonful. We can lock it up there."

"There's no way I'll let this out of my sight," Eamon replied. "My daughter's life depends on this."

"But Eamon, whatever happens, this money belongs to the insurance company," Lucky said.

"I don't give a damn about the insurance company," Eamon replied. "I just want Janie back." He turned away, the box tucked under his arm, and followed the pathway out of the chamber. He was out of sight in a moment.

"What do you think, Jack?" Lucky whispered.

"Strange doings. Must be hard for him, knowing his brother was involved in a robbery and a murder."

"Let's get out of here. I keep shivering like someone's walking on my grave, and I'm not the least bit cold. There's something terribly frightening about this place."

Single file, they climbed the path to the outside. When they reached it, Lucky breathed in deeply. The night air seemed to calm her. The wind still moaned through the rocks and darkness surrounded them, but it was a relief to be in the world again, the world they knew. She placed the lantern on the ground and shone her light in a circle. She didn't see Eamon. She turned to Jack. "Did he start back to the car?"

"Must have. But he should have waited. We need to stick together."

As she swung her light back toward Jack, something caught her eye near the edge of the clearing. A man's boot. "Oh no," she cried.

Jack followed the beam of her light. Eamon lay face-down on the ground. They rushed toward him.

Lucky knelt. "Eamon, what happened?"

He groaned and tried to raise his head.

A beam of light shot across the clearing. "Hold it right there, folks."

Lucky gasped and spun toward the sound. Her flashlight illuminated the face of Joe Conrad.

Chapter 41

CONRAD STOOD AT the edge of the clearing, a flashlight of his own in his left hand. In his right a black angular gun was aimed in their direction.

"Joe!" The name escaped from her lips. The man they had trusted had followed them. He had watched and listened to their efforts to locate Taran's stash.

"All that bull about proving yourself to the company," Jack said. "You wanted it for yourself."

Lucky gasped. Full realization dawned. "You're not Joe Conrad," she said quietly. "You're the guard who disappeared." Remembering his own story of the robbery, she said, "You're Jimmy Devlin."

"You got that right." He laughed. "I had a feeling this guy knew where his dumbass brother hid the cash," he said, indicating Eamon. "You . . ." he said, aiming the flashlight at Jack. "Open that box, old man."

Jack's jaw tightened. Lucky knew Jack wished he were still strong enough and fast enough to jump the man. Jack glanced at the box next to where Eamon lay. Eamon was slowly regaining consciousness. Eamon pushed himself away from the ground and turned over into a sitting position. Jack, with a dark glance at their captor, walked the few steps toward Eamon and bent down to open the metal container. He pushed the lid back to reveal the bundles of cash.

Devlin's flashlight illuminated the contents. "What the hell is this? Where's the rest of it?" he demanded.

"That's all that's left," Eamon spoke, slowly rising to his feet. "My brother bought land and lived off the money all these years."

Lucky kept her flashlight trained on Devlin. She was frightened by the look on his face.

"You're lying. There's more, and I know you know where it is."

"Not true," Eamon replied. "I didn't know for sure Taran was involved until just now. But now I know it was you who killed him."

Devlin didn't respond to the accusation. His silence told them all they needed to know. "Then how the hell did you know to come here?" Devlin asked.

"He once told me if anything ever happened to him, I should come to the Stones. This is all that's left. Take it. I don't care about the money. I just want my daughter back."

"You'll get her back all right . . . eventually. You . . ." he said, pointing his beam of light at Lucky. "Grab this." He reached down and picked up a rope that lay at his feet. He tossed it to Lucky. "Tie those two up and be quick about it.

"And you two," he said, indicating Eamon and Jack, "on the ground. Hands behind your back. Sit!"

"Where is she?" Eamon cried out. "For God's sake, man. Tell me where she is."

"Shut up, will ya. She's fine. She's at the farmers' market. Your corn-fed girl's right where she should be."

Lucky moved closer to Eamon. Devlin aimed the beam at Eamon's hands as Lucky wrapped the rope around his wrists and tied it with a knot.

"Tighter. Make it tighter and knot it again," Devlin snarled. "Now the old man," Devlin ordered. "Tie 'em together."

"I'll old man you, you . . ." Jack grumbled.

"Jack. Shhhh," she whispered. "You'll set him off. Move closer to Eamon."

Jack carefully lowered himself to the ground in a sitting position, staring at Devlin, as Lucky wrapped the end of the rope around his wrists and knotted it twice.

"Now their ankles." Devlin took a step forward. Lucky moved in front of Jack and Eamon as they sat on the ground. She uncurled the rope and bound first Eamon's ankles together and then Jack's with the same length of rope. "And don't try anything funny. Make sure those knots are tight.

"Now you," Devlin said. "Turn around."

Lucky's heart was beating madly. She felt her temper rising. She considered her options. She could swing at him and maybe even land a good punch, enough to knock him off balance. But she'd have to wait until he put the gun down and attempted to tie her hands. She couldn't risk Jack getting hurt. She was slight. Devlin wouldn't perceive her as a threat, not the way Eamon, a large man, would be. She turned around and caught Jack's eye. He knew what she was thinking. She heard the rustle of Devlin's Windbreaker as he placed the gun on the ground. She took a deep breath. Devlin reached out to grasp her wrists, and she ducked away. She turned quickly and gave him her best right hook. Devlin grunted and fell backward. Blood spurted from his nose.

"Way to go, Lucky!" Jack hollered.

Lucky fell to her knees, frantically feeling over the ground where she was sure Devlin had placed the gun. She wasn't fast enough. Devlin scrambled across the distance and grabbed her coat collar. Dragging her to her feet, he back-handed her across the face. Her head snapped around, and she flew across the clearing, landing in a heap near Jack.

"Son of a . . ." Devlin said. Blood poured down his face and over his jacket. "You little bitch . . ." His flashlight had fallen on a rock and broken. Their own flashlights, hers and Jack's and Eamon's, were on the ground, shining in all directions against the tree trunks. At the moment they were no help to Devlin. The lantern was bright but cast shadows all around the clearing. She heard Devlin muttering to himself as he searched for his gun. Her vision was blurred from the blow, and her ears were ringing.

Jack leaned over. "Are you all right?" he whispered.

Lucky rubbed her cheek. "I'll be okay."

Devlin stood. He had found his gun. He moved to where Eamon sat and dragged the metal box to the other side of the clearing. He grabbed one of the flashlights and shone it on Lucky. She was still dazed from the blow. Devlin reached for the end of one of the ropes and quickly tied her ankles together. Then he ran the rope around her neck once and tied her wrists behind her. She tried to struggle, but the rope only tightened around her neck, choking her.

Devlin was breathing heavily when he finished. Lucky's punch had done some damage. "Now," he said to Eamon, "you're gonna tell me where the rest of the money is. If not, you're gonna be in more pain than you can imagine."

"I told you. That's it. There is no more. Taran spent it."

"I don't believe you." Devlin aimed the gun at Eamon's leg. He moved the muzzle slightly to the left and fired once. The explosion was deafening. Lucky nearly jumped out of her skin. Eamon shut his eyes tightly but otherwise showed no reaction. An owl screeched in the treetops above them. Would the shot be heard at Eamon's encampment? Would someone come to their rescue?

"That was a test shot. The next one goes right into your knee."

"I told you, there is no more money. This is it. Take it and be gone. Just tell me where my daughter is."

"You'll never walk right again," Devlin warned. He raised the gun, moving closer to Eamon, and stood with the muzzle only two feet away from Eamon's knee. It was a deadly-looking weapon. It would blow Eamon's leg apart. Even if he survived, how would they get help to him? Lucky was afraid to breathe.

"Nothing to say?"

Eamon glared at Devlin but kept his silence.

"Hate to do this to you, big guy, but here goes." Devlin aimed the revolver slowly.

Chapter 42

A LOW MOANING sound filled the air. Shivers ran up
Lucky's spine. She looked all around, but it wasn't possible
to tell where the sound came from.

Devlin spun in a circle. "What the hell . . ." He glanced
back at Eamon who hadn't moved.

A heavy thunk and a crashing of twigs came from
the trees. Devlin turned, aiming the gun at the darkness of
the woods. "Come out now or I'll shoot." He moved next
to the trees that marked the perimeter, still aiming his gun
in the direction of the noise.

A dark figure leaped from the other side of the clearing.
Devlin spun around quickly, his flashlight illuminating
Daniel's face for a brief second. Daniel held a tree limb in
his hands, and as Devlin moved toward him, Daniel swung,
a brutal blow that sent Devlin careening sideways. Daniel
leaped on the prone man and began to pummel him with
his fists. Devlin made no move to protect himself. He was
unconscious.

"Daniel. Hold on," Eamon shouted. "Help me get free."

Daniel stood and rushed to Eamon's side. He undid the rope that bound his uncle and used it to quickly tie Devlin's ankles and wrists.

Eamon laughed in relief. "That was a good move. You fooled him." He knelt on the ground and felt for the pulse on Devlin's neck. "He's alive." He looked up at Daniel. "Can you help them?"

Daniel nodded and hurried to untie Jack, helping him to his feet.

Jack, as soon as he was steady, rushed to Lucky's side. "Are you all right, my girl?" he asked softly.

"I will be," she reassured him. "Probably just have a big bruise tomorrow."

"Too bad you didn't knock him out," Jack said admiringly. "But you did good. I sure named you right."

Daniel had found Devlin's gun. He stood over the prone man, his foot on Devlin's chest.

"Daniel!" Eamon called out. "What are you doing?"

Daniel made no response. He slowly aimed the weapon.

"Don't do it," Eamon said quietly. "Put the gun down."

"Why shouldn't I? He killed my father. He would have crippled you."

Lucky reached out and grasped Jack's hand, squeezing it tightly from fear. She prayed that Daniel would not shoot.

"If you pull that trigger, you'll be just like him. Give me the gun."

Daniel remained focused on Devlin. "It would be so easy."

"It would," Eamon said quietly. "But you do not want that stain on your soul. He will be punished. Give me the gun."

Daniel's hand shook slightly and then wavered. Eamon reached out and carefully took the gun as Daniel's arm dropped slackly to his side.

Chapter 43

EAMON HANDED THE gun to Jack. "Watch him," he said, indicating Devlin. Then he pulled Daniel close and hugged him tightly. "You did the right thing. But where have you been? Why didn't you come back to the campsite?"

"I was afraid. Afraid the police might bother you if I came back."

Devlin moaned and tried to move.

Jack raised the gun. "Stay right where you are," he ordered.

Eamon grabbed one of the other ropes and bound Devlin to a nearby tree. "Let's make sure he can't go anywhere." He glanced at Jack. "I think he'll keep for a while, don't you?"

Jack laughed in relief. "Might be a good time to let the police take over. You have your phone?" he asked Lucky.

"Yes." She reached into her jacket pocket and retrieved her cell phone.

Eamon placed a protective hand over hers. "I can't stay. Not if the police are coming. I have to find my daughter." He looked at Jack. "If he comes to, do your best to get more from him about Jane. I don't want to delay."

"Jane?" Daniel had a quizzical look on his face.

Eamon nodded to him. "I'll explain to you later, Daniel. Can you stay here with them until the police arrive? As soon as you hear them, you can take off. But for God's sake, go back to the camp. Don't disappear like that again."

Daniel nodded his agreement.

"Jack?" Lucky said. "I think Eamon's going to need some help. I'll go with him, but I'll leave you the phone. Can you call Nate?"

"What do you think I should tell Nate when he gets here and asks how we found the money?" Jack asked.

"Tell him he doesn't want to know," Lucky replied.

"Nate won't go for that, but I'll try," Jack grumbled. "You two get going. Go find Janie."

EAMON WAS SILENT as Lucky followed the Old Colonial Road back toward town. When she reached Snowflake, she drove straight down Broadway, past the Spoonful and headed west to the field where the Harvest Festival was being held.

"He said, 'At the farmers' market.' What do you think he meant?"

Lucky shook her head, driving as fast as she dared. "I don't know. That's a big area. There are lots of people around during the day. He must be keeping Janie hidden somewhere. Somewhere she can't escape. There are just the rides for little kids and the stage area and the pony corral." Lucky thought for a moment. "There is a barn past the market area at the far end of the field. It belongs to the man who owns the property, but he's semiretired now and really doesn't use it." She shrugged. "I think we should start there. It's the only place I can think of where Devlin could have hidden her."

"What if he lied? What if he . . ." Eamon was tense, terrified Janie could have been harmed. "If he's touched her, I'll . . ." Eamon didn't finish his statement but fell silent once again.

"Nate found her car out there today. Jack told me earlier tonight. I'm thinking she might have gone out there by herself, without telling anybody. Devlin could have followed her and grabbed her. I know he put two and two together and figured out the connection between you and Janie."

"How?" he asked.

"She had an attack of nerves at the restaurant when she saw you across the street. Conrad . . . Devlin . . . whatever his name is, was asking some questions. I know he spotted you and took a long look at Janie."

"It's my fault. I should never have come here. I've just brought trouble to their doorstep."

"It's Devlin who brought trouble." Lucky glanced at Eamon. She could see in the dim light from the dash that his jaw was clenched. "We'll find her," she said in an effort to reassure him. She hoped she was right.

Within a few miles Lucky spotted the gates that led to the parking lot. She hit her brakes, suddenly aware how fast she had been traveling. She slowed and turned into the parking area. It was empty of cars. She drove close to the entrance gate and stopped.

"Hurry," Eamon said, climbing out of the car before Lucky could turn off the engine. She climbed out, slamming the door, and hurried after him as he loped toward the entrance. She followed him down the walkway lined with empty stalls, their canvas coverings billowing in the wind. Only a few short hours ago this deserted area had been full of shoppers and children seeking fun. Janie couldn't possibly have been hidden in such an open area.

Lucky was forced to break into a run to stay close to Eamon. They reached the end of the road. The barn loomed ahead of them in the field; the building itself was a slightly darker shape against the night sky. Lucky reached for her cell phone to check the time before remembering she had left it with Jack. It must be close to four in the morning. She struggled to figure the time, but given the startling events at the Stones, she was afraid she'd be far off the mark.

"What time do you think it is, Eamon?" she asked.

He turned to her in the dark. "Don't know. You're thinking it'll be light out soon?"

"Yes." She nodded.

Eamon looked at the horizon. "I'd say two, two and a half more hours till sunup."

Lucky clicked on her flashlight and raked it over the building. "It just *feels* deserted," she whispered.

"It can't be. She's got to be there. What if she's tied up or hurt?"

"We'll have to get inside somehow."

"Do you know who owns this barn?" he asked.

"This acreage belongs to the farmer Ernie White rents from. Maybe they use this barn for the horses or for storage."

"We can't take the time to wake anybody up."

"I agree. Let's find a way in. If she's in there, we'll find her."

Eamon walked toward the barn. He aimed his flashlight at a small door at the side.

Lucky followed him. The door was locked with only a simple hasp. "We need bolt cutters."

"No we don't," Eamon said. He pulled a small flat screwdriver out of a back pocket and focused on removing the screws holding the hasp in place. He managed to pull out three of the screws, but the head of the fourth one broke off. Frustrated, Eamon slipped the screwdriver into the space between the hasp and the door and forced the flat plate away from the wood. "Hate to do this, but we have no choice."

Their breath was frosty in the cold night air. Lucky's hands were chilled though she tried to hold the flashlight steady. They didn't hear the footsteps approaching.

"You two—hold it right there!" A man's voice rang out. Lucky jumped involuntarily. She turned, only to be blinded by a powerful light.

Chapter 44

LUCKY SHIELDED HER eyes as the man behind the flashlight approached. Eamon cursed under his breath. He slipped the screwdriver into his back pocket and stood up straight.

"Lucky? Is that you?" the man called out. The light flashed across Eamon's face. "What are you doing?"

"Remy?" she cried with relief. "Oh, I'm so glad it's you. I could ask the same question."

"I'm staying in the trailer back there," he said, indicating the rear of the barn. "Keeping close to the horses. I thought I heard voices so I came out to check." Remy was obviously curious who Eamon was. "I know I've seen you before. You're with the Gaelic band, aren't you?"

Eamon breathed a sigh of relief. "We have to get into the barn."

"Remy, you might not know this, but Janie's disappeared. We thought she had run away again, but . . . it's a long story, but we think she's being held somewhere here. We have to find her."

Remy's look was quizzical. "Janie?" The color drained from his face.

"We don't know exactly where. But we think she's being kept somewhere around here. We have to search the barn. I'm just praying she's in there."

"I have a key," Remy replied.

Lucky shrieked, "Why didn't you say so?"

"You didn't ask." Remy reached into his back pocket, retrieving a ring of keys. "Ernie arranged for the barn so we could stable the horses here." He reached forward and, tucking his flashlight under his arm, released the padlock. He stepped inside and held the door open for Lucky and Eamon.

Inside, the smell of sweet hay and pungent manure permeated the air. Lucky heard the soft snorting of horses.

"Wait. Don't move. There's a light switch over here." Remy shone a light on the wall near the door and spotted the switch. He flicked it on, and the entire lower level was illuminated by hanging lamps. They were shaded by shiny metal coverings hanging from the eaves. "There's not much to see down here—other than the horses. It's pretty empty. There's some feed stored in the corner over there. And some tools, and that's about it. I'll check the stalls."

Remy walked the length of the barn, peeking into each stall, shining his flashlight into corners and gently murmuring to the horses. Eamon skirted the inside perimeter, looking into darkened spaces, examining old tarps hanging from beams along the wall. He reached the corner and continued along the next wall. Lucky and Remy watched him in silence.

"What's up there?" Eamon asked, pointing to the loft.

"No idea, but you can get up there on the ladder," Remy replied.

Eamon silently climbed the wooden ladder to the loft. Lucky and Remy waited, listening to Eamon's boots stomping above them on the wooden flooring. After a few minutes he descended the ladder. He shook his head. "Nothing. No one's been up there at all."

"Are you sure?" Lucky asked.

"There'd be something. Some scuff marks, things moved. If she were held in this barn, there'd be something to see. Don't think she was ever here."

Lucky's nervousness was growing by the minute. What if Joe Conrad or Jim Devlin or whatever his name was had left Janie tied up without water or someplace without enough air to breathe? Janie must have come here and been overpowered the night before. Was she outside in the elements with only a sweater or a thin jacket? It was still warm during the day, but the nights were growing colder. Lucky hated to think of Janie shivering somewhere for a second night or worse.

"Remy, you've been working here every day. Do you know if there's another barn or building nearby?"

"Just this one. It's the only one I know of."

"So you haven't noticed anyone hanging around? You put the horses in last night and tonight?"

"That's right. I'm sure no one's been in here."

"And there's no other place he could have taken her?"

"Who's 'he'?" Remy asked.

Lucky took a deep breath. "A man claiming to be an insurance investigator has been hanging around town. He's kidnapped Janie."

"What? Why?"

"I promise to fill you in. Right now there's no time to waste. Just help us."

"Of course. I will. Other than my trailer, I can't think of any other hiding places. Well, maybe behind the stage area."

"We have to search everywhere. She's got to be somewhere around here," Eamon said.

Lucky turned to him. "Eamon, you know the stage area. You take that. Remy and I will go through the vendor stalls, check any storage bins, check underneath the tables . . . everywhere. It's unlikely that she'd be there, but we have to look. Even if we call Nate in, it'll take too long. There are three of us and only one of him. Besides, I'm sure Nate's busy at the Stones with Jack right now."

Eamon turned without a word and left the barn. Lucky stayed and waited for Remy to turn off the overhead lights and lock the door behind him, replacing the padlock as best he could.

"Why didn't Nate search out here before?" Remy asked as they headed toward the vendor stalls.

"He may have done that. I don't know. He found out Janie's car was parked here, but no one even noticed it or thought to report it. He must have questioned people. Maybe he showed Janie's picture around."

"I didn't see him," Remy said. "But I had to pick up some supplies in Lincoln Falls yesterday. I might have missed him. Let's each take a side of the walkway."

"Make sure you look under the tables; it'll be hard because people store boxes and stuff underneath. We just need to make sure to check everything."

Remy followed Lucky to the vendor area. They moved slowly from one stall to the next, shining their flashlights under the tables, shifting mostly empty boxes to be sure nothing was concealed. There was no food to be found, but there were plenty of storage containers, all empty. They finally reached the end of the walkway and the vendor area.

In frustration, Lucky called out, "Janie! Can you hear me?" She waited, listening to the silence of the night. No response came.

She turned to Remy. "Let's catch up with Eamon. I have no idea how big that backstage area is." They approached the stage, and Lucky called out to Eamon. She saw a flickering light behind a makeshift wing to the right of the stage. They heard his footsteps approach.

"Find anything?" she asked. Lucky couldn't see his face, only the beam of his flashlight.

"Nothing," he said. "Looks just as we left it earlier tonight." Eamon swung down from the front of the stage and nervously ran a hand through his hair.

Lucky sat heavily on the wooden stairway that led up to the stage. "What was it Devlin said?" She rubbed her temples.

Eamon stared at her. "I'm not sure. Something about 'she's at the farmers' market.'"

"No. Not that. It was after that." Lucky closed her eyes in an attempt to remember. "He said, 'Your corn-fed girl's right where she should be.' Wasn't that it? Oh!" She gasped. "The cornfield! Is that what he meant?"

"Hey," Remy said. "I just remembered something. There's a storage shed on the other side of that cornfield."

"Where is it?" Eamon demanded.

"I'll show you. It's kind of a hike—way on the other side."

"Let's go," Eamon said.

Chapter 45

IN SINGLE FILE with Remy leading the way, they headed diagonally across the cornfield. It was slow going. Lucky felt many times as if she were sinking into the earth. She wished she had worn more serviceable shoes. They pushed their way through the tall stalks of corn, some as high as eight to ten feet. The leaves of the stalks hit their cheeks as they passed. The hike seemed to take forever but Remy appeared to know the way and cheered them on. Lucky wasn't sure where they were headed, but the line of trees was now slightly darker against the night sky, a sky that was just beginning to show the barest promise of sunrise. Her muscles ached from tension and lack of sleep, but she refused to give in. She couldn't rest until they found Janie. The ground felt harder now and easier to cross. She spotted a small rectangular building just a few yards away.

"This is the rear of the farmer's property," Remy said. "If we kept going in this direction, we'd eventually reach his house."

"Do you have a key to this building?"

Remy shook his head. "No. They just gave me the barn to use for the horses. I'm not sure what's in here. I think it's just tool storage."

"We have to get inside."

Eamon approached the flimsy door. He stopped suddenly and aimed his flashlight. The door stood open. Remy pushed ahead of Eamon and tried to rush in.

"Wait." Eamon pulled him back. "Be careful. Let me go first." Eamon stepped up to the threshold and swung the beam around the inside of the room.

"Okay," he said. "It's safe." He stepped into the dark interior of the shed. Lucky and Remy followed. A musty odor assailed their nostrils. She shone the beam of the flashlight up to the rafters. They were covered with spider webs.

Remy spoke first. "Can we find a light in here?"

"Don't know," Eamon replied. He turned in a circle, shining the light near the doorjamb and finally at the center of the tall ceiling. A thin chain hung down, too high for Lucky to reach, but Eamon pulled it easily. The interior was flooded with light. Lucky squinted, willing her eyes to adjust to the change.

Inside the storage shed were pieces of farm equipment Lucky knew she couldn't possibly name. Rakes, heavy construction hoses and tools hung on the bare wooden walls. Eamon moved to the corner of the shed. He was silent for a long minute.

"Eamon?" Lucky called. "What is it?" She suspected he had discovered something.

"Over here," he replied quietly.

Lucky and Remy picked their way around the parts and equipment and joined Eamon.

"She was here. Look." He pointed his flashlight at a section of flooring, free of dust. "And this," he said, reaching down and holding up a dark blue sneaker.

"Oh!" Lucky exclaimed. "That's Janie's shoe. She wears

them all the time. But where is she? Did she get away or was she moved?"

The overhead light was bright, but the corner of the shed was in shadow. Eamon shone the light on a length of rope wrapped around a wooden beam. "He tied her up—like an animal. He tied my little girl up. I'll make sure he pays for this," Eamon growled. He looked around and bent down. Then stood, holding a thin plastic binding in his hands. "She got free."

"What now?" Remy asked.

"We track her. That's if we haven't messed up her prints on the way in." Eamon turned away and headed back to the entry door. Lucky hurried to catch up. He stood on the threshold, aiming the beam of his flashlight on the ground outside the doorway. The dampness of the night had made several prints visible. "Don't move. Don't step outside. She's out here somewhere. We'll find her."

After a minute Eamon exclaimed, "There!"

"Where?" Lucky asked.

"Right there. Look." Eamon stepped outside. The sky was lined with a hint of lavender. Daybreak was coming. "Oh dear Lord. Her feet are tied. She's shuffling and jumping."

Lucky could now clearly see two footprints very close together. One print of a shoe with rubber striations—Janie's sneaker—the other a bare foot.

"And here. Look." Lucky and Remy followed the beam of Eamon's flashlight. Eamon looked across the field. "She went this way."

The sound of a deep throbbing motor reached their ears.

"What's that?" Remy asked.

"Oh, no!" Lucky cried. "They're harvesting. They'll never see her if she's out there."

Chapter 46

THEY STOOD TOGETHER, surrounded by the corn stalks. "I heard the farmer arguing with Ernie about the corn maze," Lucky shouted above the noise. "He said he couldn't wait any longer. His crop would be spoiled."

In the distance, two intense lights were visible at the top of the combine. A second engine roar throbbed through the ground. Lucky felt the vibrations under the soles of her shoes. Two vehicles—a combine that would slice the corn stalks off at the base and separate the cobs, grinding the rest of the crop for silage. The second truck would follow the combine in a parallel course to catch the harvest.

"How close are they?" Eamon asked.

"I can't tell. But they're coming this way," Remy said. He attempted to jump high enough to see over the stalks.

"She could be anywhere," Lucky cried. "Help me look. We have to find her."

"I'll stop the trucks," Remy said. "They can't do this now. Those blades would cut her to ribbons." Remy started running in the direction of the combine, waving his arms and shouting at the top of his lungs.

"They'll never hear him over that noise," Eamon said. "They might not even be able to see him."

"Let's follow her tracks. That's all we can do. I'll stay behind you and look in either direction. She's got to be in here somewhere," Lucky said.

Eamon stared at the ground, flashlight in hand, straining to see which way Janie had gone. A pale haze was lighting the tops of the tallest trees that stood in the distance around the field. The roar of the farm machinery was louder. The combine was headed their way. The machines were moving fast, too fast. She couldn't hear anything over the deep throb of the engines. The ground was vibrating beneath her feet. Would Remy be able to get their attention? Whatever he was doing, it wasn't stopping the mammoth vehicles.

"I've lost her trail. I can't see it," Eamon called out, panic in his voice.

Lucky could barely make out his words. She shouted, "She's got to be close. Maybe she fell, maybe she . . ." Lucky tripped and fell headlong between two rows. The breath was knocked out of her. She reached out and felt something soft, a form and some kind of fabric. She pushed herself to her knees to get a better look. It was an arm.

Lucky shouted as loud as she could, "I found her, Eamon! I found her! Help me move her." Lucky stepped over Janie's prostrate form. She felt her neck. It was warm. Janie was alive. Had she been knocked out? Was she drugged? Or had something worse happened?

"Janie! Can you hear me? Janie, you've got to wake up," she screamed.

Janie's eyes fluttered, but she made no response. Eamon pushed through the cornstalks and arrived at Lucky's side.

Lucky dug her heels in to gain purchase and grabbed Janie's shoulders. She looked up, trying to gauge how quickly the combine and the truck were moving. She heard the crunch and snap of the stalks being cut and ground up.

"We've got to get her out of here." She pulled Janie into a sitting position. Her feet were still bound. Lucky reached around and felt the binding with her fingers. It was plastic and tight. Something a professional would use. How could Devlin have done this to Janie? Lucky struggled to keep the girl in an upright position. She reached under Janie's arms and held tight, managing to drag her through the next row of corn. It took all her strength to move Janie just a few feet. She looked around for Eamon to help her, but he had disappeared. The harsh lights of the combine were bearing down on them. In another minute it would be too late. Too late for both of them.

Chapter 47

EAMON RAN STRAIGHT toward the combine, waving his arms and shouting above the noise. The brilliant spotlights cut through the early morning light. Eamon spotted Remy running along the far side of the truck. Blood covered the side of his face. He looked winded, but he tried to climb on the running board of the container truck to get the driver's attention. The truck gave a lurch, and Remy lost his grip and was thrown to the ground.

LUCKY TOOK A deep breath and pulled Janie across the soft earth and into the next row. Sweat was pouring down her face in spite of the chill. No one could possibly see them here. She dragged Janie again, managing to move her another foot. Janie's head lolled forward. Lucky was dragging a dead weight, and she didn't know how far she'd have to go to be safe from the wheels of the truck and the blades of the combine. Was she going in the right direction or was she dragging Janie straight into the path of the deadly

machine? There was no choice. She couldn't leave her here
to be mauled to death. The sound of the blades crunching
through the stalks was deafening now. Grunting, she
pulled Janie another few feet. She stopped and raised her
head. The harsh light blinded her.

A swift shadow passed in front of the lights. A moment
later all sound stopped. Silence. Eamon had somehow
stopped them. He must have climbed into the cab of the combine and shut the vehicle down. Lucky cried in relief. She fell
to her knees, still holding Janie upright. The rising sun cast
its light through the windshield of the combine. A man sat in
the high cab of the vehicle, his jaw slack, and stared at the
large man who had suddenly appeared next to him.

A few feet from where Janie lay, the light glinted off
the blades of the machinery, its metal maw constructed of
five long, almost triangular, blades. Between the long blades
were shorter thick ones topped by layers of rotating metal
teeth like a prehistoric beast—a terrifying sight. Lucky didn't
want to think what those blades could have done to them.

The farmer climbed down from his cab and with Eamon
following headed for the spot where Lucky struggled with
an unconscious Janie. Lucky recognized the same man she
had seen arguing with Ernie White at the festival.

"What the . . . ?" he said. "What's going on? You folks
have no business fooling around out here like this. You
could've all been killed. I wouldn't have seen you until it
was too late."

Remy caught up with them, breathless from running
and falling off the truck. "I tried to stop you. Couldn't you
hear me?"

The farmer turned to him. "Can't hear a thing in there.
I wear these," he said, indicating large ear covers slung
around his neck to muffle the sound. "Can't see very much
either. This corn is too tall. I'm just glad this fellow jumped
on the combine in time."

Eamon knelt and gently put his arms around Janie.

Without a word he lifted her and carried her across the field heading for the parking lot.

"You gonna take that little girl to the hospital?" the farmer called after them.

"That's where we're headed," Remy replied, running to keep up with Eamon and Lucky.

Lucky rushed ahead of Eamon and opened the back door of her car. Eamon, still holding Janie, slid into the backseat. He cradled Janie's upper body in his arms. Lucky supported Janie's legs and once both of them were safely inside, she shut the car door.

She turned to Remy. "You're coming with us?"

"Of course." He jumped into the front seat, wiping blood from his face with his shirttail. "Where are we taking her? The Clinic?"

Lucky had already considered their options. "I think we should go straight to Lincoln Falls. We don't know what's in her system or what injuries she has." Lucky was relieved she wouldn't have to see Elias, but more importantly, the emergency room at the hospital would be faster and better equipped to deal with Janie's condition. "We're almost halfway there."

"She's hit her head," Eamon said from the backseat. "She must have fallen. There's some blood. We just don't know how long she's been out in that field." He gently pushed Janie's hair away from her face. "How long will it take to get there?"

Lucky glanced in the rearview mirror. "Not long. We're five miles from the hospital. She'll need an X-ray, maybe a lot more. But they'll be able to run tests right away. And she might be in shock and dehydrated. The ER's the best place now."

Lucky followed the winding road up and over the mountain and then finally down into Lincoln Falls, passing under an umbrella of ancient trees brilliant with yellow foliage. The last time she had driven this road, she had been with Jack. Elias and the other specialists had been attempting to diagnose his health problems. She only hoped they'd be as fortunate this time with Janie.

She glanced in the rearview mirror. Eamon's jaw was clamped shut, a look of fear on his face.

"I hope you know where this place is," he murmured quietly.

"I do. Don't worry." Lucky drove as fast as she could through the first few blocks toward the center of Lincoln Falls. When she reached the corner where the post office stood, she made a right turn on the street that would lead straight to the emergency room of the hospital. Remy was just as anxious, but he remained silent. Ignoring the sign pointing to a parking garage, she pulled up at the ambulance entrance directly in front of the automatic doors.

Remy hopped out and opened the back door. He gently guided Janie's feet to the ground; one foot was still bare. Lucky ran toward the entrance, rushed inside and waved down an orderly who quickly located a wheelchair. He followed Lucky out the emergency doors to the parking lot.

Eamon said nothing, but he shook his head, refusing the help. He carried Janie through the sliding doors and, ignoring the clerk at the intake desk, headed for a small examining room. He laid Janie gently on the gurney. Remy followed in his wake.

Eamon turned to Remy. "Go find the doc. Quick."

Remy nodded nervously and scooted out of the room as Eamon covered Janie with a soft white cotton blanket he found in a supply cabinet.

Remy rushed to the clerk's window. "We need a doctor. Right away."

The clerk patiently replied, "We've already called. Dr. Norden's on call today. He'll be right out to examine your friend." Turning to Lucky, she said, "Someone will have to fill out these forms. I'll need an insurance card, some ID, whatever you have. Are you family?"

"I'll fill in as much as I can," Lucky replied. "And no,

I'm not family, but I'll get you the information you need."
She settled into a molded plastic chair and, balancing the
clipboard on her lap, started to fill in the spaces with a
ballpoint pen that didn't work very well. She completed as
many blanks as she could and then reached for her cell
phone. Belatedly, she remembered she had left it with Jack.

Remy was standing outside the door of the examining
room. She called to him, and he hurried over. "Do you have
a cell phone with you?"

Remy patted his pockets. "No. It's in my trailer. I didn't
take it with me when I went out to check on the horses."

"Never mind. I'll ask the clerk if I can use hers." She
hurried back to the intake window. The clerk hit a button,
and the door to the small chamber opened.

LUCKY QUICKLY DIALED Miriam's home number. Miriam
answered on the first ring. "We've found Janie."

"Oh, thank God," Miriam sobbed. "Where is she?"

"We're at the hospital in Lincoln Falls. The doctor's
with her now. I don't want you to panic, but she wasn't
conscious when we found her." Lucky had no intention of
describing to Miriam the close call with the combine in
the cornfield. That could wait till later.

"Where did you find her?"

"In the cornfield." Lucky hesitated. But finally decided
it would all come out in the end. "She didn't run away,
Miriam. She was abducted."

"What? Why?" Miriam cried. "Who would want to hurt
Janie?"

"It's a long story, and I'll fill you in later." Lucky felt
exhaustion creeping over her. Her muscles ached, and her
eyes burned from lack of sleep. "We don't know exactly
what happened, but she might have been drugged. We
think she tried to escape and hit her head in a fall. We just
don't know how long she'd been in that field."

"We? Who's with you?"

"I'll tell you later, okay?" Lucky peeked down the hall. "Miriam, I just saw the doctor come out of her room. I'd like to talk to him. Right now I just need her insurance information if you can give me that over the phone."

"Of course. Of course. Hang on. I'll go find the card." Lucky heard the telephone receiver bang heavily on a table and then Miriam's heels clacking as she ran down the hall. She was back in a minute. "Here it is." Miriam recited the company name and policy number.

"Thanks, that's all I need."

"I'll be right there," Miriam answered.

Lucky hesitated. "Miriam?"

"Yes?"

"You should know. Eamon's with her."

"Eamon?" Miriam's voice had dropped several registers.

"Yes. If it hadn't been for him, we wouldn't have found her."

Miriam was silent for a long moment. "I'm on my way."

"Drive safely. There's no need to panic. She's in good hands," Lucky replied, but Miriam had already hung up.

ALL THREE OF them were seated on hard plastic chairs that lined the corridor. Waiting. Janie had woken up, confused and disoriented. She had been given an IV saline drip and now had been wheeled away for a CAT scan. Eamon had insisted on going with her, but the nurse was very firm and barred him. When Janie realized who was in the room with her, the light of recognition filled her eyes, but she said nothing.

Remy had found a nearby coffee shop and returned with three cappuccinos. The coffee was making Lucky's hands shake, and it still wasn't doing a very good job of keeping her awake. She had managed to call Jack who was at the police station with Nate. She wanted to tell him they were fine and they had found Janie. Jack had been up all night as well, but he sounded a lot more chipper than she could have managed. Daniel, he said, had taken off for the travelers' campsite as soon as he heard Nate's siren, and Jack didn't mention Daniel's involvement in subduing Devlin, who was now in custody.

Next, Lucky called Meg to tell her she had an unexpected day off. And finally, she called Sage, already at the restaurant, to say the same thing. She filled him in as briefly as possible, promising to explain more later.

"Really?" he said. "That's great news. Don't worry about me. I can get some soups ready for tomorrow, and then I'll take the rest of the day off too. You need any help out there?" he asked.

"No. Thanks, Sage. We'll be fine now. Miriam's on her way. We just don't know yet if they'll want to admit Janie."

Lucky took a last sip of her cappuccino, doing her best to scoop the frothy milk from the bottom of the paper cup, and leaned her head against the wall behind her. She felt her eyelids grow heavy, and before she knew it, she had slipped into a light sleep. She was dreaming of spinning metal blades and woke with a jolt when Remy nudged her gently. She looked up to see Miriam standing in the entryway.

Eamon rose from his chair.

Miriam stared at him. Her face was white. "Where is she?"

Eamon walked toward her. "She's getting some tests right now. She's groggy, but she's coming to."

Miriam stood rigidly. "Who did this to her?"

"It's a long story," Eamon replied. "Why don't we sit outside, and I'll tell you all about it."

Miriam turned to Lucky. "Can you come get me as soon as she's back?"

Lucky nodded in agreement. "I'll find you right away."

"Lucky?" Remy asked. She turned to look at him. "Who *is* that guy?"

Lucky smiled, realizing that Remy had been with them all night yet had never asked. "That's Janie's father." She watched Remy's eyebrows shoot up. "Her real father. I guess there's no harm in telling you now. I don't think any of this will be a secret any longer." She outlined the barest of facts for Remy. When she finished, Remy whistled and collapsed against the back of his chair.

"I had no idea all this stuff was going on. Sage never mentioned anything, but I guess he wouldn't. Did Sophie know all about it?"

"She picked up on some stuff when we were with Janie at the Harvest Festival, so I had to tell her part of it."

Remy nodded. "I always thought Janie was real cute." He smiled sheepishly at Lucky. "I still do, but I knew she'd never give me the time of day, at least not when I first met her. I was a real jerk then, so I don't blame her."

"I think Janie's got some growing up to do herself right now." Lucky reached over to squeeze Remy's hand. "You never know what can happen."

The elevator doors at the end of the hall opened, and a different orderly emerged, pushing Janie down the corridor in a wheelchair. Her complexion had regained some color. She was conscious, and she smiled when she saw Lucky and Remy. Remy stood up nervously to greet her.

Lucky walked toward her. She leaned over and kissed Janie on the cheek. "Your Mom's here. I'll go get her." Lucky turned away and headed for the door to the emergency entrance. Before she stepped on the mat that would release the glass doors, she saw Miriam sitting on a concrete barrier. Tears were running down her face. Eamon's arm was around her shoulders. Lucky hesitated, not wanting to interrupt them, but she had promised Miriam she would let her know immediately when Janie was back. She took a step, and the doors whooshed open. She hoped that maybe now the healing could begin for all of them.

Chapter 48

JACK DROPPED A heavy log onto an already flaming hearth and shifted the fireplace screen back into place.

Janie sat next to Eamon on the cushioned sofa. Miriam was across from them in a rocking chair, gazing at them both. Seated together, the resemblance between father and daughter was unmistakable.

Remy was excitedly relaying the events of their early morning search for Janie while Janie sat wide-eyed. When he reached the part of his story where Lucky and Janie were almost trapped by the combine, Miriam looked as if she were about to faint.

"But it was really Eamon who saved them. He just hopped on that combine, pushed the farmer out of the way and managed to shut it down. You wouldn't believe what those things look like. Layers of metal blades. They wouldn't have stood a chance."

"That's enough," Jack grumbled. "You're scarin' everybody half to death. You're scaring me half to death too."

Lucky was greatly relieved Remy didn't continue to

describe in gruesome detail what could have happened. A shiver ran up her spine. Jack had had enough of violence in the war to last him several lifetimes. He still had a great deal of trouble at the sight of blood, and she didn't want anything to bring back dreadful memories for him.

They had all agreed to gather at Jack's house that evening. Lucky was glad of the suggestion. It was neutral ground for both Miriam and Eamon. Jack had plenty of room for everyone plus a fireplace to keep them warm. Janie had been given a clean bill of health—no fractures, no dehydration, no concussion—and had been sent home with her mother. The doctor felt that under the circumstances there was no need to admit her. She had been drugged, but the dosage was wearing off as they reached the hospital. Once Janie was back in Snowflake, she had no objection to returning to her mother and her own house. Remy had spent that day checking on the horses while Lucky headed back to her apartment for a hot shower and a long nap.

On the way to Jack's house that evening, she had stopped at the Spoonful and picked up a large container of Sage's pumpkin soup and enough supplies for sandwiches for everyone. Jack had made three large bowls of popcorn and offered beers to everyone.

Lucky passed on the beer, but she consumed a giant sandwich of turkey meat and dried cranberries. She realized it was the first thing she had eaten all day.

"Won't they miss you tonight at the Harvest Festival, Eamon?" Jack asked.

"They'll be fine without me. They're all good musicians. They can carry the show. Spending some time with Janie is far more important to me." He looked across the room at Miriam. "As long as her mother has no objection."

Miriam smiled. "None at all, Eamon."

"We have two more performances. One tomorrow

afternoon and the last one tomorrow night. And then we'll be on our way."

"Well, I hope you return soon," Jack said. "You're welcome in Snowflake any time."

"Thank you." Eamon nodded gravely. He turned to look at Janie. "As long as Janie's willing to talk to me."

Janie reached over and squeezed his hand. "I'm sorry I was so horrid." She looked over at her mother. "And I'm so sorry I made you worry, Mom."

Miriam took a deep breath. "If you ever do that again, I'll . . ."

Jack reached over and placed a hand on Miriam's shoulder. "Let's not think about that. She's home now, safe and sound."

Chapter 49

"I STILL CAN'T believe it," Nate said. "Look at this." He pushed the driver's license used by Jim Devlin across the desk. He shook his head. "I got taken. I got taken real bad. And here's a picture of the real Joe Conrad."

"There's a definite resemblance," Lucky said. "The same shaped face, gray hair, blue eyes. Nose is very similar."

"I even called Union Fidelity and talked to one of his colleagues. The man knew Joe real well. In fact, Conrad had even trained him. He confirmed the story that Devlin gave us. Said Conrad was a guy who could never let go of a trail. It'd be just like him to keep chasing an old case in his retirement." Nate shook his head. "I even tested Devlin with the name of the guy at the insurance company, but he didn't miss a beat. What a fool I've been." He slammed his hand against the desk, making Lucky jump.

"So is this driver's license a fake?" Jack asked.

"Yes and no. It's a real driver's license, but this is Devlin's picture on it. That's how he managed to fool me," Nate continued. "See, Jimmy Devlin got to know Conrad pretty well when Conrad was investigating the original robbery. It was really Conrad's persistence that caused the detectives to keep looking at Devlin for the robbery. That's when they went back and kept digging. Then, of course, Devlin took off when the police got too close to the truth. About a year later . . . by the way, I did manage to contact the real Joe Conrad. He's a widower, and he's been on a cruise for a month with his kids and grandkids. Anyway . . . a year later after the robbery, Conrad was forced to retire. Had some trouble with his eyes, detached retina, something like that, so he didn't drive anymore. Devlin carried a grudge against Conrad. He blamed Conrad for his troubles, and Devlin's a vengeful son of a gun. He had been keeping an eye on Conrad—from a distance. He thought about the resemblance and thought it might be useful to him. So he kept tabs on Conrad, watched the house now and then, and must have figured out Conrad wasn't driving anymore.

"I got the story out of him. This is what happened. Devlin rented a post office box in a false name. He hired someone to follow Conrad around and lift the poor guy's wallet. Conrad cancelled the credit cards when he realized his wallet was missing but didn't bother notifying the motor vehicle division, because he couldn't drive anymore anyway. Conrad never thought his wallet was stolen because Devlin was smart enough not to use any of the credit cards. Conrad just thought the wallet was lost. He figured the license was about to expire so no harm done.

"With the ID in hand, Devlin filled out a change of address card for Conrad's home, changing it to the post office box. Then he applied for a lost driver's license and gets a new picture taken. It's now Devlin's picture on Conrad's license, and the new driver's license gets mailed to the PO box. Conrad's none the wiser.

"I've talked to Conrad on the phone. He remembered a time when he stopped getting mail a few years ago, and he went to the post office to complain. When they looked into it, they just figured somebody mixed up an address."

"Pretty smooth," Jack remarked.

"I'll say. And I feel pretty dumb. I've been leaning on Ernie White. Had him in here for questioning when I discovered he had been at the accident scene. He swore up and down he had nothing to do with the accident. I didn't believe him, but it turns out he was tellin' the truth." Nate shook his head. "Then when I saw the security tape from the impound lot, I was convinced Ernie was as guilty as sin. He was right there, in the lot, drinking beer with the guard the night the van was stolen. That clinched it for me."

"I can understand that. I'd think the same thing if I were in your shoes," Lucky offered.

Nate sighed. "Turns out that guard had worked for Ernie before, and he was just trying to get him to fill Daniel's spot at the pony corral."

"Did Remy finally tell you about the woman from the band who was attacking Ernie?"

"Yeah, he did. The travelers didn't know why Daniel hadn't come back to them. At first they thought he had been arrested, and then they started to suspect Ernie might have had something to do with it. They didn't know what to think. Believe me, Ernie and his sidekick are no choirboys. Probably guilty of a lot of things, but this murder isn't one of them. It's a good lesson for me, though, not to let personal feelings get in the way. I never liked the guy, and I woulda been happy to nail him for this."

"Don't be too hard on yourself, Nate. You did everything you reasonably could. If the Conrad family was away, or out of the country, what else could you have done?"

"I think Devlin got a kick out of using the old investigator's name. He probably had other ones he'd used over the years, but this was a perfect cover for being in Snowflake and looking for the missing cash."

"So he killed the man you found in the van?" Jack asked.

"He claims he didn't. Claims it was an accident. Devlin says he was trying to force the guy to tell him where the loot was, and the guy we found on the road jumped him. They struggled, and the gun went off by accident. Our guy was wounded, but he managed to get in the van to escape. Devlin might be tellin' the truth. I think that's why I found the newer indentations on that old van. He was trying to force the guy off the road before he could escape and get help. Why would he want to kill him if he still didn't know where the money was hidden? And he thought the money might have been hidden in the van. That's why Devlin stole it from the impound. When there was nothing there, he got desperate and went after Janie. Anyway, that's outta my hands. Up to a judge and a jury to decide now. How they're gonna do that without a body, I don't know. But we've got him for the robbery and the kidnapping charge."

Lucky hesitated. She shot a quick look at Jack. "His name is Taran MacDougal, and he's Eamon's twin brother. But Eamon had nothing to do with that robbery years ago."

Nate raised his eyebrows. "Funny how he knew where to find that money."

"He didn't really. His brother once told him if anything ever happened to him, Eamon should go to the Stones. It took us a good while to find that box. I believe him."

"The theft of a human body is a criminal offense, but I have no way to prove it. I plan to go out there today and have a talk with our wandering friends." Nate sighed. "I already know it's a waste of time. They're not gonna tell me anything."

"Probably not," Lucky offered, stealing a glance at Jack.

"Anyway, the important thing is that the money or what's left of it will go back to the insurance company, the statute hasn't run out on the robbery—a couple of weeks to go. Unfortunately for Mr. Devlin. A judge'll have to decide about the death of that man in the van. And most important, Janie's home with her mother, safe and sound, thanks to you." Nate nodded in Lucky's direction.

"And don't forget Eamon. If he hadn't jumped on that combine . . ." Lucky shuddered to think about it.

"And Eamon," Nate agreed. "Devlin's locked up in Bournmouth for now. The travelers will be on their way soon, and you and Jack are doing just fine."

"It's kinda funny, Nate." Jack looked thoughtful. "The case is solved and Conrad, the real Conrad, didn't have to do a thing. It was Devlin himself who blew it wide open. If anyone else had found that money, anytime in the last seven years, they'd never even have known where it came from."

"That's a fact," Nate said. "There's one thing I'm curious about. If Devlin had a gun and you and Eamon Mac-Dougal were tied up, how did you ever overpower him?"

Lucky held her breath, hoping Jack wouldn't slip and mention Daniel. Even if he did, there really was no harm done, but she respected Eamon's wishes to keep Daniel away from the police.

Jack, a guileless look on his face, said, "It was Lucky. She knocked him out—sent him sprawling. She's got a great right hook."

Nate raised his eyebrows. "Well, I'm impressed. I never woulda thought a little slip of a thing like you could do that." He glanced at Lucky. "But I saw the blood all over his shirt," Nate continued. "Now, I just need you two to sign your statements, and you can be on your way. I'm sure you'll have to talk to the prosecuting lawyers some time down the pike, but for now you're done."

Chapter 50

LUCKY AND JACK walked slowly down Broadway. The air was crisp, the sky a deep cerulean blue. Dried red and golden leaves crackled under their footsteps as they headed back to the Spoonful.

"I was wondering if you were gonna mention the land in Nova Scotia to Nate," Jack whispered.

Lucky turned to him and grinned. "What land?" she asked, as she slipped her arm through Jack's.

"That's my girl." He smiled back.

As they passed the Off Broadway ladies' clothing shop, Lucky glanced in the window. Marjorie was pinning a rust-colored dress, a new arrival, on a mannequin. She looked up and waved when she saw them.

"Jack." She turned to him. "You go on ahead. I'll catch up in a few minutes. I'd like to stop and chat with Cecily."

"Good idea," Jack agreed. "Might be a little bit of a bruised heart there."

Lucky entered the shop and saw Cecily at the glass counter at the rear folding sweaters. "Hi, Cecily."

"Hello there," Cecily said. She made a wan attempt at a smile.

Lucky approached and leaned over the glass.

"I'm so sorry, Cecily."

Cecily bit her lip and nodded. She had obviously been crying. "I heard all about it. The news is all over town."

"I know you liked him."

"Yes, I did." She shook out the sweater she held in her hands and refolded it. "And now everyone will know what a fool I've been—again."

"Don't say that." Lucky reached across the counter and stilled Cecily's hands. "How could you possibly have known? He used us all. Even Nate. Nate feels terrible too. We all liked him. He was very charming."

"A scoundrel and a murderer." Cecily burst into tears.

Lucky moved around the counter and led Cecily through the curtained doorway to the storeroom. She grasped her hand and pulled Cecily down onto a stool. She glanced around. A box of tissues sat on a worktable. "Here." She passed several tissues to Cecily and waited while Cecily blew her nose loudly.

"I was very attracted to him. You know, at my age, there aren't a lot of opportunities—not like you. You're just a young thing. Lots of men will cross your path."

Lucky shrugged. She wasn't so sure of that. The only man she had ever wanted was Elias, and she was probably losing him. She had to steel her heart. There was no other choice.

"My sister is fine on her own. She doesn't miss having a husband or a man in her life. She's always been like that. But I'm different, Lucky. I never thought . . . I never thought I'd end up alone, and I don't want this to be all there is."

"I think . . ." Lucky thought a moment. "I think when it comes to that part of life, none of us has a choice. We're given what we're given. We can go out and look and then try to pound a square peg into a round hole, but that usually doesn't work. And both people end up going their separate ways. I don't mean that it's impossible," Lucky continued, "but I think when the time is right, the right person falls into your lap."

"But I thought Joe . . . whatever his real name is, might be that person. I thought this could be it, Lucky." Cecily looked up. Lucky reached over and wiped a tear off Cecily's cheek.

"Don't give up hope, Cecily. Keep your eyes open and keep looking."

"I'm just an old maid," she replied.

"No you're not! Love has nothing to do with age or beauty or brains or anything for that matter. Love is love. It comes to us when it comes to us, and I wonder if we really have a lot of choice in the matter. The only important thing is not to become bitter . . . to keep your heart open."

Cecily nodded. "Maybe you're right. Maybe I was pounding a square peg into a round hole. Obviously Joe wasn't right for me, or anybody else for that matter. But I just feel like such a fool."

"Forgive yourself. We were all taken in."

"Thanks, Lucky. You're a sweetheart."

"I better get back. I just stopped in to see you and make sure you were okay. I'm really sorry it all came out like this."

Cecily took a deep breath. "Had to. The truth had to come out. And you and Janie, you could have been killed because of that awful man. And your poor face." Cecily reached out. Her fingertips gently touched Lucky's cheek, still aflame in shades of red and purple.

"But we weren't. We're alive and well."

"Thank heavens." Cecily leaned closer and whispered, "And I hate to admit this, but here I was, looking down my nose at the travelers, and they turned out to be the best of the lot."

Chapter 51

LUCKY STEPPED ACROSS her threshold and shut and locked the apartment door behind her. She took a deep breath. Blessed privacy. She turned on a lamp in the living room and pulled the drapes closed. The sun had set hours ago. Now the days had grown very short. Soon bitter winter would be upon them. The first anniversary of her parent's death was around the corner—less than two months away. How her life had been turned upside down by their accident. And how was it possible almost a whole year had passed? There wasn't a day that went by when she didn't feel they were with her. It was more than seeing their photos on her bureau and filling the apartment with keepsakes from her old home. It wasn't because she made a point of visiting their gravesites regularly. She missed them terribly, but they lived still in her heart. Was it just the memory of them? Or do the dead hover and watch over the living left behind?

She looked around the apartment. Janie and Miriam had come by at some point during the day and packed up all of Janie's things. Lucky walked down the hallway. Miriam had straightened everything up. Janie's sheets and blankets were clean and folded in the linen closet. Someone had even dusted. The sink was scrubbed, and the dishes stacked in the kitchen cabinet. Lucky was sure an experienced housewife had done most of the work. She only hoped Janie had helped her mother with some of it. A small vase of yellow and orange marigolds sat on the kitchen table, a folded note next to the flowers. The extra key she had given Janie sat on top of the paper. Lucky opened it. It said, *"We can never thank you enough."* Janie's signature was scrawled underneath, and next to that was Miriam's in a neat script.

Lucky collapsed into a chair, not bothering to slip out of her jacket. She felt completely drained. It had taken a lot of energy to keep up a cheerful front over the past few days. No one had even asked her once how Elias was. And what hurt even more was the fact that Elias had not even tried to make contact. Sophie was correct. The gossip that they were no longer together, that Elias was seeing someone else, had spread all over town. Lucky felt humiliated. Angry and hurt. She pushed herself out of the chair and trudged to the bathroom. She wrenched the faucets in the bathtub open and let hot water pour in, filling the tub. She dumped a copious amount of bubble bath into the stream. A nice hot soak would help her aching muscles. Aching not just from work, from being on her feet all day, but from all the tension over the past several days. But how could Elias just ignore her? If he no longer had feelings for her, if he had fallen back in love with Paula, couldn't he have been decent enough to simply tell her? Why did she have to hear this from someone else? She cringed inwardly when she realized what a fool she must have looked like, arriving at his office to find him close to Paula both times. Cecily had absolutely nothing to be ashamed of. She, Lucky Jamieson, could take the prize for being the chief fool.

The phone started to ring. Lucky groaned. She didn't want to talk to anyone. She had had to repeat the story of Janie's kidnapping and rescue to everyone who had come into the restaurant—minus the true story of Janie's connection to Eamon. She couldn't go through it one more time. The phone continued to ring. Maybe it was Jack. If Jack was calling, she'd answer. She shut the faucets off and went back to the kitchen. She glanced at the caller ID and recognized Elias's home number. Her face flushed. Obviously he was calling because he had heard of the close call at the Stones and in the cornfield. Someone must have told him about it. Or maybe he's received Janie's medical report from the hospital in Lincoln Falls and, wondering why he hadn't been informed, had started asking questions. Whatever. How he found out didn't concern her. She ignored the ringing phone and returned to the bathroom. She stripped off her clothes and stepped gingerly into the steaming tub, sinking under the bubbles. She heard garbled speech on the answering machine as Elias left his message. She didn't want to hear the message, and she didn't want to talk to him. She didn't care what he had to say. She was finished. She closed her eyes and held her breath and sank under the bubbles, not wanting any human sound to reach her ears.

Chapter 52

LUCKY SNUGGLED INTO her bathrobe and pulled the comforter up to her chin. The apartment had been so cold when she woke, she turned up the thermostat, made a quick cup of strong coffee and carried it back to her bed. She sipped it slowly, relishing the comfort and the warmth. Her bruised cheek was turning from a purplish blue to a greenish yellow. She touched it gingerly. It was still sore.

She took a last sip of coffee and padded back to the kitchen. The apartment was warm enough now to get into the shower. As she headed down the hall to the bathroom, she heard a knock at the front door. She stopped in her tracks. It wasn't even seven o'clock. Who would be at her door at this hour? Perhaps it was Miriam having an anxiety attack. She tied her robe tighter and cracked open the front door. Elias stood in the hallway.

Her first reaction was anger. What right did he have to come to her apartment with no warning at this ridiculous hour? And why now? He hadn't stopped by the Spoonful in over a week, not since Paula had joined the Clinic. He had done a very good job of ignoring her and the rumors flying around town.

"Elias!" Her tone was distant if not icy. She couldn't help it.

"Can I come in?"

She hesitated. "I was just about to get in the shower. Is this important?"

"Yes, I think it is."

"Very well." She opened the door wider and returned to the kitchen, aware that her hair was sticking up in various places, her face was unwashed and discolored, her teeth weren't brushed, and she was in an old bathrobe that had seen better days. Elias followed her down the hallway.

"Would you like some coffee?" It wouldn't kill her to be civilized, she thought.

"No. Thanks. Lucky, I just wanted to apologize."

"For what?" *Make him spell it out*, she thought.

"For a number of things. For not calling all week. For . . . I just found out late last night about what happened with you and Janic. I'm so sorry I wasn't there to help you." He stared at her bruised cheek and jaw. "And . . . I also found out about some of the rumors going around about me and Paula. I want you to know they're not at all true."

Lucky sat at the kitchen table, still gripping her coffee mug. "How did you hear?"

"Rosemary finally told me. She's been pretty mad at me because she thought the rumors about me and Paula were true too." He paused. "I've been terribly busy, but I know that's no excuse. I meant what I said the other night. That my former relationship with Paula was over."

Lucky closed her eyes, willing herself not to fling the mug across the table at him. "I saw you with her in the office, Elias. You were about to kiss her. There's no need to lie about it."

"What?" He flushed a bright red. "That's not true, Lucky. Not true at all."

She hesitated, not willing to tell him all the gossip that Sophie had conveyed. "I had heard rumors too. That's why I went over there to talk to you. To find out what exactly was going on." She didn't want to admit to him that the entire week she had felt like a one-ton stone was lodged in her chest. "After you left the office, Paula said . . . implied that something was going on between the two of you."

"And you believed that?" Elias raised his voice. "Why didn't you talk to me?"

"That's exactly what I was trying to do when I went to your office," she shouted back.

"Lucky." He reached for her hand across the table. She had to stop herself from pulling away. "Please believe me. Nothing was going on—at least not on my part. That day, Paula said she had something in her eye and asked me to have a look. That's why we were standing by the window."

"That's a good one!" Lucky replied.

"It's true. Stop trying to make me look like the bad guy here."

"What's that supposed to mean?" Lucky shot back.

"It means that I'm not the one dragging my feet in this relationship. We've been together for how long, and you won't even tell me why Jack calls you 'Lucky.' How crazy is that?"

His words stung. He had a point. Lucky took a deep breath. "Virgil Lukorsky . . . Lucky," she said.

"What?"

"Jack named me after a Navy boxer because of my right hook. I didn't want you to know. I was embarrassed. I wanted you to think I was feminine."

Elias was completely silent. He stared at her and blinked. Finally he said, "Oh."

Lucky waited.

"I never thought you weren't feminine. Look, I'm sorry I shouted. I didn't mean to. But you have to believe me. Nothing, absolutely nothing, happened between me and

Paula." He hesitated then sheepishly said, "At least not on my part."

Lucky was having a difficult time letting go of her anger. Part of her yearned to believe Elias, and part of her was still hurt and furious.

"You're telling me that what Paula said to me that day wasn't true?"

"She . . ." Elias hesitated. "Because she . . ." He sat heavily in the kitchen chair across the table from her. "I might as well tell you the whole story. I realized she was being overly friendly, overly familiar." He looked at Lucky quickly. "I did *not* encourage it. In fact, I did my best to discourage it. I just wanted someone to take the load off my shoulders. She told me she had no issue with the fact that I would be her boss essentially, in spite of our prior relationship. That's what she said. What was happening, I finally realized, was her actions didn't match her words."

"And the rumors around town—that you and she were seeing each other, that we had broken up?" Lucky was struggling to understand the motives of a woman who would behave in such a way.

"Obviously started by Paula. Who else? Certainly not me. And I realize now, it was deliberately done to drive a wedge between us."

Lucky thought Elias himself had certainly contributed to the situation by not being more present, but she didn't voice her opinion. "Why would she say one thing and do another?"

"She needed to involve me in a relationship. I understand why now. I think she thought I would go for it. She didn't plan on there being someone else in my life. She thought she could . . . seduce me, I guess, and that would give her added leverage."

"Leverage for what?" Lucky was mystified.

"She was let go from her last position . . . in Bennington— there were two malpractice claims by patients against the hospital's insurer. And that wasn't all. I got the whole history from my insurance agent. Before the malpractice claims in Bennington, she had been working in Boston. She left Boston because of a wrongful-death action." Elias sighed. "It was my own stupid fault. I agreed to hire her without running it past my insurance carrier because I knew her, knew her work, how good a doctor she is. But she lied to me—a huge lie of omission."

"You said the claims were against the hospital in Bennington?"

Elias nodded. "Yes. Usually the hospital carries the insurance and, in fact, often advises doctors not to carry their own, so they're not personally vulnerable to a claim."

"If she's such a good doctor, why the malpractice accusations?"

Elias shrugged. "I don't know. I really don't know the details of each case. But I did start to notice that she had a rather cavalier attitude—dismissive—toward a few of my patients. I asked her about it, but she refused to discuss it. None of the Clinic's patients have complained to me—at least not yet, but . . . I don't know what to say. Emotional problems? A disconnect? Maybe she shouldn't be treating patients at all."

"And the wrongful death in Boston?"

"That can happen to any doctor, even when they've done everything possible to save a patient. Families are sometimes angry. They want to lash out at the person they blame for a loved one's death. But in that case she misdiagnosed acute appendicitis and a young woman died."

"How could she miss that?"

"Appendicitis is strange. It can present in many different forms, and this young girl had no elevated white count, no fever, none of the classic signs. Frankly it could have happened to anyone. Paula's mistake was that she didn't keep looking for an explanation of the pain."

"That's terrible!" Lucky said. "How did you find all this out if she didn't tell you?"

"From my insurer. I blame myself for not running her through the system before I agreed to hire her. She knew I'd find out eventually, and what I think is, she hoped to involve me in a relationship again, and once involved, maybe she figured I'd be willing to overlook it, to pay the premium on the malpractice insurance, assuming they'd cover her. Even if I were so inclined to keep her on, the Clinic doesn't have that kind of budget. A large hospital couldn't pay that kind of exorbitant sum. I never realized . . . how manipulative a woman she is. Her plan was to rekindle our old relationship and put me in a position where I couldn't renege on our agreement."

"Does that mean she can't work anywhere?"

"She'll find work. I think she just took the easy way out by coming to Snowflake until the case in Boston is settled one way or the other. When I confronted her about not telling me, we had a very ugly scene. Then yesterday one of my patients told me they were sorry you and I had broken up. I was stunned. I had no idea she had managed to create all those lies and distractions and innuendoes. I had no idea she was doing her best to cause trouble between us. I was so stupid. I still can't believe she was so calculating. She's not the woman I thought she was." Elias rubbed his forehead. "She's gone now. She's left Snowflake. Can you forgive me, Lucky? I should have stayed in better touch with you this week. I should have come to see you as soon as I realized things were getting weird. And I should have been with you that night in the cornfield. I heard all about it from several people. They just looked at me as if I were lower than dirt—abandoning you when you were in trouble."

Lucky stared into her half-full mug. "Elias . . . I'm not really sure how I feel right now. I thought you had turned your back on me. It was obvious what she was doing the day I walked into your office."

"I was embarrassed that day. I know what it looked like, but I thought you'd . . . I don't know . . . have trust in me. I'm so sorry. I wouldn't hurt you for the world. I was very clear with her. That I am involved with you. That I have feelings for you."

"I just can't sort all this out right now."

Elias's face had grown pale. "Lucky . . ."

"I'm sorry. Please. I just can't talk about this right now. What's happened this week has been very hurtful, even if it wasn't really your fault. But it's made me think, about myself, about my life, about what I'm doing, about . . . I know that whoever I'm with has to be someone I can trust totally. Trust and respect are the most important things to me."

Elias's face was grim. "You *can* trust me, Lucky. I've never lied to you. I've never led you on. I thought that you loved me. That we could have a real future together."

What was holding her back? He had poured out his heart, and yet she still held on to the hurt? Why was it so hard to forgive him for the insults that had taken place? Was he the right man for her? Regardless of how attracted to him she still was, she needed time to think. She remained silent at the table.

When she didn't speak, Elias sighed and rose from his chair. "I don't blame you for being upset. I was blind. I was an idiot not to see what Paula was up to. But I've never lied to you, Lucky."

She looked up at him.

"You know where I am if you change your mind." The hurt was apparent on his face. He walked down the hall and closed the door quietly behind him.

Chapter 53

MIRIAM REACHED OUT to Janie's hand and squeezed it tightly as they approached the encampment. Janie held a small suitcase in her other hand. Miriam's anxiety was palpable. Lucky couldn't imagine how daunting this meeting must be for her, a woman who had torn herself away from everything she knew. Close to twenty years had passed since she had seen her family, her clan, spoken a language she had almost forgotten.

Lucky slipped her hand through Jack's arm as they followed Miriam and Janie up the hillside. Miriam's back was ramrod straight, as if she expected punishment for her exodus. They entered the clearing. Eamon stood in the center, apart from everyone else. The entire clan—men, women and children—stood waiting for them. The vans were packed and ready, the area cleared, and the campfires extinguished. Eamon smiled broadly as they approached. Janie's eyes held a barely suppressed excitement as she looked first at one person and then another.

One woman took a step forward. Her hair was a deep

auburn, like Janie's. She wore a bulky sweater over a long brightly colored skirt. Hesitant at first, she rushed toward Miriam and grasped her hands. "Morag! Do you remember me?" she asked.

Miriam's eyes filled with tears. "Aislinn. Yes, yes, of course I remember you."

The woman reached out and enveloped Miriam in her broad arms. "*Fàilte dhachaigh, mo sheann charaid.* Welcome home, old friend." She smiled and took Janie's hand. "And you must be Janie. We've been hearing a lot about you for the past few days." She smiled broadly. "Would you like to meet everyone?"

Janie nodded excitedly. "I doubt I'll remember everyone's names, but I'll try."

Eamon walked toward them. He spoke to Miriam. "Are you sure you won't change your mind?"

"No." She shook her head. "Perhaps another time. This has all been so overwhelming."

"We'll take good care of her. There's no need to worry."

"She has her cell phone if she needs me. I'll see you in Halifax in a month. I just hope she'll still want to come home with me then."

"We won't steal her away. Don't worry."

Miriam nodded. She looked about to cry once again. "She has a home. And I want her to get an education. Don't forget that, Eamon."

"I won't. I respect your wishes, Morag. Forgive me if I call you that. I've whispered your name so many times in the dark. I always hoped you'd heard me."

Before Miriam could respond, Janie called out, running across the field. "Mom. Mom, they're ready to go. Give me a big hug and don't worry about me. I'll be fine."

Miriam nodded and held Janie tightly. "I love you," she whispered. Tears filled her eyes. "I love you . . . with all my heart and soul."

Janie extricated herself from Miriam's arms. "I'll be fine, Mom."

"*Gus an coinnich sinn a-rithist*. Till we meet again," Eamon said, leaning down to kiss Miriam on the cheek. He looked into her eyes for a long moment then turned away to lead Janie to his van.

"And you better help me learn more Gaelic when I come home," Janie called out as she ran to the van that would carry her to Cape Breton.

Lucky and Jack stood on either side of Miriam. Jack placed a protective arm around Miriam's shoulders. Lucky knew it took every ounce of strength for Miriam to let Janie go, even if it was only for a brief time.

The engines revved, and each vehicle pulled slowly out of the field, heading down the hill toward the highway. The three of them watched as the van Janie rode in passed by. Janie waved excitedly from the window. Miriam stood ramrod straight until everyone was gone.

She turned to Lucky. "The hardest lesson. They're not really yours—you only rent them for a little while."

Chapter 54

THE AFTERNOON SUN filtered through the yellow café curtains. The Spoonful was ready for Halloween, thanks to
Janie's decorations and electric candles. It was too bad she
couldn't be here to see the fun. Miriam had stopped by to
help out in Janie's absence. Jack had found an old fireplace
cauldron and filled it with dry ice that wafted around the
front room. Lucky had plugged in a CD with "Monster
Mash" and another one of scary Halloween sounds—
creaking doors, shrieks and cackling witches.

The evening before, after the travelers had gone, Lucky
took Miriam back to Jack's house where he cooked steaks
in his old cast-iron frying pan. Lucky had carried logs in
and built a roaring fire and poured wine for herself and
Miriam. Jack grabbed a beer from the refrigerator, and
they ate their dinners in front of the hearth.

She and Jack had decided Miriam shouldn't be alone on
the first night of Janie's trip. Lucky couldn't bear the
thought that Miriam would return to an empty house, not
after the anxiety she had suffered when Janie ran away and

then was abducted. When the evening wound to a close, Lucky had driven Miriam home and then returned to her apartment.

This evening, because of the promotional bowl of free soup from three to five, the restaurant was full. Many of the customers had brought their children along, now finished with school for the day and done up in costumes, some store-bought, some homemade. The adults were ready for trick-or-treating too, and several were in costumes themselves. Lucky looked around the restaurant and spotted Tommy Evans sitting by himself in a far corner, dressed in his everyday clothes, hidden behind Hank and Barry at their regular table. She grabbed a bowl of soup and placed it on a dish with a half sandwich and carried it over to Tommy. She nudged Barry as she went by. "This young man needs a real seat and a place to eat," she said, indicating Tommy. "May he join you?"

"Oh. Oh, of course," Barry said, looking up from his game and peering around Hank. "Come over here young man, and have a seat."

Tommy looked up hopefully. Lucky was sure he was hungry and didn't have money to buy anything.

"Where's Guy tonight?" she asked.

"He'll be here in a few minutes. He's closing up the shop now."

Lucky smiled and pulled over a chair for Tommy. "That's good. We'll be doing the pumpkin contest pretty soon. Your entry stands a very good chance."

Tommy's eyes widened, but his expression seemed to say he wasn't hoping for very much.

"Do you know how to play Connect Four, Tommy?" Hank asked.

The boy smiled. "Sure. Can I play with you?"

"Certainly can. Soon as you finish your soup and sandwich."

Lucky was sure Tommy was in good hands with the

men. She returned to the counter. The restaurant was so noisy she could barely make out any conversations. Some of the older kids were singing along with "Monster Mash." She glanced over at Jack at the cash register. He made a thumbs-up sign to her and smiled. Their Halloween promotion was a success.

The pumpkin entries with their numbers were lined up on the long table against the wall. The secret ballots were folded pieces of paper placed in a covered bean jug by the cash register. Every customer at the Spoonful that week had had a chance to vote for his or her favorite. Lucky had been rather disappointed there hadn't been more entries in the contest. Both Hank and Barry had donated their jack-o'-lanterns, as had Janie. Sage had carved one, and Sophie entered one that Lucky knew had been carved by Sage. There was Guy's entry and Horace's. Sage had given the fairy-tale pumpkin to Guy, and Guy had helped Tommy with the sharp knives, but Tommy had been adamant that his pumpkin had to be his design. Neither Marjorie nor Cecily had been interested in the contest. They were willing to vote but not willing to actually carve a pumpkin. There was Meg's pumpkin and Jack had created one just to add to the mix. Remy had found some time after his ordeal in the cornfield to contribute his entry. In all there were eleven carved pumpkins. Since the prize, three free all-you-can-eat meals for two, was something that would only be helpful to a paying customer—Jack, Sophie, Sage, Janie, and Meg already ate for free—it boiled down to the fact that the real entrants were Hank, Barry, Remy, Horace, Guy and Tommy.

Lucky had called all of them and explained Tommy's situation. And to their credit they had all readily agreed they had no problem with the pumpkin-carving contest being rigged in Tommy's favor. Sophie was in charge, and she planned to make a show of counting the votes and announcing Tommy as a winner.

Lucky glanced at the clock. It was almost four. Time to announce the contest winner. She was about to call out to Sophie, who was in the kitchen helping Sage prepare dishes, when she felt a hand on her arm. She turned around. It was Cecily. She hadn't seen her arrive.

"Lucky, you're a dear. Thank you for cheering me up the other day. You were right. I was making a mountain out of a molehill."

Lucky smiled ruefully. "We all do when feelings are involved."

"Well, it was totally silly of me. I mean, we're talking about one dinner date. That's nothing. And no one seems to be treating me like the fool I feel like. At least I hope they're not laughing behind my back."

"I doubt that very much. First of all you're well liked and well respected in town. And besides probably nobody even noticed you having dinner with Joe . . . I mean Devlin, up at the Lodge. No one who knows you anyway."

"You're right. It's made me realize how wonderful it would be to have that in my life. You probably can't understand. You're young. You don't see the window of opportunity closing at your tender age."

Lucky felt a pang in her chest. Little did Cecily know how miserable she felt about Elias right now. She didn't respond.

Cecily squeezed her arm. "But, no matter what age you are, if love lands on your doorstep, don't let it go." Cecily smiled and moved away among the crowded tables.

"Pssst," Sophie hissed through the hatch. "What are you doing out there?"

Lucky spotted Guy at the front door. She waved to him and pointed to where Tommy sat. She turned around. "Sorry. I'm losing track of time."

Sophie gave her a quizzical look. "It's time for my star turn, Ms. Jamieson." She laughed and disappeared. A moment later she pushed through the swinging door from the kitchen. She took a position near the cash register and the bean jug. Lucky turned down the volume on the CD player behind the counter so Sophie could be heard.

Sophie picked up a spoon and banged it against a glass. "Everyone. It's time. It's time for the counting of the ballots." The restaurant fell silent. "Jack here will make sure there's no cheating."

Sophie lifted the lid of the bean jug and one by one opened the folded slips of paper. She whispered a name to Jack, and Jack slipped the ballots into a drawer under the cash register and made a note on a pad of paper. When they had finished, Jack passed the notepad to Sophie.

Sophie looked at it carefully, a serious expression on her face. Lucky was admiring her acting skills. "Well, everyone did very well, actually. Hank, you received twelve votes. Barry, you received thirteen." Lucky glanced over at the men. Barry jabbed Hank in the ribs in victory. Hank ignored him. Tommy still sat at their table, his expression intent. "Remy . . ." Sophie looked around the restaurant. "Remy's not here, but he's coming later. Remy got eleven votes. Guy . . ." She looked around the restaurant and finally spotted Guy Bessette. "You got fifteen votes. Horace Winthorpe . . ."

"Here," Horace called out, waving a hand.

"Horace, you received the same number as Barry— thirteen. But . . ." Sophie took a dramatic pause. "None of you has received more votes than the winner." Sophie raised her eyebrows and looked around the room.

Lucky noticed Tommy, his brow furrowed, staring at the long table of jack-o'-lanterns. She was sure he was trying to remember how many votes had been announced and mentally counting the pumpkins.

"The winner is . . ." Sophie spoke more loudly. "Tommy Evans! Tommy Evans received seventeen votes!" She began to clap, and everyone in the restaurant followed her lead. The teenagers cheered.

Guy was grinning from ear to ear and winked at her. She smiled back.

"Let's get Tommy up here to collect his prize. Where are you, Tommy?" Sophie called out.

"Here! I'm here!" Tommy raised his hand and scooted off his chair. He rushed to the cash register, a huge smile on his face.

"You have won three all-you-can-eat meals for two at the Spoonful any time of your choosing." Sophie looked over at Lucky. "Isn't that right?"

"Sure is," Lucky said. "Congratulations, Tommy."

Tommy received another round of applause. He grasped the prize card—a printed piece of cardstock that Lucky had created on the computer, and she and Jack had officially signed—and slipped it into his shirt pocket. Tommy, excited, rushed to Guy's side, and Guy reached out to give him a high five.

"Great job, Sophie," Jack said. "Couldn't have done better myself."

Sophie winked at Jack, smiled at Lucky and headed back to the kitchen.

Chapter 55

"ARE YOU AN idiot or what?" Sophie shouted. Lucky flinched, remembering how Elias had called himself an idiot. She couldn't respond to Sophie's accusation. They had retired to the office with mugs of coffee after the customers had left for home or for trick-or-treating with their children. Guy had offered to take Tommy out for Halloween, but Tommy couldn't wait to tell his mother about winning the prize. Only Horace, Hank and Barry were still in the restaurant with Jack.

"I thought you were crazy about Elias. What's going on, Lucky?"

Lucky took a deep breath. "I'm not really sure. It's like a part of me just shut down. It's hard to explain. When I thought Elias might have lied to me, when I thought the rumors might be true"—She glanced at her friend; Sophie's face was heavy with concern—"a part of me just couldn't believe it, but another part of me was sure it was true. It's not that easy to just say, 'Oh, yes, that's fine. I'm still in love with you. The fact that Paula had decided she wanted you is just fine with me. I understand. I understand that, of course, you had to hire her. That you didn't tell me you had had a relationship before. Never once mentioned it, in fact." Lucky shook her head. "I felt needy and dependent. And I hate feeling that way. That's not me."

"Ha!" Sophie laughed derisively. "That's everybody who's in love. Get over yourself. You're just afraid of being hurt."

Lucky didn't answer.

Sophie shook her head, a disgusted look on her face. "Advice from a good friend?"

"What?" Lucky lifted her chin defiantly.

"Get off your damn high horse!" Sophie exclaimed.

"What's that supposed to mean?"

"It means I was right. You are an idiot. A stubborn idiot." Sophie reached across and grasped Lucky's hand. "Okay, so even if his head was turned a little bit, which I don't believe, not really, I don't think he was getting reinvolved with Paula. I think Paula was a calculating witch, and you can spell that with a *B*." She continued, "I think he was blindsided. I don't think he ever meant to hurt his relationship with you."

"So why was he so distant and dismissive when I got upset?"

"'Cause he knew he hadn't really been forthcoming about his past. He felt defensive. And in truth had you actually asked him about prior romances?"

"No," Lucky replied grudgingly.

"Well, there. Think about it. You're angry because he never mentioned something that *you* had never asked him about. That's twisted logic if I ever heard it." Sophie paused for breath. "What Paula did was pretty obnoxious but not illegal. She was worried about her own survival. If this case goes against her, it'll certainly hurt her career. She used Elias. She hurt you, but the way she saw it, she had to survive." Sophie waited, but Lucky didn't respond. "Are you listening to anything I'm saying?"

"Yes, of course I am."

"Bottom line is, you're angry at Elias because of what Paula's done. He may have been a real jerk, but he didn't do anything *totally* unforgivable."

"I guess you're right."

"I know I'm right. So stop sulking and go after the guy."

Chapter 56

LUCKY PULLED HER collar up and snuggled into her jacket. Indian summer was over. It was cold enough tonight that her nose was red and her fingers were chilled. It didn't help that she was sitting on the hard wooden steps in front of Elias's house. She was waiting for him. Perhaps it was Cecily's words, or perhaps it was seeing the love in Eamon's eyes when he gazed at Miriam. She couldn't begin to conceive of the pain that he and Miriam had borne for so many years. To love so deeply and to have that love ripped away. To spend years wondering and railing against the fates. No matter how closed Miriam's heart had become, she hadn't been able to completely deny the love she had for Eamon, the love she had hidden, even from herself, for so many years. While she, Lucky, had rejected Elias when he opened his heart to her.

She had called the Clinic and spoken to Rosemary and learned Elias had spent the day at the hospital in Lincoln Falls. Eager to gossip, Rosemary had babbled for almost a half hour with the latest juicy news about Paula. Lucky did not let on she had already heard the story—mostly because she didn't want any questions asked about her relationship with Elias.

Sophie was right. She was an idiot. She had been doing the very thing that Miriam had been forced to do her entire life—deny her heart. Why? Why had she hesitated when Elias declared his feelings? Fear? Uncertainty? She had used her parents' death as an excuse, but it was only an excuse. She had told herself she wasn't ready, that it was too soon after too many life changes, but it hadn't stopped her from falling in love.

When will he ever arrive? she thought, shivering inside her jacket. She could have waited another day to see him, but she felt an urgency, a necessity to tear down the barriers, to not delay in telling him how she felt. If only he would listen.

A car was approaching. It slowed to turn into the driveway. She stood, suddenly illuminated by the wash of headlights that raked across the yard. She only hoped she wasn't too late.

Recipes

BEET MUSHROOM BARLEY SOUP

(Serves 4)

½ medium onion, chopped
6 mushrooms, sliced
1 teaspoon olive or vegetable oil
4 cups chicken broth
3 beets, peeled and cubed
1 apple, peeled and cubed
½ cup pearl barley, uncooked
½ cup feta cheese, crumbled

In a large pot, sauté chopped onion and sliced mushrooms together in olive oil.

Add chicken broth. Add the beet and apple cubes to the pot with the barley. Bring to a boil, reduce heat and simmer for 20 minutes. Remove from heat and let the soup sit for 30 minutes, making sure barley is thoroughly softened.

Garnish each bowl with crumbled feta cheese.

PUMPKIN RICE SOUP

(Serves 6 generously)

1 small pumpkin (approximately 20" in circumference)
2 tablespoons vegetable oil or walnut oil
½ medium onion, chopped
4 cups chicken broth
1 apple, peeled and diced
¼ teaspoon cinnamon
¼ teaspoon nutmeg
¼ teaspoon ground cloves
A few dashes of white pepper
½ cup uncooked white rice (jasmine rice can also be
    used for a more interesting flavor)
1 cup water
½ cup walnuts, chopped

Cut a circle around the pumpkin stem and remove it. Cut the pumpkin into large sections and remove the seeds and fibrous material. Brush oil on the pumpkin sections (reserving a small amount to sauté the onion) and place the pumpkin sections on a cookie sheet or pan, skin side down. Bake for 1 hour at 350°. Remove from oven, and when pumpkin has cooled, peel away the skin and scrape the meat of the pumpkin into a bowl. This should yield approximately 4 cups of pumpkin meat.

Sauté the onion in a large pot, add pumpkin meat, add the chicken broth, rice, apple, cinnamon, nutmeg, cloves and white pepper. Heat almost to boiling, lower heat and let simmer for 20 minutes. Turn off the heat, cover and let stand for 30 minutes until the rice is completely soft. The soup may be quite thick at this point. If so, add 1 cup of water, stir and then purée with a food processor or wand. Reheat and serve garnished with chopped walnuts.

If you like to experiment, as Sage DuBois does, you can make your own spice mixture in place of the nutmeg, cinnamon and cloves listed above. Advieh, according to Wikipedia, is a spice mixture used in Persian and Mesopotamian cuisine often with rice, chicken or bean dishes. Common ingredients include turmeric, cinnamon, cardamom, cloves, rose petals or rose buds, cumin and ginger. It may also include golpar (seeds of the Persian hogweed), saffron, nutmeg, black pepper, mace, coriander or sesame.

Some of these ingredients might be hard to obtain, but following is a much simpler recipe for advieh:

1 teaspoon ground cinnamon
1 teaspoon ground nutmeg
1 teaspoon ground rose petals
1 teaspoon ground cardamom
½ teaspoon ground cumin

Add one teaspoon of this mixture to the pumpkin rice soup in place of the other spices, and save the rest of the mixture for use with other dishes.

BEEF AND BERRY SOUP

(Serves 4)

2 tablespoons vegetable oil
1 pound tender beef steak
1 large onion, thinly sliced
2 tablespoons butter
4 cups beef stock or beef bouillon
½ teaspoon salt
½ cup fresh blueberries, slightly mashed

½ cup fresh blackberries, slightly mashed
1 tablespoon honey

In a large pot, add the vegetable oil and quickly brown the steak on both sides over medium high heat. Remove the steak from the pan. Add onions and butter to the pan, and sauté on low heat until the onions are softened. Add beef stock or bouillon and salt, and bring to a boil, continuing to stir. Add the berries and honey. Simmer for 20 minutes. While the soup is simmering, cut the steak into very thin slices. Add the steak pieces to the pot and cook for another minute or two. Add a bit more honey or salt to taste and serve hot.

ZUCCHINI BREAD

(Serves 10)

1½ cups flour
1 cup dark brown sugar
½ teaspoon baking soda
¼ teaspoon salt
¼ teaspoon baking powder
1 teaspoon cinnamon
¼ teaspoon nutmeg
1 cup shredded peeled zucchini
¼ cup cooking oil
1 egg
1 cup water
¼ teaspoon lemon peel, shredded
¼ cup walnuts, chopped

In mixing bowl, combine flour, sugar, baking soda, salt, baking powder, cinnamon and nutmeg. Mix well. Add shredded zucchini, cooking oil, lemon peel and egg. Mix

"[McKinlay] continues to deliver well-crafted
mysteries full of fun and plot twists."
—*Booklist*

FROM *NEW YORK TIMES* BESTSELLING AUTHOR

Jenn McKinlay

Going, Going, Ganache

A Cupcake Bakery Mystery

After a cupcake-flinging fiasco at a photo shoot for a local
magazine, Melanie Cooper and Angie DeLaura agree to make
amends by hosting a weeklong corporate boot camp at Fairy
Tale Cupcakes. The idea is the brainchild of Ian Hannigan, new
owner of *Southwest Style*, a lifestyle magazine that chronicles the
lives of Scottsdale's rich and famous. He's assigned his staff to a
team-building week of making cupcakes for charity.

It's clear that the staff would rather be doing just about
anything other than frosting baked goods. But when the
magazine's features director is found murdered outside the
bakery, Mel and Angie have a new team-building exercise—find
the killer before their business goes AWOL.

INCLUDES SCRUMPTIOUS RECIPES

jennmckinlay.com
facebook.com/jennmckinlay
facebook.com/TheCrimeSceneBooks
penguin.com

M1287T0313

well, and add 1 cup of water to the mixture. Stir the batter until completely mixed, and add the chopped walnuts.

Pour the batter into a greased 8×4×2 inch loaf pan. Bake at 350° for 60 minutes or till a knife inserted at center comes out clean. Remove from pan and cool on a wire rack. Once cooled, wrap and store the bread overnight in the refrigerator before slicing.

ROSEMARY BISCUITS

(Serves 12)

2 cups self-rising flour
½ teaspoon salt
1 teaspoon baking powder
2 tablespoons fresh rosemary, chopped (If using dried
    rosemary, soak the leaves in hot water for a few
    minutes to soften.)
¼ cup butter or margarine, melted
⅔ cup milk
1 egg, beaten

Preheat oven to 450°. Grease a baking tray with a small amount of butter or cooking spray. Mix flour, salt and baking powder together. Add the chopped rosemary, butter and milk, and mix thoroughly to form a soft dough. Knead the dough lightly on a floured surface. Roll it out to approximately ¾" thick, and cut out biscuits with a biscuit cutter. This should provide 12 biscuits. Brush the tops of the biscuits lightly with the beaten egg, and bake for 8 to 10 minutes until golden. Cool the biscuits for a few minutes on a wire rack.